KILLED
IN THE
RATINGS

▶   ▶   ▶   ▶

Wheeling, West Virginia, was rated the safest city in America.

Number One.

New York, New York, was rated the most dangerous city in America.

Number 329.

Chicago, Illinois—Matthew Hope's hometown—was rated 205.

And crime-free Calusa, Florida, was rated 162, virtually midway down the Rand McNally list, only forty-three slots higher than big bad Chicago, and apparently not as safe as the citizens here *dreamt* it to be.

To hear them talk about the murder of Otto Samalson, you'd have thought this was the first time anyone had ever been killed down here . . .

▶

CINDERELLA

CINDERELLA

BY
ED McBAIN

THE MYSTERIOUS PRESS

New York • London

MYSTERIOUS PRESS EDITION

This Mysterious Press Edition is published by arrangement with
Henry Holt and Company, 521 Fifth Avenue, New York, N.Y. 10175

Cover design by Barbara Buck
Cover photo by Dan Wagner

Mysterious Press books are published in association with
Warner Books, Inc.
666 Fifth Avenue
New York, N.Y. 10103
A Warner Communications Company

Printed in the United States of America

First Mysterious Press Printing: August, 1987

10 9 8 7 6 5 4 3 2 1

This is for Jane Gelfman

Otto knew he was being followed.

Thirty years in investigation, he'd never had anybody following him. Such a thing never happened to him. He guessed he was getting too old for this business, fifty-eight and closing fast, smoked too much and ate too much junk food, but those were occupational hazards. Didn't carry a gun, never had, private detectives carrying guns were for the movies. Even if he'd had a gun with him tonight, he wouldn't have known how to use it. Guns scared the hell out of him.

Anyway, nice Jewish guys didn't carry guns unless they were Louis Lepke or Legs Diamond—he could remember the newspapers full of them when he was a kid. His mother would shake her head and mutter "Jewish gangsters, wot a ting!" and then would spit twice on her extended forefinger and middle finger, ptui, ptui! Nice Jewish guys weren't supposed to drink, either. There'd been tests made and Indians came out highest and Irishmen next highest on the scale of heavy drinkers and

Jews came out lowest, which showed there was some truth to the clichés. He personally drank a lot, though, which meant it was a bunch of bullshit.

The tail must have picked him up leaving the Sea Shanty half an hour ago.

Everything here in Florida had a cute name. The Sea Shanty. Like it was supposed to be the Sea *Chanty*, you know, so they got cute and made it Sea Shanty because the place looked like a shack. Had three drinks sitting there at the bar and watching two chesty girls in tube tops playing PacMan. Never too old for watching chesty girls in tube-top shirts. He'd worked divorce cases where there were ninety-year-old men fucking around outside the marriage.

So that's where the tail must have picked him up.

When he was leaving the Sea Shanty.

Stop for a couple of drinks, next thing you knew you had a tail on your ass. Maybe the two tube-top broads had decided his bald head was very cute and were following him back to the condo to introduce him to all kinds of kinky sex, fat chance. The last time he'd had any sex, kinky or otherwise, was with a black hooker in Lauderdale who was scared of catching herpes and who washed his cock with what must have been laundry soap. Lucky she didn't wring it out later. She was good, though. Hummed while she blew him. Very nice.

He kept wondering what she was humming.

It had sounded like Gershwin.

Matthew didn't recognize her at first.

She was wearing red, which had always been her favorite color, and that should have been a tip-off, but she'd done something to her hair, and she'd lost he guessed ten or twelve pounds, and she looked taller than when he'd last seen her, and tanner, and he honestly didn't know she was Susan. He was, in fact, staring at her as she came into the room. Actually staring at her. Standing on a deck with his back to the Gulf of Mexico, and staring across the room at his own wife from whom he'd been divorced two years earlier, and wondering who she might be, and thinking he would like to cross the room right away and corner her before somebody else did. And then her dark eyes flashed, and all at once he was back on Lake Shore Drive in Chicago, strolling hand in hand with the most beautiful girl he'd ever met in his life and the girl was Susan and she was here and now, but she wasn't his wife any longer.

Smiling, he shook his head.

She was coming toward him.

Fire-red gown held up by her breasts and nothing else. Dark brooding eyes in an oval face, brown hair cut in a wedge, a full pouting mouth that gave an impression of a sullen, spoiled, defiant beauty. Black pearl earrings dangling at her ears. He had given her those earrings on their tenth wedding anniversary. Three years later, they were divorced. Easy come, easy go.

"Hello, Matthew," she said.

He wondered who she was going to be tonight. The Witch or the Waif? Susan had a marvelous way with the art of transmogrification. Ever since the divorce, you never knew who she was going to be next.

He could not take his eyes off her.

"You cut your hair," he said.

"You noticed," she said.

He still couldn't tell whether to expect a mortar attack or a shower of rose petals.

"Are you still angry?" she asked.

"About what?" he said. Warily. With Susan, you had to be very wary.

"Joanna's school."

Joanna was their fourteen-year-old daughter, whom Matthew saw only every other weekend and on alternate holidays because Susan had custody and his daughter lived with her. The last holiday he'd spent with Joanna had been Easter. Since then, he had seen her a total of four times. Today was the eighth of June, and he was supposed to have seen her this weekend, but since *next* weekend was Father's Day, he and Susan had agreed to switch weekends. They had similarly switched weekends when Mother's Day rolled around. The logistics of divorce. Like generals planning pincer attacks. Except the battlefield was a young girl growing into womanhood.

In April, Susan had come up with her brilliant idea to send Joanna away to school next fall. *Far* away. Massachusetts. Their separation agreement gave her that right. Now she was asking him if he was still angry.

He did not know whether or not he was still angry.

Oddly, he was wondering if she was wearing panties under the red silk gown.

Once, years ago, when they were much younger and actually happy together, she had startled him in church one morning by telling him she wasn't wearing any panties. This was when Matthew still went to church. He had thought at the time that the roof would fall in on them. Either that, or a little red creature with horns and a forked tail would pop out from under Susan's Presbyterian skirts, grinning lewdly.

She was looking at him, waiting for an answer.

Was he still angry? He guessed not.

"Actually it might be good for her," he said.

Susan raised her eyebrows, surprised.

"Getting away from *both* of us," he said.

4

"That's what I was hoping," she said, and they both fell silent.

Two years since the divorce and until this moment they could barely manage civil conversation. It was Joanna who bore the brunt of it. Away from them, she wouldn't be forced to take sides anymore. She was fourteen. It was time for her to heal. Maybe time for *all* of them to heal.

Beyond the deck, the beach spread to the shoreline and a calm ocean. A full moon above laid a silvery path across the water. From somewhere below the deck, the scent of jasmine came wafting up onto the night. Some kids up the beach were playing guitars. Lake Shore Drive again. Except that on the night they'd met, it was mandolins and mimosa.

"I knew you'd be here tonight," Susan said. "Muriel phoned and asked if it was okay to invite you. Did she tell you I'd be here?"

"No."

"Would you have come? If you'd known?"

"Probably not," he said. "But now I'm glad I did."

The tail was still with him.

He had deliberately turned south on U.S. 41, away from his condo, the last thing he wanted was to get cold-cocked in an apartment that had only one way in or out. He figured he'd find another bar, go in there, hope the tail would follow him in, see if he couldn't make the guy, play it from there. Maybe do like they did in the movies. Walk up to whoever it was, tell the guy "Hey, you gonna stay with me all night, why not sit down and have a drink?" Eddie Murphy did that once, didn't he? In that movie where he played a Detroit cop?

Could see the lights of the car in the rearview mirror.

Following.

5

Steady.

Twenty, thirty feet behind him. Very ballsy.

Not anyone's car he knew.

He'd spotted the car three blocks after he'd left the Sea Shanty. Stopped to buy himself some cigarettes at the Seven-Eleven on 41, noticed the car pulling in behind him. Still there when he came out with the cigarettes. Car was a black Toronado with red racing stripes and tinted windows, couldn't make out the driver through the almost-black glass. Pulled out almost the minute he did, though, the guy had to be an amateur. Or somebody just didn't give a shit.

Otto himself was driving a faded blue Buick Century. The whole thing in surveillance work, you wanted the car to blend in with the surroundings. You drove something showy, they made you in a minute. If automobile dealers sold pre-faded cars, he'd buy a dozen of them. This one had faded by itself over the years and was perfect for making itself disappear.

It wasn't doing too hot a job of that tonight, though, because the guy in the black Toronado was still on his tail.

It was a black-tie party. Muriel and Harold Langerman's twenty-fifth wedding anniversary. All the men were in white dinner jackets, the women in slinky gowns. The band's drummer had gone up the beach to disperse the kids playing guitars, and then had come back to join the piano player and the bass player on the patio below the deck. They were now playing "It Happened in Monterey." The moon was full. The Gulf of Mexico glittered beneath it like shattered glass.

"What are you thinking?" Susan asked.

"I'd get arrested," he said, smiling.

"That bad?"

"That good."

". . . a long time ago," the lyrics said.

"You look beautiful tonight."

A shy smile.

"You look handsome."

"Thank you."

He was an even six feet tall (though his sister Gloria insisted he had once given his height as six-two, to impress an adolescent girl), and he weighed a hundred and seventy pounds, and he had dark hair and brown eyes and what his partner Frank called a "fox face." He did not consider this handsome. This was adequate. In a world of spectacularly handsome men in designer jeans, Matthew Hope thought of himself as simply and only okay.

". . . lips as red as wine," the lyrics said.

He wanted to kiss her.

"But then, Matthew, you always *did* look marvelous in a dinner jacket."

She had called him Matthew from the very beginning.

Back then, people were calling him Matt or Matty. In fact, his sister Gloria used to call him Matlock, God only knew why. But Susan had called him Matthew, which he preferred. Nowadays, hardly anyone called him Matt. He guessed he could thank Susan for that. In fact, he guessed he had a lot of things he could thank her for.

He was staring at her again.

"Something?" she said.

"Yes, let's get out of here," he said in a rush.

The black Toronado was closer now.

Fifteen feet behind him maybe.

And then, all at once—like the scene in *Close Encounters* where the headlights in the rearview mirror are almost on the guy, whatever his name was, the guy who was also in *Jaws*, and they swerve up and away and you know it's a spaceship behind him—just like that scene except that the lights in Otto's mirror swerved to the *left*, and all at once the Toronado was alongside him, and the smoked window on the right-hand side of the car glided down and Otto looked over at a gun.

He thought Oh, shit, and that was the last thing he thought because the gun went off once, and then another time, but he didn't hear or feel the second shot because the first one took him clean in the left temple and his hands flew off the steering wheel like a pair of startled birds and the Buick swung out of control onto a sidewalk outside a television repair store and went through the plate-glass window of the store and smashed into a dozen or more television sets and the Toronado continued driving south on 41, the smoked window on the right-hand side gliding up again.

He could not believe later that he was in bed with Susan when he first heard the news about Otto Samalson.

His daughter would have thought they were both crazy.

Maybe they were.

The bed was a brierpatch of memories.

The radio was playing softly in his bedroom. Music of the fifties. Their music.

Memories of her.

Susan as he'd first seen her, sitting on a Styrofoam ice cooler, the lake behind her, singing along with a boy playing a mandolin, her legs widespread, skirt tucked between them, long brown hair blowing in the wind off the lake, dark eyes flashing as Matthew approached.

The pool lights were on outside. He could see her naked body in the reflected light.

A tangle of memories.

Susan as virgin queen, radiant in white, billowy white skirt and white sandals, white carnation in her hair, gleaming white teeth, face flushed as she rushed to him, hand outstretched, reaching for him, reaching. . . .

She whispered that she liked his house.

He whispered that he was renting it.

Memories.

Susan as wanton hooker standing in their bedroom door, black garter belt and panties, seamed black nylons and high-heeled black shoes, dark hair hanging over one eye, Come fuck me, Matthew. . . .

She asked him if he enjoyed living alone.

He told her he didn't.

So many years together, you learned the hollows and curves, you learned the spaces, you molded yourselves to re-membered nooks. . . .

"In Calusa tonight—"

The news.

He looked at the bedside clock: 11:03 P.M.

He kissed her.

"—killing the driver. The car swerved off the highway and into the front window of a television repair—"

Her mouth the way he remembered it when she was young.

Breasts still firm.

Legs. . . .

"—identified as Otto Samalson, a private investigator with offices on Highgate and—"

"*What?*" Matthew said.

Susan gasped, startled.

"Did you hear that?"

"No. What? Hear what? *What?*" she asked, frightened, and sat up, clutching the sheet to her naked breasts.

"Shhh," he said.

"In Sarasota, the county commissioners have outlined a plan to open—"

"Did he say Otto *Samals*on? Did you hear . . . ?"

"No," Susan said. *"Who?"*

"Jesus," he said, and got out of bed.

"Matthew, what . . . ?"

"I have to . . . I'd better call . . . Susan, if it was Otto . . . look, you'd better . . . listen, I have to make a call, excuse me."

He went into the room he'd set up as an at-home office, and called the Public Safety Building, and asked for Detective Morris Bloom. A detective named Kenyon told Matthew that Bloom was on vacation, but yes, the man who'd been shot and killed on U.S. 41 was indeed a private investigator named Otto Samalson.

Matthew thanked him and hung up.

When he came back into the bedroom, Susan was already dressed.

"I just remembered why we got divorced," she said, and walked out.

It was nightmare time.

A nightmare of flashbacks.

Invading Matthew's bed, invading his sleep.

I just remembered why we got divorced.

Susan's words. Opening a floodgate of memories that triggered the first of the nightmare flashbacks: Matthew coming home at a quarter to one, the lights on in the study, Susan sitting naked behind the desk in the house they used to share. "I just had a phone call," she says, "from a man named Gerald Hemmings," and Matthew's throat goes suddenly dry.

He and Aggie have rehearsed this scene a thousand times. They are lovers, Aggie and he, and therefore liars of necessity. They are lovers, he and Aggie, and therefore killers by trade, strangling their separate marriages. They are lovers, Aggie and he, he and Aggie, and therefore conspirators in that they are sworn to secrecy and know exactly what to say in the event of a trap.

This is a trap, he knows it is a trap.

But he knows in his darkest heart that it is nothing of the sort.

She has spoken to Gerald Hemmings, she has talked to Aggie's husband, it is one o'clock in the morning, and Susan knows everything, Susan knows all.

In the horror chamber of his mind, as he tries to sleep, the scene replays itself.

Denial, denial, denial, for surely this is a trap.

It is not a trap.

She is suddenly laughing. He comes around the desk swiftly, wanting to stop her manic laughter before it awakens Joanna down the hall. He puts his hand on her shoulder and she recoils from it as if a lizard has crawled up her arm, and suddenly there is more to be afraid of than hysterical laughter. Without warning, her hand reaches out to grab for the scissors, clutching it in her fist like a dagger, and lunges at him, lunges again, tearing the sleeve of his jacket. She is naked in the emptiest hour of the night, a woman scorned, a deadly weapon in her fist, and she comes at him again and again, he cannot catch her wrist. The tips of the scissors flick the air, retreat, flick again, catch the lapel of his jacket, cling there an instant till she rips them free with a twist and comes at him again. He brings up his left hand in defense and a gash magically opens from his knuckles to his wrist. All at once he feels

11

faint. He falls against the desk for support, knocking the telephone to the floor. She is on him again . . .

And suddenly there is a scream.

For a moment, he thinks it is he himself screaming.

His bleeding hand is stretched toward Susan, his mouth is indeed open—it is possible that he is the one screaming.

But the scream is coming from behind him.

He spins to the left, partially to avoid the thrusting scissors, partially to locate the source of the scream.

His daughter, Joanna, is standing in the doorway.

She is wearing a long granny nightgown, her eyes wide, her mouth open. Her scream hangs on the air interminably, overwhelming the small room, suffocating murderous intent.

The scissors stop.

Susan looks down at her own hand in disbelief. It is shaking violently, the scissors jerking erratically in her fist. She drops them to the floor.

"Get out," she says. "Get out, you bastard."

In nightmares there is no fade out/fade in, there is no matching shot, no attempt at continuity, flashback overlaps flashback and there is horror in chaos. The naked woman dropping the scissors, the little girl rushing to her and throwing herself in her mother's arms, both are rudely and abruptly replaced on the screen of Matthew's mind by a slender woman wearing a wheat-colored suit and a wide-brimmed straw hat, pantyhose to match the suit, tan high-heeled shoes, dark sunglasses covering her eyes.

Time outdistances time.

Two years ago is suddenly two weeks ago.

This is the twenty-third day of May, *anno domini*, the Friday before the Memorial Day weekend, and in his nightmare Carla Nettington has come to the law firm of Summerville and Hope, ostensibly to discuss the drawing of a will.

Ten minutes later, she is telling Matthew that she suspects her forty-five-year-old husband is having an affair. That is why she is really here. She did not want to go personally to a private detective; there is, she feels, something sleazy about private detectives. So she is here to ask if Matthew can help her secure the services of someone who can ascertain (these are her exact words, nightmares do not lie) ascertain whether her husband's frequent absences from home are truly occasioned (the exact words) by a heavy work load or are instead attributable to the favors of another woman.

"Because if the bastard's cheating on me," she says, "I want a divorce."

The bastard is Daniel Nettington, her husband.

Get out, you bastard.

In the distance, beyond the fringes of Matthew's unconscious, beyond the nightmare, *offscreen* so to speak, there is the sound of an automobile. He knows consciously—he is half asleep, half awake, he can hear for example the sound of raccoons outside, rummaging in his garbage cans, can hear a forlorn train whistle, for sometimes in the middle of the night Calusa gets trains bound for God knows where—he knows consciously, his *conscious* mind tells him that this offscreen automobile is Otto Samalson's. His conscious mind is a *raisonneur*, wide awake, explaining to half-asleep Matthew that this flashback nightmare will soon replay scenes he has never witnessed. The offscreen car is Otto Samalson's and soon Matthew will be subjected to the horror of his death, an event he can only blindly conjure, but such is the magic of nightmare.

He is talking to Otto on the telephone. He is asking Otto if he can take on a surveillance case. Otto is saying he's working another case right now, but if Matthew doesn't mind a little time-sharing he can start maybe Tuesday, will that be all right?

"What I'm doing," he says, "I'm taking Monday off like a normal human being."

The sound of the car is closer, it nudges the unconscious, demands to be driven onscreen. Matthew knows the car is a blue Buick Century, he has seen the car before. That he can only *hear* it now, cannot *see* it now, is frustrating. And yet he does not *want* to see it. He knows that once it enters the dream, he will know true horror, he will witness a close friend dying. He wants Otto to stay alive, to *be* alive, he wants the car to drive all the way to Tampa on I-75, bypassing Calusa, bypassing the nightmare.

Friday.

Is it Friday already?

Friday, the sixth day of June, 4:00 P.M. or thereabouts, Otto Samalson sitting in Matthew's office, smoking a cigarette. It is difficult to imagine this man as a private detective. He is no Sam Spade, no Philip Marlowe. He looks instead like a tailor or a shoe salesman. Short and slight of build, mostly bald with a halolike fringe settling above his ears, twinkling blue eyes, his mouth in a perpetual smile, he is the Eli Wallach of the sleuthing profession, enormously likable, immensely sympathetic, a man you would trust to drive your youngest sister to Napoli. Matthew suspects that Otto, with his wonderful bedside manner, could coax a devoted mother into revealing the whereabouts of her ax-murderer son.

The sound of the car.

Closer.

Louder.

Matthew tosses in half-sleep, half-wakefulness. Outside, the raccoons argue heatedly among themselves, their voices shrill.

"The guy's been fucking this widow lives in Harbor Acres," Otto is saying. "I've got him going in and out every night since

I started tailing him. That was Tuesday a week ago, I got him going in and out nine days already. Nice pictures, Matthew, he gets there when it's still light, I catch him with the long lens. I also got a tape I want you to hear. This lady, she thinks this is still Calusa twenty, thirty years ago, she goes out, leaves doors unlocked all over the place. I been in and out twice already. I put my recorder right under the bed, voice-activated. I got some very hot stuff, Matthew, wait'll you hear it. I couldn't bring the tape today 'cause I only got the original, it's in the safe. I'll make a copy, let you hear it next time I see you. Very beautiful stuff, Matthew, the two of them talking very dirty, she's a widow, nice-looking woman in her late—"

The Buick suddenly roars into view.

The office is gone.

There is only U.S. 41 and the blue Buick.

Otto is behind the wheel. He is smiling.

Turn back, Matthew thinks.

"Pictures of them in action are gonna be impossible, I think," Otto is saying, "because so far they only been makin' it with the drapes closed. You maybe have all you need on the tape, anyway, names, everything, a guided tour of what they're doing there in the lady's bed. I shoulda brought it today, but I didn't want to risk it 'cause I'll tell you the truth, if anything happens to that tape I'm not sure I can get in the house so easy again. I think he's on to me, Matthew, and I think the two of them are gonna start being very careful in the not too distant—"

Otto is still smiling.

This is a close shot of him behind the steering wheel. He has no idea what's coming. Only Matthew knows what's coming. Matthew hears a repeat of the news broadcast he heard only hours ago, while he and Susan were making love, *Get out, you bastard,* hears the broadcast as if it is coming from very far away, like a short wave broadcast, Otto's smiling face filling the screen, *In Calusa tonight*—

Turn back, he thinks.

"Reason I think he's made me," Otto says, "is there's something on the tape, I think he's referring to me. I couldn't be sure 'cause it wasn't an *absolute* reference. But he *could've* been talking about me, about me following him. And last night when he's coming out of her house, this must've been along around eleven, he stops dead in the street, he does like a take, you know, and looks straight at the car. So I think my days are numbered. What I'd like you to do is hear the tape and then decide whether you want to stay with this. You ask my opinion, he's gonna go underground a while, maybe surface again in a few weeks, but meanwhile cool it till he's positively sure nobody's watching him. What I thought, maybe Monday I can—"

—killing the driver. The car swerved off the highway and into—

"Turn *back!*" Matthew screamed aloud.

He sat up in bed, wide awake.

He was drenched with cold sweat.

Morning was here.

He could still hear Otto's voice.

So I think my days are numbered.

16

2

There were flies buzzing around the cheese Danish on Frank Summerville's desk. He was drinking coffee from a soggy cardboard container, and he was glaring sternly at Matthew over the rim of it.

"I don't want you getting involved in this," he said.

"Otto was a friend," Matthew said.

"Otto was a private eye who occasionally did work for us."

"No, Frank, he was a *friend*. I liked him."

"I liked him, too," Frank said. "But now he is dead, Matthew. He was shot in the head, Matthew. Twice, Matthew. His murder has nothing whatever to do with *us*, and I want you to stay away from the Public Safety Building *and* Detective Morris Bloom, do you hear me, Matthew?"

"Morrie's on vacation," Matthew said.

"Good," Frank said.

He was a half-inch shorter and ten pounds lighter than Matthew. They both had dark hair and brown eyes, but Frank's face was somewhat rounder, what he himself called a "pig face."

In Frank's physiognomical filing cabinet, there were only two kinds of faces: pig and fox. Frank also believed that there were only two kinds of names: Eleanor Rigby names and Frère Jacques names. Benny Goodman was a Frère Jacques name. "Benny Goodman, Benny Goodman, *dormez vous, dormez-vous?*" Robert De Niro was an Eleanor Rigby name. "Robert De Niro, puts on his face from a jar that he keeps by the door . . ." Frank further believed that there were only two kinds of people in the world: the Tap Dancers and the Touchers. He considered himself a tap dancer because he was very agile at gliding away from any sticky situation. He considered Matthew a toucher because he was always getting involved in situations he had no business getting involved in.

"I'm going over to his office later today," Matthew said.

"Whose office?" Frank said. "You just told me he's on vacation."

"Otto's."

"What for?"

"I want to hear what was on that tape."

"Otto's murder has nothing to *do* with us, Matthew."

"You don't know that for sure."

"He was working a lousy *surveillance!*"

"Maybe somebody didn't like the idea, Frank."

"Matthew . . . please. Do me a favor . . ."

"I want to hear that tape."

The people of Calusa, Florida, liked to believe there was no crime here at all; the uniformed cops and detectives who worked out of the Public Safety Building were concerned only with such things as citizens stubbing their toes.

Public safety.

Not crime.

But in Rand McNally's most recent *Places Rated Almanac*, there was a section that rated metropolitan areas from safest—the number-one position—to most dangerous—the 329th position.

Wheeling, West Virginia, was rated the safest city in America.

Number One.

New York, New York—Frank's beloved Big Apple—was rated the most dangerous city in America.

Number 329.

Chicago, Illinois—Matthew's hometown—was rated 205.

And crime-free Calusa was rated 162, virtually midway down the Rand McNally list, only forty-three slots higher than big bad Chicago, and apparently not as safe as the citizens here *dreamt* it to be.

To hear them talk about the murder of Otto Samalson, you'd have thought this was the first time anyone had ever been killed down here. Oh my, how shocking. Shot twice in the head. Unthinkable. Tsk, tsk, tsk. Blue-haired ladies shaking their heads and refusing to believe that public safety meant anything more than avoiding banana peels on the sidewalks. Such an embarrassment. It annoyed Matthew that Otto Samalson had become an embarrassment to Calusa, Florida—where homicides never happened except on a motion picture or television screen.

He did not get to Otto's office until a little after noon that Monday. By then he had spoken on the telephone to at least a dozen people who clucked their tongues (and undoubtedly wagged their heads, which Matthew could not see) over the unfortunate death on a public thoroughfare of a man whose profession was questionable at best. It took him ten minutes to walk from his own office to Otto's office in downtown Calusa. Downtown Calusa. The words somehow conjured a giant metropolis. Like downtown *Calusa*, man, you dig? Same as downtown New York or downtown Chicago. Downtown Detroit. Downtown L.A.

Well . . .

Downtown Calusa was exactly nine blocks long and three blocks wide. The tallest buildings in downtown Calusa, all of them banks, were twelve stories high. Main Street ran eastward from the Cow Crossing—which was now a three-way intersection with a traffic light, but actually *had* been a cow crossing back when the town was first incorporated—to the County Court House, which, at five stories high, was the tallest building anywhere on Main. The other buildings on Main were one- and two-story cinderblock structures. The banks were on the two streets paralleling Main to the north and south. So when you said "downtown Calusa," you weren't talking about a place that also had an *uptown*. There *was* no uptown as such. There was simply *downtown* Calusa and then the *rest* of Calusa.

Similarly, when you saw a frosted glass door and the lettering on it read—

SAMALSON INVESTIGATIONS
SUITE 3112

—you expected to open that door and find behind it a *suite*, which by strict definition was a series of connected rooms and which in the popular imagination (like downtown *Calusa*, man!) conjured grandness, a suite at the Plaza Athenée, right?

Well, when you opened the frosted glass door to Otto's office, you found yourself in a reception room measuring six by eight feet and crammed to bursting with a wooden desk, and a typewriter on it, and In and Out baskets to the left of the type-writer, and papers all over the desk, and a wooden chair be-hind it, and an upholstered easy chair opposite it, and green metal filing cabinets, and bookshelves, and a Xerox machine, and a coatrack, and walls hung with pictures of presidents of the United States, only two of whom Matthew recognized. On the wall opposite the entrance door, there was another door, presumably leading to the rest of the "suite."

A Chinese woman was sitting behind the reception room desk. She did not look at all like the Dragon Lady. She had black hair and eyes the color of loam, and she was wearing a Chinese-style dress with a mandarin collar, but that was where the resemblance ended. Matthew guessed she was in her fifties, as plump as a dumpling, as tiny and as squat as a fire hydrant.

"Yes?" she said. "May I help you?"

Perfect English. Not a trace of sing-song.

"I'm Matthew Hope," he said. "Summerville and Hope. Mr. Samalson was doing some work for us."

"Oh, yes," she said. "I'm May Hennessy. Otto's assistant."

He had spoken to her on the phone more times than he could count, but he had never once guessed she was Chinese. Always figured Otto's assistant was a big redheaded Irish lady who carried a blackjack in her handbag. May Hennessy. That's what a May Hennessy should have looked like. He glanced at her left hand resting on the typewriter. No wedding band. So where'd the Hennessy come from? Had her mother been Chinese, her father Irish? Or was she divorced?

"Hell of a thing, isn't it?" she said.

"Yes."

"Nicest man who ever lived."

"Yes," Matthew said, nodding.

There was an awkward silence.

"Miss Hennessy," he said, "when I saw Otto on Friday, he mentioned a tape he'd made. On the Nettington case. He said it was in the safe." He paused and then said, "Could I possibly have that tape?"

May Hennessy looked at him.

"I don't know," she said.

"Would there be any problem with that? I know my client—"

"Well, I can't see any *problem* as such," May said. "Your client was paying Otto to *make* that tape, so I guess you're entitled to it. It's just . . ."

"Yes?"

"Well, the detectives asked me . . ."

"Oh? Have they been here?"

"Been here all morning," May said. "Left just a few minutes ago."

"Who? Which ones?"

"Hacker and Rawles."

"Have they sealed the office?"

"Well, this isn't a crime scene, I don't suppose they'll be sealing it, do you? It's just . . . they want me to gather all the current files, the cases Otto was working on when he got killed." She shook her head. "I still can't say those words. I get a lump in my throat if I even *think* those words."

"Yes," Matthew said.

"So I guess that includes the tape, don't you?"

"I would guess so. When will they be coming back for the files, did they say?"

"I told them it'd take me a while. The phone's been ringing off the hook all morning. He had a lot of friends, Otto."

"But will they be coming back later today?"

"I told them around five, five-thirty."

"I wonder if you'd do me a favor, Miss Hennessy."

"You want to hear that tape, don't you?" she said. "Before I give it to the police."

"Please."

"I can't see any harm in that," she said.

"May I take it with me? I'll bring it back in an hour or so."

"You can listen right here," she said. "If you're worried about me, I've already heard anything that could be on that tape a hundred times before. I've been working with Otto for ten years now, Mr. Hope. There's no more dirty surprises for me."

Matthew hesitated.

"You can go in his office and close the door if you think I'll be embarrassed," May said. "The recorder's on his desk. I'll get the tape for you."

"Thank you," he said. "And Miss Hennessy . . . these cases Otto was working? The current ones?"

"Yes?"

"How many were there?"

"Just yours and one other."

"Both here in Calusa?"

"Yes."

"Are the files very thick?"

"How could they be? He only started working yours a few weeks ago and the other one around the end of April."

"Miss Hennessy . . . I wonder . . . after I hear the tape, would you mind very much if I Xeroxed those files?"

"It's a free country," May said, "and so far nothing's been impounded."

"Thank you," he said.

"I'll get that tape," she said.

A taped conversation somehow always sounded more immediate and real than a live one. Matthew didn't know why that was so. He guessed that when people were actually engaged in a conversation, they didn't notice how sloppy and ragged it was. Like life itself, he guessed. But listening to a conversation on tape, you realized that continuity and order were for novels and movies. In real-life conversation, people invariably meandered far afield, sometimes returning to a point minutes later, often seeming to forget it altogether. Interruptions were frequent, overlapping was common, entire passages sometimes made no sense at all. Listening to a taped conversation was compelling because, first of all, it *was* so shockingly real, and second, the listener was unquestionably eavesdropping. The conversation between Daniel Nettington and a woman identified on Otto's hand-lettered cassette label as Rita Kirkman (but only as "Rita" on the tape itself) was even more compelling because the people talking were lovers.

Otto's private office was larger than the reception area—eight by ten as opposed to six by eight—but just as cluttered. It enjoyed the advantage of a window, however, which, combined with its few extra feet, made it seem spacious by comparison, even if the only view from the window was of a bank building across the street. The desk, a twin sister to the one in the reception room, was piled high with papers. There were bookshelves and filing cabinets and a standing electric fan and a small-screen television set and a radio and two wooden chairs with arms and a typewriter on a stand and, on the wall opposite the desk and surrounded by charcoal drawings of nudes, Otto's framed Class-A license to operate a private investigative agency in the state of Florida.

In accordance with Chapter 493 of the Florida Statutes, such a license granted to its recipient the right to investigate, and to gather information on, a wide range of matters that included:

- The credibility of witnesses or other persons . . .
- The whereabouts of missing persons . . .
- The location or recovery of lost or stolen property, and . . .
- The causes and origin of fires, libels and slanders.

The license further permitted the investigator to:

- Secure evidence to be used in the trial of civil or criminal cases, and . . .
- When operating under express written authority of the governmental official responsible, to investigate crimes or wrongdoings against the United States or any state or territory of the United States.

All for a hundred bucks.

Which was what the license cost annually.

Renewable before midnight on the thirtieth day of June.

This year, Otto Samalson would not be renewing his license. Nor would he be posting the five-thousand-dollar bond required by subsections 493.08 and 493.09.

Matthew took the cassette May had given him, inserted it into the recorder, sat down behind Otto's desk—facing the wall with its framed license and its charcoal nudes—and pressed the play button.

. . . of getting away for at least a weekend.

I don't know, Rita. I'll have to see.

I don't want to force you into doing anything you—

He hit the stop button. Obviously, he'd started the tape

someplace beyond the beginning. He rewound it now, pressed the stop button again, and then the play button.

. . . of getting away for at least a weekend.

I don't know, Rita. I'll have to see.

I don't want to force—

He hit the stop button again. Okay, he had it now. The recorder Otto had planted under the bed was voice-activated. It probably had a good pickup range, and it had begun taping as they came into the bedroom, Rita continuing a sentence she had already started before entering the room. Nodding, Matthew rewound the tape, and started it all over again.

. . . of getting away for at least a weekend.

I don't know, Rita. I'll have to see.

I don't want to force you into doing anything you don't want to—

You're not forcing me into—

It's just . . .

That's the thing of it.

Meeting here all the time.

I know.

Silence.

Matthew listened.

Suddenly:

Mmm.

Yeah.

And another long silence.

He guessed they were kissing.

The silence lengthened. Then:

Don't you think I *want* to get away?

I know you do, Dan.

Take this off, okay? But I don't have the kind of job . . .

I know.

Some guys travel all the time, you know.

It's difficult for you, I know.
Guys in sales . . .
They go all over, I know.
The bra, too.
I'm not saying we should go away for two, three weeks . . .
Two, three. . . ?
I know, did I. . . ?
Impossible.
Did I *say* two, three weeks?
Two, three weeks, whoo.
Impossible, I know.
Impossible.
I said a *weekend* is what I said.
Another silence.
Matthew listened.
Murmurs on the tape.
Then:
God, you're gorgeous.
Silence again.
Then the woman's voice:
Ooooo, yes.
And more silence.
Matthew sighed.
Careful, they're a little sore.
Sorry.
I'm about to get my period.
Silence.
Then the man's voice:
I'd better take these pants off.
Yeah.
Don't want to go home wrinkled.
That's what I mean.
What do you mean?

About a weekend.

Yeah, what?

All I'm asking is a weekend.

I know that. Look, if I had Freddie's job—

Because if we went away, you wouldn't have to worry about getting wrinkled or getting lipstick on you or smelling of perfume or—

Away three, four months out of the year, Freddie.

Yeah, but you haven't.

I know I haven't. Los Angeles, Houston, Phoenix.

Sure, that'd be ideal.

You could meet me anywhere.

Maybe I oughta give *Freddie* a call, huh?

Oh, sure.

Meet *him* in Los Angeles sometime.

Yeah, sure.

Silence.

Then the woman's voice:

Oh my, where'd *that* come from?

You like that, hmm?

I love it. Bring it over here.

The creak of bed springs.

Mmmm.

And again . . . silence.

Matthew looked at the charcoal drawings of the nudes. He looked at Otto's framed license. He looked at the bank building across the street. He listened to the sounds coming from the recorder. Suddenly—

Nettington's voice:

Don't stop, Rita.

And more sounds.

Deeper, honey.

And heavy breathing.

That's it.

And a gasp.

Jesus. Oh, Jesus. Oh, God.

And a moan.

And a sigh.

And silence.

The tape kept unreeling.

Silence.

Another sigh. Heavier.

Then Rita again:

Was that good, baby?

Nobody does that like you.

How about Carla?

Make me so fuckin'—

How about your wife, baby?

—big.

Mmm.

Silence.

Matthew listened.

You want a cigarette?

Please. What do you think of the Fourth?

The sound of a match striking.

Someone exhaling.

Thanks.

Let me get an ashtray.

For our weekend. The Fourth falls on a Friday this year.

Silence.

Then Nettington's voice, distant at first:

I don't think we ought to . . .

And then coming closer, probably as he carried an ashtray
back to the bed:

. . . take any chances right now.

We could leave late Thursday night, come back late Sunday.

Too risky.

Be a nice long weekend, Dan.

Not right now. I think she's getting suspicious.

Oh?

Yeah, I think she suspects some . . .

What makes you . . . ?

Just a feeling.

Has she said anything?

No, no.

Anyway, who gives a fuck, actually?

Well, I don't want to . . .

I mean, I just don't *give* a fuck if she knows or she doesn't know.

This isn't the right time, that's all. I just don't want her to find out right now, that's all.

When *is* the right time, Dan?

Not now. If we're gonna do this, we have to prepare for it.

Sure, prepare.

Otherwise she walks off with everything I've got.

You'll *never* be ready to leave her.

That's not true, Rita.

It's true. You can't take me away for a weekend, you're going to leave her?

Well . . .

You can't even take me out to *dinner*.

Not right now, Rita.

I must be dreaming.

It's too dangerous right now.

Why? If she hasn't *said* anything . . .

She hasn't, but . . .

Then what makes you think . . . ?

Just a feeling. I thought I saw somebody.

What do you mean?

I don't know. Just a feeling.

You saw somebody? Here? Tonight?

I'm not even sure.

But here?

No. The past couple of days. Just a feeling.

Silence.

Then:

I don't want to get caught, Rita.

We won't get caught.

I don't want to.

We won't.

A deep sigh. Silence.

Matthew listened.

How much time have we got?

The woman. No answer from Nettington.

Dan?

Mmm.

What are you doing there?

Looking.

At what?

That car across the street. Was it here when I got here?

What car?

Across the street.

What kind of car?

I can't tell from here.

Well, what color is it?

Blue? Green? Come take a look.

I don't want to take a look.

Does anybody across the street own a blue car? Or a green one?

I don't know what they own. What time do you have to leave?

I've got an hour or so.

Then come here.

Silence.

The tape unreeled.

There were only sounds on it now.

Harsh breathing.

Rita moaning.

And at last:

Oh, Jesus, *give* it to me!

And she screamed.

And the tape ended.

3

At three o'clock that Monday afternoon, the Cubans who'd been looking for Alice Carmody finally found her. One of the Cubans asked her, "Where's Jody?" but his accent was so thick that Alice didn't know who he meant at first. She said, "*Who?*" and he smacked her.

She thought Boy, what a shame it is, these fucking spics taking over Miami Beach, next thing you know they'll be taking over Kansas. She didn't even know where Kansas was. She was in a cheap hotel on Collins and Sixth, that's where Alice was when they found her. Alice was a junkie, and she hadn't had a fix since ten o'clock this morning, and they were asking her questions she couldn't understand, these two fuckin' spics.

"You seest'," one of them said.

"*What?*" Alice said.

"*Tu hermana,*" the other one said.

Alice gathered he didn't speak English, the other one. Fuckin' spic, she thought, and he smacked her, as if he could

33

read her mind. He said something in rapid-fire Spanish to the one who spoke English. Must've been three thousand words he spewed at him, but all Alice caught was the name Ernesto. She figured the one who spoke English—not that he'd get a prize, but at least it was English—was named Ernesto. The greaseball she didn't know his name yet.

Ernesto said, "Listen, okay?"

"I'm listening," she said.

"Wha' we *wann* to *know* ees *where* ees you seest'."

"My *what?*" she said.

"You seest', you seest'," he said, patiently.

"Oh," Alice said.

"Ah," he said.

"My *sister*, you mean?"

"Ah," he said, and spread his arms wide to the greaseball.

"Which sister?" Alice said. "I got two. One's in Orlando, the other's in L.A."

Ernesto smacked her again.

"*Here*," he said, "Miami. Never mine nowheres else."

"I got no sister here in Miami," she said.

This time the greaseball smacked her. They were taking turns smacking her.

"Listen," she said, "stop hitting me, okay? Who the fuck are you? What right do you have . . . ?"

One of them smacked her again, she didn't know which one.

"Listen," Ernesto said. "You unnerstan' English?"

What a fuckin' question, she thought. Coming from him. She just looked at him.

"Okay," he said. "You got a sister, she's a blonde, she's here in Miami, and we want to know *where*, okay, 'cause we got to find her, okay? So—you want your teeth knocked out, or you want to tell us?"

She was beginning to understand him. All at once, it sounded as if he was talking almost perfect English. Even "seest'" sounded like "sister."

"Oh, you mean *Jenny*," she said.

Ernesto looked at the fucking greaseball. "Domingo?" he said. "*Se llama Jenny?*"

The greaseball shrugged. Domingo. A fuckin' dance team, she had here. Ernesto and Domingo.

"We're talking about a girl named Jody," Ernesto said, "we know she's your sister, so where is she?"

"That's a name she uses," Alice said.

"What name?"

"Jody. But Jenny's her real name. But you won't find her under Jenny, either, 'cause she uses a lot of different names."

The two men looked at her.

Ernesto nodded at Domingo.

Domingo took a switchblade knife from his pocket and snapped it open.

"So what's that supposed to be?" Alice asked, but all at once she was scared.

"Jenny *what*?" Ernesto said.

"That depends. You want her square handle or the hundred other names she's been using? Her last name ain't the same as mine, you know, she's my step—"

Ernesto smacked her.

"*Por favor*," he said patiently and pleasantly. "No bullshit."

"She's my fuckin' *step*sister! Listen, you smack me one more time—"

He smacked her one more time. Her lip split open. Blood spilled onto her blouse. She thought, Boy.

"Listen," he said. "You want to get cut?"

"No," she said. Like a little girl. Looking at the knife in Domingo's fuckin' fist. Eyes wide. "No," she said again.

"Okay." Pause. "Jenny, Jody, whoever." Pause. "Your sister."

"Yes." Eyes still wide, entire face attentive.

"Her last name is *not* Carmody?"

"She was born Santoro," Alice said quickly, "that was my stepfather's name, Santoro, Dominick Santoro, he was a big contractor here in Miami, ask anybody. The Santoro Brothers? That was my stepfather."

"*Es Latino?*" Ernesto said. "Santoro? *Es un nombre Latino?* He's Spanish, your stepfather?"

"No, Italian," Alice said. "My mother's Italian, maybe that's why she married him when my father died, who knows? My father was Irish," she said proudly. And immediately thought, My father would kill me if he knew I was doing drugs. But her father was dead.

"Jenny Santoro," Ernesto said, trying the name for size. Even though she could understand his English now, it still came out "Henny," as if he was clearing his throat to spit.

"Yes," Alice said, nodding, eager to please. "That's what she was when she came to us. That was her father's name, a wop, and he married my mother, but me and my sister didn't take the name, we kept our own names. So that's the story. I'm Alice Carmody, and my sister is Kate Carmody, and Jenny is Jenny Santoro, but sometimes she calls herself Jody Carmody. So now you got what you want, right?"

"Where is she?" Ernesto said.

"Jenny? She's in L.A.," Alice said. "I told you."

"No," he said.

"I'm telling you that's where she is," Alice said.

"You're full of shit," Ernesto said, and nodded at Domingo, and Domingo cut her.

Not a serious cut. Just a touch with the blade. Feather light, burning for an instant, and then wetness on her cheek, her hand coming up to touch the wetness, fingers coming away red, and all at once she felt a loosening of her bowels and thought she had soiled herself.

"Listen," she said.

They looked at her.

There was blood on the knife blade.

"Listen, really," she said. "Jenny's a hooker, the last time I heard she was in L.A., I mean it. If she's back here in Florida, this is the first I'm hearing, I mean it. I talked to my sister yesterday, she didn't mention nothing about Jenny being back, either. So, I mean it, I'm telling you the truth, put away the fucking knife, okay? I'm telling you the truth. I swear to God. Put away the knife, okay?"

Domingo did not put away the knife. He kept looking at her. There was a very sad expression on his face, as if it had pained him to cut her.

"Please put it away," she said. "Okay? Please? You make me nervous with that knife, I mean it."

"You want to get cut again?" Ernesto said.

"No," she said quickly, "no, I don't. Really." She put her hands up defensively, fingers widespread, palms out. "Really, you don't have to cut me," she said.

"We don't want to cut you again," Ernesto said.

"I know you don't," she said, "So don't, okay?"

"Where is she?" Ernesto said.

"I don't know where she is, I mean it," Alice said. "If she's in Florida, that's news to me. Look, if I knew where she was I'd tell you in a minute, why wouldn't I? I never liked her, I'd tell you in a minute. I just don't know, that's the truth. So, guys, you know, I'm supposed to meet somebody, I'm late now, I'm overdue, you know what I mean? So if we're finished here . . ."

"The sister in Orlando," Ernesto said. "Where?"

"Aw, come on, guys," Alice said.

"Her address," Ernesto said.

"*She* don't know, either," Alice said. "You don't want to bother her."

"Cut her," he said to Domingo.

"No, don't!" Alice said. "She lives near Disney World, I'll get you the address, I've got it in my book, put the knife away, okay?"

"Get the address," Ernesto said.

David Larkin didn't like fags. They made him nervous. He always suspected they were trying to touch him. Or stand too close to him. He believed all the stories people told about homosexuals, that if you didn't watch your eight-year-old son, they would take down his pants and bugger him. He believed there was a great homosexual conspiracy to turn the whole world gay. Homosexuals were worse than Communists in that respect.

The worst thing about Larkin's fears was that he could never be absolutely sure who was gay and who wasn't. He'd get a bead on some guy he thought was a fairy, and next thing you knew he'd see the guy in a restaurant and the guy was with a gorgeous blonde whose tits were spilling out the front of her dress. Down here, the girls wore next to nothing, it drove a man crazy. It was Florida did it to them. The sun boiled their brains, they right away ripped off all their clothes.

Once, Larkin met a guy he thought was as straight as an arrow, tried to fix him up with a girl who would fuck a sea slug, the guy said, "Thanks, I dress to the right." Meaning he wore his cock on the right-hand side of his pants. Meaning he was a fairy. Not that all fairies wore their cocks that way, this was just the guy's way of speaking. At least, Larkin didn't *think* they wore their cocks that way, he sure as hell didn't *know*. But maybe they did. Maybe that was a way all the fairies of the world had of identifying each other, the way they dressed their cocks, right or left. Who the hell knew? It was all very complicated.

Vincent Hollister was a fag, no doubt about that. This was only the third time he'd cut Larkin's hair—well, he'd only been working here at Unicorn since the beginning of April— but Larkin knew definitely that Hollister was a fag. Still, he was the kind of fag Larkin could get along with. Not the flouncy type, you know? Not mincing. No limp wrist. Talked like anybody would, no lisp. Dressed like a normal human being. No jeans tight across the buns. A very interesting person, too. The things he talked about were very interesting. Like which hotel to stay at in Positano, Italy. Or where to buy good amber in London, England. Also, if he'd been a woman, Vincent had what a man would consider a very pretty mouth. Larkin wondered if he ever dressed up like a woman. He wondered what fairies did when they got together, other than blow each other and fuck each other in the ass. He was almost tempted to ask. He felt he knew Vincent well enough to ask. But then Vincent might take it the wrong way. You never knew with fags.

"So," Vincent said, "what have you been up to?"

"Oh, I been busy," Larkin said.

"Always busy, busy, busy," Vincent said and smiled, and began combing out Larkin's hair, his eyes on each separate strand as it passed through the comb, searching each strand the way Larkin's mother used to search her fine tooth comb when he was a kid growing up in New York City. Larkin was fifty-three years old. When he was growing up, you'd go to school in the morning, come back that afternoon with a head full of lice. His mother used to fine comb his hair, looking for nits. Every time she found a nit, she'd squash it against the comb with her thumbnail. Vincent was maybe twenty-six, twenty-seven years old, he didn't know about nits. Christ knew why he studied the hair that way.

Maybe it was an act.

Make the customer think you were paying great attention to the way the hair fell or whatever. Fags were great actors. In fact, some of the best actors in the world were fags. It always came as a shock when somebody told Larkin this or that actor was a fag. Last month sometime it must've been, he told this girl he had in bed with him—she was nineteen years old, this juicy little girl down from Atlanta, ass like a brewer's horse and an appetite for coke that was astonishing—he told her Burt Reynolds was a fag. She almost started crying. She should have realized he was lying, Burt Reynolds used to have that big thing going with Dinah Shore, didn't he? And then Sally Field. So unless every woman in Hollywood was a beard, then how could Burt Reynolds be a fag? Her eyes going big and round, misting over, he really thought she was going to start crying. Hey, I was only kidding, he said. It's Clint Eastwood who's the fag. Had to smile even now, just thinking of it.

"What's comical?" Vincent asked.

"Oh, just remembering something," Larkin said. "Just remembering something."

In Miami Beach, Domingo thought Alice Carmody wasn't getting the address fast enough to suit him.

He cut her again, on the arm this time.

She said, "Hey, come on, I'm dancin' as fast as I can."

A minute later, while she was opening the top drawer of the dresser across the room, he cut her again, over the eye this time. She said, "Shit, what's the matter with you?" and angrily threw her address book on the dresser top and stamped off into the bathroom to get a towel. There were only two rooms, the bathroom and the other room with the daybed and the dresser in it. As she turned on the water in the sink, Ernesto and Domingo began talking in Spanish about whether or not they had to kill her. It was Ernesto's contention that Domingo had now cut her a few more times than were necessary to scare her, and she might go to the police once they were gone. Alice didn't know what they were talking about out there, jabbering away in Spanish. She was trying to stop the flow of blood from the cut over her left eye. It didn't occur to her for a minute that they might try to kill her. She had already given them her sister's address, hadn't she? All she was thinking was that she had to get out of there fast because her connection sure as hell wasn't going to wait on Collins Avenue and Lincoln Road forever.

In the other room, they decided they had to kill her.

When she came out of the bathroom with a Band-Aid over her left eyebrow, Domingo had the knife in his hand again. There was a funny look on his face.

Ernesto was standing just inside the door to the apartment, blocking it. He had a funny look, too.

She ran right back into the bathroom, and locked the door.

It was very quiet out there.

All she could hear was the sound of her own heart.

And then, all at once, they began whispering in Spanish.

What she had to do was get the bathroom window open. Get through it and jump down to the street. She was on the second floor, she knew she'd hurt herself if she jumped, but not as much as they were going to hurt her if she didn't. The lock on the door was one of those push-button things on the knob, a Mickey Mouse lock, they could kick open the door in a minute if they wanted to. She figured if they hadn't done it already they were afraid it would make too much noise. She once had a dealer kick in her door because she owed him money, man, it woke up the whole building. So she figured that's why they weren't doing it. Just whispering outside there in Spanish instead.

The window was painted shut.

She looked around for something she could work the paint with.

Nothing.

She looked around for something she could smash the window with. She had to get the fuck *out* of there!

Nothing.

She heard a sound at the door behind her.

A scraping sound.

They were trying to loid the door. They were sliding a credit card between the doorjamb and the door, working the spring lock, trying to force back the bolt with the card. She picked up the towel she'd used earlier to stanch the flow of blood over her eye. She wrapped the towel around her right hand. She hit out at the window with it, smashing the glass, and just then the door behind her opened. She screamed even before she turned.

Domingo was standing there with the knife in his hand.

Hair fell on Larkin's shoulders, on the faded blue smock they gave you when you came in, it was impossible to figure out how to tie the thing, you had to be a magician. Same kind of smock they gave the women on the other side of the salon. He wondered if Vincent ever wore women's clothes. Some of these fairies, Larkin bet they dressed up like girls when they were alone together. Wore lipstick and everything. Larkin looked at himself in the mirror and wondered how his mouth would look with lipstick on it. Brown hair, dark eyes, wide forehead, prominent nose, strong mouth—an overall impression of rough-hewn good looks. Put lipstick on that mouth, it'd be like painting a gorilla's toenails. Vincent's face was more delicate. A pale oval. Hazel eyes. High cheekbones. The pouting feminine mouth. Black hair done like a fairy's, though, that was the clue.

"Been hot enough for you?" Larkin asked.

"Please," Vincent said, and rolled his eyes. "Don't ask." *Sounded* like a fag, too, sometimes.

"You still plan on going to Europe this summer?"

"I may leave Calusa permanently," Vincent said.

"Oh? How come?"

"Just tired of it."

"Where would you go? You just *got* here."

"Oh, I don't know."

(In Miami Beach at that moment, a medical examiner leaning over the body of the blood-smeared woman lying on the bathroom floor ventured the learned opinion that she was the victim of multiple stab and slash wounds and that the cause of death was severance of the carotid artery.)

"Profession like yours, you can settle anywhere, I guess."

"Oh, sure."

"Just take a pair of scissors with you," Larkin said, and smiled.

"Sure. Actually, though, I may leave the business altogether. I just don't know yet."

"Quit being a barber?" Larkin said.

"A stylist, yes," Vincent said.

"What would you do?"

"Live the good life," Vincent said. "Become a degenerate. Who knows?"

"Takes money to live the good life," Larkin said.

"Well . . . I've saved a bit," Vincent said.

"Where would you go?"

"Asia maybe," Vincent said.

Larkin could just imagine him in Asia. Bunch of hairless Chinese fags smoking dope, Vincent in the middle of them wearing a long blue gown, ice-blue gown like the one Cinderella was wearing at the Jacaranda Ball. He could never get used to saying it the way the Cubans did—Hacaranda. To him it was Jack be nimble, Jack be quick, Jack Aranda. Listen, what's in a name? His own maiden name was David Largura. All his wop cousins had names like Salvatore and Silvio and Ignazio and Umberto, his mother comes up with David, a Jewish name. Largura meant "space" in Italian. Changed it to Larkin back, oh, thirty years ago must've been. You called him Mr. Largura now, he wouldn't know who the fuck you meant. He'd been Larkin longer than he'd been Largura.

How do you do, my name is David Larkin.

Hi. I'm Angela West.

Want to have your picture taken, Angela?

Sure, why not?

"Sri Lanka," Vincent said. "Or Goa. Or Bali in the South Pacific. Lots of places a person can go."

(In Miami Beach at that moment an ambulance was carting away the body of the knifing victim. A man picking his teeth outside the hotel said the lady who got juked was Alice Carmody, the junkie who lived in 2A.)

"Lots of places to go if you've got the money," Larkin said.

Want to come home with me, Angela?

Sure, why not?

All so simple. Gorgeous girl in her twenties, he's fifty-three, it never occurs to him she might be a pro. Well, listen, he kept himself in good shape, jogged on the beach, worked out at Nautilus. He'd even been to bed with *teenagers* who said he looked terrific, *two* of them together one time, took care of them both very nicely, thank you, no complaints. *Pizzichi e baci non fanno buchi*—his mother used to say that. It meant you could kiss and pinch all you wanted, it wouldn't leave scars. *Pizzichi e baci no fanno buchi*. Wrong, Mama.

Want your picture taken? Sure, why not? Watch the birdie, click, click, click.

Want to come home with me? Sure, why not? Pinches and kisses. But plenty of scars later, Mama. *Molti buchi*.

Angela West, my ass.

Catch up with her, he'd give her Angela West.

"Or Thailand," Vincent said. "Lots of places."

As Vincent's scissors snipped away, the men continued talking about Asia. Neither of them had ever been there, and they were full of speculations about it.

In Miami at about that time, Ernesto and Domingo were just entering the Sunshine State Parkway, driving a red Chrysler LeBaron convertible on their way north to Orlando.

Domingo confessed that he had found Alice Carmody quite charming and attractive. What he said, actually, was "*Me gustaría culiarla.*"

4

During the summer months, the weather forecasts in Calusa were the same day after day after day. Temperature in the nineties. Humidity in the nineties. Showers in the afternoon. Clearing before evening. Temperature in the nineties again. Humidity the same as it was before the showers. There was, Matthew supposed, something to be said for dependability. On the other hand, there was nothing quite so boring as predictability.

He had put on a tan tropical-weight suit when he'd left for the office that Tuesday morning. By two o'clock that afternoon, as he started the drive out to Sabal Key from downtown Calusa, the suit was rumpled and limp. He drove with the windows of the Karmann Ghia closed tight, the air-conditioning up full blast. To his left was the Gulf of Mexico, the water still green under broken clouds close to shore, the sky much darker to the west where thunderheads were already building. By three, three-thirty—four at the very latest—it would rain.

Visitors, of which there were only a handful during the summer months, always thought the rain would mean a break in the humidity.

He had already driven past most of the Gulfside condos; the remainder of Sabal Key, running northward, was virtually as wild as when it had been inhabited by the Calusa and Timicua tribes of Indians back in the good old days. Flanked on the west by the Gulf and on the east by Calusa Bay, the key here at the northern end narrowed to a tangle of mangrove and pine and sabal palm in which only a few isolated houses nestled. Carla Nettington lived in one of those houses.

A woman in her thirties, not spectacularly beautiful—what a discreet journalist might have called "handsome"—she had come to the offices of Summerville and Hope on the twenty-third of May, elegantly dressed, slender and tall, somewhat flat-chested, and wearing a telltale sorrowful look that had nothing to do with preparing a will. There had been something very old-fashioned, almost Victorian, about Carla Nettington. At the time, Matthew had found it difficult to visualize her in a swimsuit.

She was, nonetheless, wearing a swimsuit when he arrived at the house that afternoon. She expected him, he had called first. In fact, she had told him on the phone that she'd probably be out back. Matthew rang the front doorbell. When he got no answer, he started around back, past a garden lush with red bougainvillea and yellow hibiscus. As he came around the corner of the house, Carla rose from a lounge chair and walked toward him with her hand extended.

The swimsuit was a black bikini, a bit more than nothing in its bra top, its black panty bottom snugly brief below her angular hips. She looked tall and leggy, her skin very white against the patches of black, the whiteness totally unexpected here in Florida, a stark paleness of flesh that caused her to appear somehow fragile and vulnerable and inexplicably sexy. He had not supposed she would look more exciting with her clothes off than she had with them on. With most women, in fact, the opposite was usually the case. But undeniably sexy she was, in spite of her virtually adolescent figure, the angular hips and collarbones, a coltish look—well, boyish to be more exact—dark hair cut close to her narrow face, eyes hidden behind overly large sunglasses, no lipstick on her generous mouth, lips wide in a smile now as she came closer.

"Mr. Hope," she said, "how nice to see you."

Her voice was somewhat husky, a cigarette-smoker's voice, or a drinker's, he couldn't tell which.

She took his hand.

"I hope this isn't a bad time for you," he said.

"No, no, not at all. Well, as you can see, I was just sitting here reading." She released his hand and gestured languidly to the lounge chair she had just vacated, and to the magazines strewn on the table beside it. A pitcher of lemonade and an ice bucket were on the table. Two empty glasses, both upside down, rested on a tray beside the bucket.

"Some lemonade?" she asked.

"Please," he said.

She filled both glasses with ice cubes. She poured lemonade. All angles in the sun. Black and white and yellow in the yellow sunshine. His shirt and jacket were sticking to him. She handed him one of the glasses. He waited for her to fill her own glass.

"Please sit down," she said.

He sat on the chaise beside hers. They sipped at the lemonade. A pelican swooped in low over the mangroves, settled on the water. The pool was a rippled blue under a patchy blue sky, the patio and pool ending at the line of mangroves, the bayou water beyond that a grayish green. In the distance, the storm clouds were closer. There was the smell of rain in the air. But the sun was lingering, if tentatively, for yet a little while. She crossed one ankle over the other, white on white.

"So," she said, "has your man learned anything?"

All business now. She had not known the name of the private investigator he'd hired; she had come to him specifically to *avoid* personal contact with such a scurrilous breed. Ergo, she did not know that the man he'd hired was dead, the victim of gunshot wounds inflicted on a hot summer night, though the eighth day of June couldn't be considered summertime except in the state of Florida. In the state of Florida, summertime sometimes came at the end of April. In the state of Florida, violent death sometimes came, too, and it had come on Sunday night to a nice guy named Otto Samalson who smoked too damn much, and coughed a lot, but who did a good job. "Your man," she had called him. Matthew wasn't so sure Otto would have enjoyed being called *anybody's* man. If nothing else, Otto was his *own* man.

"My *man*," Matthew said, "is dead."

"What?" she said, and took off the sunglasses.

She'd been wearing sunglasses on the day she came to the office, hadn't taken the glasses off during her entire visit. Her face had looked long and sorrowful, the glasses adding a further dimension of mournfulness, black against her pale white skin, as impenetrable as a crypt. On the day of her visit, she had told Matthew that her husband was forty-five years old, and he had assumed she was in her mid- to late-thirties. Her eyes, revealed now, were a glade green, youthful and alive with intelligence, easily her best feature. Without the glasses, she seemed a decade younger. The adolescent body now seemed entirely appropriate.

"He was shot to death on the Tamiami Trail," Matthew said. A blank stare from her. "This past Sunday night," he said. "A man named Otto Samalson." The green gaze un-wavering. "You may have read about it in the papers. Or seen it on television."

"No," she said.

"In any event, he's dead," Matthew said.

"I'm sorry to hear that," she said, and then, almost at once, "Does this mean I'll have to find another detective?"

Me, me, me. Matthew thought, how does this affect *me*? Does Otto Samalson's untimely and inconsiderate demise mean I will now have to seek the services of *another* private detective, equally faceless and anonymous?

He almost sighed.

"If you feel you still want one," he said.

"Well, if the man is *dead* . . ."

"He is dead, yes, Mrs. Nettington."

"Then how can we continue . . . ?"

"I'd already had a report from him, Mrs. Nettington. And yesterday I heard a tape that—"

"Why didn't you tell me this?" she said. "When did you have this report?"

"Late Friday afternoon."

"And you didn't call me?"

"Otto was making a duplicate copy of the tape. I thought I'd wait till—"

"What tape? What do you mean?"

"Otto was able to plant a recorder . . ."

"Who is she?" Carla said at once. "Who's the woman?"

"Someone named Rita Kirkman."

The same blank green-eyed stare again. The name meant nothing to her.

"She lives in Harbor Acres," Matthew said. "That's where the tape was made. In her home there."

"Where is it?" Carla said. "I want to hear it."

"The tape? In Otto's office. The police—"

"You don't have it with you?"

"No, I don't. The police are investigating a homicide, Mrs. Nettington—"

"You mean the *police* will be listening to that tape?"

"There's a good possibility of that, yes."

"Oh God," she said. "What's on it?"

"Everything you wanted," Matthew said.

"When can I hear it?"

"I'll check with the police. I'm sure—"

"I wish the goddamn *police* weren't in this," she said.

"Yes, it's unfortunate that Otto was killed," Matthew said dryly.

She looked at him, uncertain whether sarcasm had been intended.

"Was your husband home on Sunday night?" he asked.

She hesitated.

"Mrs. Nettington?"

She put the sunglasses on.

"I don't know," she said. "I was out myself. I went to a movie with a girlfriend."

"You didn't call home at any time Sunday night? From the theater? Or anyplace else?"

"No."

"Then you don't know whether your husband was here or not?"

"I'm sorry. I don't."

"What time did you get home, Mrs. Nettington?"

"At a little past midnight. We stopped for a drink."

"You didn't try calling your husband from where you were, did you? The bar, or the restaurant, or wherever."

"We were at Marina Lou's. No, I didn't."

"Was your husband here when you got home?"

51

"Yes, he was in bed. Asleep."

"But you have no idea if he was here all night or if he—"

"No."

"What movie did you see?"

"*Dr. Zhivago*. For the fifth time," she said, and smiled. "They're showing it again at the Festival."

"Up on the North Trail?"

"Yes."

"Good movie," he said.

"Very romantic," she said.

"Yes," he said.

There was a long silence.

"Mrs. Nettington," he said, "do you think your husband *knew* he was being followed?"

"I have no idea."

"He didn't say anything to you about it, did he?"

"Nothing."

"Didn't accuse you of hiring—"

"No."

"Didn't *hint* that he knew—"

"No, nothing like that," she said, and then, in sudden realization, "You're asking exactly what *they'll* ask, aren't you? Daniel will be a *suspect* in this, won't he? Because he was being *followed* by the man who was killed!" She swung her long legs over the side of the chaise, facing him now, lips compressed in a tight angry line, sunglasses reflecting the approaching storm clouds, towers of storm clouds hiding her green eyes, a cool wind blowing in suddenly off the bayou. "They'll ask Daniel where he was Sunday night, and Daniel will want to know *why* they want to know, and they'll have to tell him that a private investigator was killed, and my husband will ask what a private investigator has to do with *him*, and they'll say he was being followed by this man who was killed, your wife *hired* this man to follow you—and there goes my goddamn marriage down the drain!"

"Mrs. Nettington," Matthew said, "I thought the reason you came to me—"

"Not because I wanted *this* to happen!"

"But . . . you told me . . . I'm sorry, but you said you were thinking of a divorce. You said that if your husband was in *fact*—"

"Never mind!" she said sharply.

Matthew almost flinched.

"Forget it," she said. "Thank you very much, Mr. Hope, please send me your man's report, *and* the tape, and of course your bill."

He looked at her, still puzzled.

"Go now, would you? Leave me alone, okay?"

"Mrs. Nettington . . ."

"Would you please *go*?" she said.

Two men were sitting in Kate Carmody's living room when she got home from work that Tuesday afternoon. Both of them Hispanic. One of them clean-shaven and as slender as a toreador, the other one a huge man with a slick little mustache. The clean-shaven one was reading a copy of *People* when she came in. The one with the pencil-line mustache was cleaning his fingernails with a switchblade knife. Kate took one look and turned to run out of the apartment.

The one with the knife was off the couch in a wink.

He grabbed her shoulder, spun her away from the door, hu...ed her back across the room, and closed and locked the door. The other one put down the magazine and said, "Miss

Carmody?" Heavy Spanish accent. She immediately thought *Miami*. She next thought *Alice*. This had something to do with her dumb junkie sister in Miami.

"What do you want?" she said. "Who are you?"

"Ernesto," he said, smiling. And then, indicating his pal, "Domingo."

The one with the knife said nothing, and he didn't smile, either. He was the one who bothered her.

"So what do you want here?" she said. She was frightened—two strange spics in her house, a knife that looked like a saber—but she was also annoyed. Come home after a day with Mickey Mouse, you wanted to grab a beer, change into some shorts and sandals. She was living in this really tiny place—closet-sized living room, kitchen too small even for roaches, a bedroom the size of a shoebox—six miles from Disney World, where she worked as a ticket taker for Jungle Cruise. She did not like working for Disney World, and she didn't like Orlando, Florida, either, but she kept telling herself this was only temporary. Florida was supposed to be water and boats, not the middle of a damn desert like Orlando. Wasn't for Disney World, nobody would've ever heard of Orlando. Orlando sounded like some kind of magician doing tricks in a sideshow. And *now*, ladies and germs, we are proud to introduce the *Great* Or-*lan*-do! Plus his two assistants, Ernesto and Domingo, who will show you how to break and enter a small apartment without using brute force. "How'd you get in here?" she asked Ernesto.

"Jenny Santoro," he said. "Your sister."

Accent you could cut with a machete. Jenny came out "Henny" and sister came out "seest'."

"What about her?" Kate said. "Jenny, you mean? What about her?"

"Where is she?"

"How the hell do I know?" she said, and was starting to walk into the kitchen when Domingo stepped into her path.

"I'm only going for a beer," she said. "You want a beer? *Una cerveza,*" she said. "You want one?" She turned to Ernesto. "How about you? You want a beer?"

"I want to know where your sister is. Jenny Santoro. That is her name?"

"Give or take," Kate said, thinking Jenny, Henny, six of one, half a dozen of the other. She went to the refrigerator, opened the door, took out a bottle of Bud, twisted off the cap, and drank straight from the bottle. "And she's not my *sister,* she's my *step*sister. *Mi hermana política.*"

Not many Anglos knew the Spanish word for stepsister. Ernesto looked at her admiringly and then said, "*Usted habla español correctamente.*"

"I picked some up in Puerto Rico," Kate said in English—no sense showing off and making mistakes. "I used to be a cocktail waitress in a casino down there."

Ernesto nodded. Domingo was looking her over, appraising her legs, her ass, her breasts, his eyes roaming insolently. Ernesto hoped Domingo wouldn't cut her the way he had the other one. He was thinking she had no idea her sister was dead. Maybe this could be useful, her ignorance. He didn't know how yet, but he thought perhaps it could be.

"You have two sisters, *verdad?*" he said, testing her.

"Two," she said, nodding. "But only one of them's my *real* sister. *Mi propia hermana.* Alice. She lives in Miami Beach. The other one, I don't know where she is. Last I heard, it was L.A. Why?" she said, and looked first at one and then at the other.

"We have to find your *hermana política,*" Ernesto said.

"That's the one in L.A. Have you tried L.A.?" she asked, making a joke—L.A. was so far away—but nobody smiled. "I haven't seen her in six years, it has to be. She left Miami when she was sixteen, went to New Orleans, I heard, and then Houston, and then L.A. is what my mother told me. *Seven* years, in fact."

"Where does your mother live?" Ernesto asked.

"In Venice."

The two men looked at each other.

"Not Venice, *Italy*," Kate said. "Venice, *Florida*. Near Sarasota. About fifteen, twenty miles south of Sarasota."

"Does *she* know where your sister is?"

"Jenny? I got no idea."

"But she was the one who told you Jenny was in Los Angeles, *verdad*?"

"Yes," she said. He pronounced it so pretty. *Los Angeles*. The Spanish way. *Los* to rhyme with "gross," the first syllable of *Angeles* sounding like "ahn," all of it so pretty. But the other one had a knife.

"Did she also tell you when your sister was in Houston?"

"I guess it was her told me, yes," Kate said.

"Your mother, *verdad*?"

"Yes."

"Whose name is?"

"Annie."

"Carmody?"

"No, Santoro. She remarried. I told you, Jenny's my—"

"And she lives where? Your mother?"

"I told you where."

"Venice, you said."

"Yes."

"Do you have the address?"

"Yes," she said.

"Will you give it to me, please?" Ernesto said.

Kate looked at the knife in Domingo's hand.

56

"Yes," she said, and went into the bedroom for her address book.

Ernesto gestured with his head for Domingo to follow her. Domingo went into the bedroom. The telephone was on the bedside night table, and Kate was sitting on the edge of the bed, leafing through her address book when he came into the room. The telephone rang as he walked through the door. Without once thinking they might not want her to answer the phone, she picked up the receiver.

"Hello?" she said.

Domingo came across the room at once.

"Katie?"

"Yes?"

He was standing in front of her now.

"It's Mother."

"Oh, hi, Mom," she said, and covered the mouthpiece. "My mother," she said to Domingo. She uncovered the mouthpiece and was about to say that two men were here asking for her address when her mother said, "Alice is dead."

"What?" she said.

"Alice. She was killed yesterday in Miami Beach."

"Oh my God!" Kate said.

"She was stabbed," her mother said, and suddenly the phone was trembling in Kate's hand. "The police called me five minutes ago. Took them all that time to locate me. Because my name is different, you know? My last name. They think it was drug-related. They really don't know, Katie. They see an addict, they automatically figure drug-related."

"Oh God, Mom," Kate said.

She got up suddenly, moving away from Domingo, trying to find some room for herself in the narrow space between the bed and the wall, Domingo still there crowding her, the open knife in his right hand.

"I have to go to Miami to identify the body," her mother said. "Can you meet me there?"

"When?" Kate asked.

Domingo was watching her, listening to her end of the conversation.

"I thought I'd drive over there tonight. They're holding her body in the morgue, they need a positive ID."

"I . . . uh . . . I don't know, Mom. I have to go to work tomorrow, tomorrow's a workday. If you can handle it alone . . ."

"This is your *sister*," her mother said.

"I know she's my sister . . ."

Domingo looked suddenly alert.

"So?" her mother said.

"I'll have to call you back later," Kate said.

"I'm going to need help with the funeral arrangements, too."

"Let me see what I can do about work, okay, Mom? Can I call you back?"

"I won't be leaving for a while yet."

"All right, I'll get back to you," she said, and put the receiver back on the cradle.

Ernesto was standing in the doorway to the room. She wondered how long he'd been there.

"Your mother?" he said.

"Yes."

"What did she want?"

Kate hesitated.

"Yes?" Ernesto said.

"She . . . she . . ."

"*Le contó de su hermana*," Domingo said.

"No, she didn't!" Kate said.

58

"*Did* she tell you about your sister?" Ernesto asked. "That your sister is dead?"

Kate said nothing. If they *knew* her sister was dead . . . oh my God, if they *knew* . . .

Ernesto sighed deeply, and nodded to Domingo.

Kate broke for the door, screaming, tripping over Domingo's immediately extended leg and foot, falling headlong across the room, twisting so she wouldn't land square on her face, her left cheek nonetheless colliding with the floor. Pain rocketed into her skull but she started to get to her feet at once, coming up like a runner, palms flat on the floor, legs behind her and ready to push off, ready to propel her toward that bedroom door and into the living room, and out the front door and down the stairs to the street, screaming all the way. But Domingo jumped on her back and knocked her to the floor again, straddling her like a rider on a fallen animal, his left hand grabbing for her long hair, twisting it in his fist, pulling back on it, head and chin rising, his right hand—the hand with the knife—coming around her body instantly and slashing swiftly across her throat.

Her eyes opened wide.

She saw blood gushing from her throat in a torrent.

A scream bubbled soundlessly in her mouth.

In an instant, she was dead.

Domingo wiped the blade of his knife on her skirt, and then ran his hand up her thigh to her panties. Ernesto watched him and said nothing. He tore the page with Anne Santoro's address and phone number from the address book, and then walked toward the bedroom door.

"*Vienes?*" he asked.

Domingo nodded.

5

At ten o'clock on Wednesday morning, Matthew remembered that he had to call Susan about the Father's Day weekend. He did not much feel like making this particular call. On his desk were copies of the two files he had Xeroxed at Otto Samalson's office on Monday. Matthew wanted to read those files more thoroughly than he had yesterday, when he'd only briefly glanced through them. He had asked Cynthia Huellen, the firm's factotum, not to put through any calls. But now he was about to make one. To Susan. Who, on Sunday night, had left his bedroom in a huff.

Years ago, when there were still some laughs left in their marriage, he and Susan had defined a "huff" as a "small two-wheeled carriage." A person who went off in a huff was therefore a somewhat lower-class individual who could not afford to hire or own a "high dudgeon." A high dudgeon was one of those big old expensive four-wheelers. A person who went off in "high dudgeon" was usually quite well off. A person who was in a "tizzy," however, was truly rich since a tizzy was a luxurious coach drawn by a great team of horses to a stately mansion called "Sixes and Sevens." All at Sixes and Sevens were in a tizzy save for Tempest, the youngest daughter, who was in a "teapot." A teapot was even smaller than a huff, about the size of a cart, but fitted with a striped parasol that . . .

And so it had gone.

In the days when their marriage was still alive.

These days, their marriage was as dead as old Aunt Hattie, who had left Sixes and Sevens in a "trice," which was a flat-bedded vehicle used to transport coffins. Dead and gone. Like all things mortal. Which is why he had no burning desire to talk to Susan today. But place the call he did. Dialed the number by heart—used to be *his* number, after all—dialed all seven numerals, and waited. Listened to the ringing on the other end. Waited. Five . . . six . . . seven . . . all at Sixes and Sevens . . .

"Hello?"

Susan's voice.

"Susan, hi, it's Matthew."

"Matthew! I was just about to call you!"

"I wanted to discuss arrangements for the weekend," he said. Business as usual. Forget the foolish hugging and kissing on Sunday. "You do remember it's . . . ?"

"Father's Day, yes, of course," she said. "But, Matthew, first I want to apologize for Sunday night."

"There's no need."

"I'm so ashamed, I could die."

"Well, really . . ."

"That's why I was calling," she said. "To apologize. I'm genuinely sorry, Matthew."

"So am I," he said, and guessed he meant it.

"Walking out," she said. "Dumb. Just plain dumb." She hesitated and then said, "Just when it was getting good, too."

There was a sudden silence on the line.

Matthew cleared his throat.

"Uh, Susan," he said, "about the weekend . . ."

"Yes, the weekend," Susan said. "Here's what I thought, if it's okay with you. Can you pick her up here at about five on Friday?"

"Sure, that'll—"

"And if you have a little time, maybe you can come in for a drink."

Another silence on the line.

"Yes, I'd like that," Matthew said.

"So would I," Susan said.

"So . . . Friday at five, right?"

"Right. See you then. And Matthew . . . ?"

"Yes?"

Her voice lowered. "It really *was* getting good."

There was a small click on the line.

It sounded like a maiden's blush.

Smiling, he put the receiver back on the cradle and pulled the first of the two folders to him. Both folders had been labeled here at the office yesterday morning, after he'd given the photocopied pages to Cynthia. Both folders contained Otto's standard contract form, signed by himself and the party or parties hiring him, stapled to which was a two-paragraph rider. The first paragraph stated *why* Otto was being hired, and the second was a disclaimer to the effect that whereas Otto would investigate diligently and in good faith, there was no guarantee, stated or implied, that he would necessarily achieve results. That Otto had felt it essential to add this rider to his basic contract indicated that he'd been burned before and was taking no chances on collecting his fee. Each folder also contained Otto's daily notes on the case, all of them typed clean.

The first folder was labeled DAVID LARKIN.

Whether you approached the place by land or by sea, it didn't make any difference. Either way, you could see the sign announcing Larkin Boats. Big white double-sided sign with ice-blue plastic lettering on each side, Larkin Boats. Biggest retailer of boats in all Calusa, sold them new, sold them used, sold them from dinghies to yachts—Larkin Boats, his TV commercials said, The Way to the Water. The showroom was on the Trail itself, but behind that was a deepwater canal and enough dock space to accommodate fifteen, twenty boats, depending on the size. Bird sanctuary just beyond the canal, and beyond that the Inland Waterway, man wants to take a boat out for a spin, be my guest. Larkin Boats, The Way to the Water.

Late that Wednesday morning, Larkin was sitting with Jimmy the Accountant on the foredeck of a fifty-seven-foot Chris-Craft Constellation, a boat maybe twenty years old but still in terrific shape, could take you clear to the Bahamas if you wanted it to. Larkin was wearing jeans and Topsiders, and a white T-shirt with blue lettering on it: Larkin Boats, The Way to the Water. Jimmy the Accountant was wearing a green polyester suit and pointy brown shoes and a white shirt with a tie looked like somebody vomited on it and mirrored sunglasses and a narrow-brimmed straw fedora. Jimmy was five feet eight inches tall and he weighed a hundred and eighty pounds, and Larkin thought he looked more like a fat spic than the Italian he actually was. Jimmy's real name was James Anthony Largura but almost everybody called him Jimmy the Accountant or Jimmy Legs, both names having to do with his

63

occupation. Jimmy the Accountant came to see you when there was an accounting due. Jimmy Legs *broke* your legs if you didn't account to his satisfaction. Or your arms. Or your head. Or sometimes only your eyeglasses.

Jimmy was Larkin's younger brother.

Jimmy was here to ask if Larkin could let him and some friends of his use one of the boats for a little trip they had to make on Friday, the twentieth of June. The kind of boat Jimmy had in mind was a cigarette. Which could outrun the Coast Guard, if Larkin followed his drift. Larkin followed his drift perfectly, not for nothing were they brothers. Jimmy and his friends were expecting another shipment, of what Larkin didn't want to know. Larkin made a point of never asking Jimmy about business. That way, Larkin stayed clean. Every once in a while, Jimmy asked him for the use of a boat. Larkin always said what he said now.

"If somebody accidentally left the keys in one of the boats, and somebody came in and used it, I wouldn't know anything about it. It comes back safe and sound, that's terrific. It gets blown out of the water, I didn't even know it was gone."

"Yeah, that's cool," Jimmy said.

Forty-two years old, Larkin thought, and he looks like a fat spic, and he buys his clothes in the discount joints lining 41, and he still talks like a teenager. Yeah, that's cool. Jesus!

"Then we pick it up that night sometime, that's cool with you, huh?"

"If I don't know anything about it," Larkin said.

"But the keys'll be in one of the cigarettes, huh?"

"It's possible keys could get left in a boat by mistake."

"Sure, I dig," Jimmy said.

I *dig*, Larkin thought. Jesus!

The men sat in the sunshine drinking beer.

"I hear you're searchin' for some broad," Jimmy said.

64

Larkin looked at him.

"A Miami hooker," Jimmy said.

Larkin said nothing.

"Stole your watch," Jimmy said.

"Where'd you hear that?" Larkin said.

"You remember Jackie? Jackie Pasconi, his mother used to run the candy store downstairs when we were kids in New York? Jackie? Pasconi? Whose brother got stabbed up in Attica? Don't you remember Jackie?"

"What about him?"

"What he does sometimes, he works—he *used* to work—for this guy got shot here last Sunday. This Jewish guy, I forget his name. Jackie done work for him in Miami."

"What kind of work?"

"Like listening around, you know? Like a snitch, sort of, but not really, 'cause this wasn't for the cops, it was for this Jewish private eye, what the fuck's his name, I can't think of his name right now."

"Samalson," Larkin said.

"Yeah, right, Samuelson."

"So?" Larkin said.

"So I run into Jackie at the dogs, he starts tellin' me my brother hired this private eye to find this hooker ran off with his solid gold Rolex, that's what Jackie tells me."

Larkin looked at him again.

"Is it true?" Jimmy asked. "That a hooker took you for five bills *plus* the gold Rolex?"

"No, I didn't pay her nothing," Larkin said. "I didn't even know she was a pro."

"But she got your watch though."

"Yeah."

"Walked off with the watch, huh?"

"It was on the dresser."

"You musta been sleepin', huh?"

"Yeah."

"This was when, in the morning?"

"Yeah."

"She was gone when you woke up, huh?"

"Yeah."

"With the watch."

"Yeah."

"So why'd you go to a private eye? Whyn't you come to me? I'm your brother, I coulda taken care of this for you."

"Well."

"Better'n any fuckin' private eye, that's for sure. Who got himself killed, by the way."

"Well."

"You think she mighta done it?"

"I *know* she did," Larkin said.

"Killed him? No shit?"

"No, no, I thought you meant—"

"Oh, the watch, sure. But you don't think she killed him, huh?"

"Who the fuck knows *what* she did," Larkin said.

One thing he knew for sure, she'd stolen his watch. The other thing he knew for sure . . . well, the other thing was something he hadn't even told Samalson, and he sure as hell wasn't going to tell his brother, either. Nor anybody. Ever. Fucking little bitch! He wondered now, sitting in the sunshine on the foredeck of a sleek Constellation with his fat brother Jimmy Legs the Accountant in his polyester suit, wondered if maybe she *had* killed Samalson. Because suppose Samalson was getting close? And suppose she knew this was something more than a solid gold Rolex, this was something could get a pretty girl's face rearranged in a way you'd never recognize her again. And suppose she knew the minute Samalson zeroed in she'd be having company who didn't want to hear no shit about what a big gorgeous cock you got, honey. It was possible. Desperate people did desperate things.

"You want me to go on the earie?" his brother asked.

"What?" Larkin said.

"You want me to listen around, see I can get a line on her? Bust her fuckin' head and get the watch back for you?"

"You've got other things to do," Larkin said.

"No, I ain't too busy just now," Jimmy said. "You want me to, or not?"

"Well, I'd like to find her," Larkin said.

"Then consider it done," Jimmy said. "What's her name?"

"Angela West. That's the name she gave me. But I don't think that's her real name."

"You got a picture of her?"

"I gave it to Samalson."

"Then tell me what she looks like."

"Blonde hair, blue eyes, about five feet nine inches tall . . ."

"How old?"

"Twenty-two, twenty-three. Tits out to here, legs that won't quit . . ."

"They'll quit when I find her," Jimmy said.

What he told her, he said there was dope in the house there.

Coke in the house, he said it had to be worth on the street something like seven hundred and fifty K. Six kilos of pure, something like that. This customer of his had seen them—half a dozen of those white plastic bags—when he opened the safe. Well, seven including the one that was already open and on the dresser. Figure he'd already used a few bags, or sold them off, whatever, so say there were still four in the house, maybe three, shit, even *two* would make it worthwhile.

You came away with two kilos of pure, that was a bit more than seventy ounces, you stepped on it till you got it to street strength, you could ask a hundred and a quarter a *gram*. Something like twenty-eight grams to the ounce, you multiplied that by your seventy ounces, you got nineteen hundred and sixty grams times a hundred and twenty-five bucks, you came away with two hundred and forty-five thousand bucks, almost a quarter of a million, that's if there was only *two* kilos in the house.

You could add, say, another hundred and a quarter, give or take, for every kilo you came away with. Come out of there with *four* kilos, for example, you had half a million bucks right there in your hand. You were talking two point two pounds per kilo. You were talking carrying eight, ten pounds the most in your tote bag when you left the house. Walk away with it, disappear in the night.

She told him it sounded dangerous.

Also, how did he know this customer of his wasn't full of shit?

He said For Christ's sake, I've known her for ages, she's a hooker same as you, she had no reason to *lie* to me, she was just telling me an interesting *story*.

Listening to him tell her all this, she was thinking amateurs shouldn't fuck around with dope deals.

She told him she knew a hooker in L.A., a working girl like herself, who got involved bringing dope in on an airplane. They were paying her fifty thousand bucks to bring the dope in from Antigua where it had come from London by way of Marseilles. All she had to do was carry in this false bottom bag with the dope in it. So they brought out the police dogs that day, and she was now doing twenty in San Quentin, and the guys who hired her were still having a nice time on their yacht on the French Riviera. Amateurs shouldn't fuck around with dope deals, she told him.

Also, you shouldn't try to cross guys dealing dope.

That's how amateurs got their brains blown out. Crossing guys who were dealing dope for a living. Nobody likes his rice bowl broken, she told him. You mess with a guy's rice bowl, he's gonna come break your head.

So I don't think I want to do it, she said.

But at the same time she was thinking Oh God, this could be my way out.

This was back in March.

They were at this house he was renting in Hallandale. They were sitting by his swimming pool. This was the beginning of March, it was still too cold to swim here no matter what anybody said. She'd flown to Miami from L.A., got there on the twentieth of January. A girlfriend on the Coast told her she heard they were paying two, two-fifty for an hour's work in Miami, she ought to go down there, check it out. Any given city, you wanted to know what call girls were getting you looked in the Yellow Pages under "Massage" or "Escort." In L.A., Jenny was registered with an outcall massage service that advertised in the Yellow Pages and accepted credit cards. You dialed the number, you got somebody who told you what the agency fee was and asked if you wanted a girl to call you. What Jenny did when she called, she reminded you that the agency fee was fifty bucks, and then she mentioned that she usually got a hundred an hour. So what it was, it was a hundred and fifty bucks an hour, did you want some company or not? Some nights, she turned seven, eight tricks and went home with a thousand bucks when you figured the guys who tipped extra for an, ahem, exceptional blow job. Some nights she watched Johnny Carson. Miami was supposed to be two hundred, two-fifty an hour, which was a lot of bullshit as it turned out. She figured she'd get a few days' sun—actually it was also rainy and cold—and then head back to the Coast.

The day before she was supposed to leave, she met a girl on the beach, told the girl she was an insurance investigator working for a company in L.A., here settling a big claim, be leaving tomorrow. She always made up stories about what she did for a living. A lot of her friends were straight, and you couldn't just say Hey, guess what, I'm a hooker. So she either worked for a bank, or an insurance company, or she did research for a computer company, or she was office manager for a textile firm, all bland jobs nobody would ask her much more about. She liked playing different roles. Well, that was why she'd gone out to L.A. in the first place, to become a big *movie* star, sure, some star. A hooker was what she was, plain and simple. But even so, she thought of hooking as playing different roles, sort of.

Anyway, she'd hit it off right away with the girl on the beach—Molly Ryder was her name—and Molly was saying like Gee, what a shame it is you're leaving so soon, just when we're getting to know each other, it's a shame you can't stay a little longer, get the feel of the place, 'cause it's real nice here, it really is. And then she told Jenny that there was gonna be a party tonight at this guy's house in Hallandale that had a swimming pool and everything, and there'd be some interesting quite far-out people there, if Jenny would like to come along.

So Jenny went to the party and met a lot of interesting far-out people who were doing coke and stuff and decided to hang around Miami a while, see if she couldn't drum up a little trade at the fancier hotels on the beach, maybe even find some old geezer she could play house with, because Miami seemed to have less phonies here than there were in L.A.

where they came a thousand to the square inch. What came a thousand to the square inch down here were the cockroaches. She remembered them from when she used to be a kid living down here. They called them palmetto bugs down here. They were as big as your forefinger, some of them. You stepped on them, you jumped up and down on them, they crawled away all crippled and broken but they wouldn't die unless you hit them with a sledgehammer. Also, they knew how to fly. Staying with Molly the first few weeks she was in Miami, she almost wet her pants when one of them flew right up into her face.

That had been back in January.

By the beginning of March, she was sitting by a swimming pool and listening to talk about a quarter of a million dollars for a single night's work.

What she usually got for an all-night stand in L.A. was five hundred, sometimes only four if things were slow.

This was a quarter of a *million*.

Split it with him, it still came to a hundred and a quarter.

That's if there were only two kilos in the safe. If there was more . . .

How do I get *in* that safe? she asked him.

Because this was her way out.

Matthew disliked him on sight. Big beefy man with a wide forehead and prominent nose, coming across the deck to greet him, hamhock hand extended, blue jeans, and a T-shirt that had "Larkin Boats, The Way to the Water" printed on its front. The man was probably a saint, and yet—instant animosity. That happened sometimes. Even with women. Even with gorgeous women. Something clicked in the unconscious, who the hell knew? Maybe Larkin reminded him of a high school geometry teacher who'd given him an F. Or maybe there were just certain combinations of sights and smells that signaled to the brain and triggered defense mechanisms, watch out for this guy. Whatever it was, he didn't like Larkin.

But there were some questions he needed to ask him.

And, after all, when he'd called, the man had been gracious enough to invite him to his home for an early afternoon drink, hadn't he? Instead of asking him to stop by at his place of business. Gorgeous house on Fatback Key, all wood and glass

72

and stone, sitting right on the Gulf. Matthew and Larkin sitting on lounges facing the water. Thunderheads building up out there the way they did every day at this time.

"It wasn't *Otto* started calling her Cinderella," Larkin said. "It was me."

"When was that?" Matthew asked.

"When I hired him."

"Which was when? I'm sorry to be asking all these questions, Mr. Larkin . . ."

"No, no, listen, I'm happy to help. What happened was I went to this ball in April sometime . . . well, down here there are more balls than you can count, I'm sure you know that."

"Yes," Matthew said.

"Over on the East Coast, in Miami, it's your Cubans throwing a ball every time one of their daughters turns fifteen. That's a custom with Spanish-speaking people," Larkin said, educating Matthew. "The daughter turns fifteen, they dress her like a bride and throw a ball. All the friends rent lavender tuxedos and come to the party to wish the kid well on her fifteenth birthday because pretty soon she'll be on her back on the beach with her legs spread and not too long after that she'll be a fat old lady with a mustache."

Larkin laughed.

Matthew said nothing. He was not liking Larkin any better.

"*La quinceañera* they call her," Larkin said, "a lot of bullshit. Anyway, here in Calusa, we got balls to mark the seasons of the year, which is even *more* bullshit. Around Christmastime, you have your Snowflake Ball for the American Cancer Society, and in the spring, when the purple jacaranda trees are blooming, you got your Jacaranda Ball for Multiple Sclerosis or Muscular Dystrophy, I always mix them up. That's where I met her. At the Jacaranda Ball."

"This was . . . ?"

"In April."

"When in April?"

"Beginning of the month sometime. The jacarandas were just starting to bloom. In she walks, a pretty young thing in a blue gown the color of her eyes, slit high up on her right leg and scooped low over a very good chest. Danced with her all night long. Had her picture taken by a photographer who was charging fifty bucks a pop for charity. That's the picture I gave Otto. The one I had taken at the ball. Did you see that picture?"

"Yes, it's in the file," Matthew said.

"Gorgeous girl, am I right?"

"Very pretty."

"Sure, that's the picture I gave him. Plus twenty-five bills as a retainer. Find her, I told him. Find Cinderella for me. That's the first time I called her that."

"Why was that?"

"Well, because I met her at a *ball*, didn't I? Dressed like a princess, sapphire pin on her chest, high-heeled shoes looked like glass, all she's missing is a tiara. Plus by morning the princess turned into a fuckin' whore who stole my Rolex cost eight thousand dollars at Tiffany's in New York."

"Which is why you hired Otto."

"Yeah."

"To get your watch back."

"To find *her*, never mind the watch. The watch is probably in Alaska by now, you think she's gonna hang onto a hot watch engraved with my initials on the case?"

"You merely wanted him to find her."

"*Merely?* You think I was giving him an easy job or something? *Merely*, the man says. I didn't even know her name."

"I thought she—"

"Yeah, she told me Angela West, but I looked in the phone

74

book before I called Otto, and there were six Wests in it, none of them Angela. So all I had was this picture of a young blonde girl—Cinderella, right? Of which maybe there are fifty thousand such young blonde girls in the city of Calusa, so Otto's supposed to run down to the beach and find her. That's not such a *merely*, Matt, is it okay if I call you Matt?"

"Most people call me Matthew."

"Matthew then," Larkin said and shrugged as if to say there was no accounting for taste. "The point is, this was a hard job I gave Otto, and he wasn't making a hell of a lot of progress, I can tell you that."

"Why'd you go to him in the first place?"

"Why? Because I heard he was a good—"

"I mean, why didn't you go to the police?"

"I didn't want to."

"Why not? She stole your watch."

"I felt this was a personal matter. Between her and me. I didn't want the police in this. Anyway, the police are full of shit, Matthew, I'm sure you know that."

Matthew said nothing. Far out on the water, a trawler was silhouetted against the gray of the sky. Sandpipers skirted the waves as they nudged the shore. Overhead, a flight of pelicans hovered and then dipped into an air current. Matthew wondered if birds knew when it was going to rain.

"So when did you go to him?" he asked.

"Around the end of the month."

"The end of April."

"Yeah, sometime around the end of the month."

"Why'd you wait so long?"

"What do you mean?"

"She stole your watch early in April, but you didn't go to Otto till the end of the month. How come?"

"I was thinking it over," Larkin said.

Domingo said since the mother wasn't home they should go to the beach. Ernesto said the beach could wait. Neither of the men were terribly impressed with Venice, which was where Mrs. Santoro lived, in a cinderblock development house not too far off U.S. 41. Domingo said he liked Miami Beach better. He said Venice looked "crommy." That was one of the few English words he liked, crommy. He didn't think Miami Beach was crommy. Miami Beach was like a small province in Cuba, and therefore gorgeous.

The men were waiting outside the house in the red LeBaron convertible. They had decided on a high profile here because all these crommy little houses were very close together and they couldn't risk a break-in. Otherwise, they'd have preferred being inside the house when she got home. As it was, they had gone to the front door, and rung the bell and a neighbor next door had told them Annie wouldn't be back from Miami till later today. They had not anticipated *that* high a profile, being talked to by a nosy neighbor who should've been inside watching a soap opera. A moment before Mrs. Santoro drove up— at about twenty after three that Wednesday afternoon—Domingo was complaining that there were no Spanish-speaking radio stations in this crommy town. Ernesto nudged him in the ribs as her car, a brown Dodger Caravan, pulled into the driveway. They got out of the convertible at once, and were walking toward her as she unlocked the kitchen door at the side of the house.

"Mrs. Santoro?" Ernesto said.

She turned, surprised. Mother of the two other women, Ernesto thought, no question about it. Same eyes, same mouth, bleached blonde hair trying to hide the gray, yes, but no doubt the mother. Same firm breasts, well they were somewhat heavy, true, but she had to be fifty, fifty-five, something like that, a bit thick in the waist, also, but good legs like the two daughters, she was the mother, no question.

"Miami Police Department," he said, snapping open his wallet and flashing his driver's license, and then snapping the wallet shut again. "We have some questions about your daughter."

Annie heard an accent like a tortilla, words that came out as "Miami Polee Deparm, we ha' some question abou' you' door," but she supposed there were a lot of Hispanic cops in Dade County, and anyway he'd just shown her his ID card, hadn't he?

"Yes, come in," she said.

They went into the kitchen behind her.

She put her parcels down on the kitchen table and then led them into the living room. Venetian blinds closed, the room dim and cool, Florida in the summertime, up the street the sound of a lawn mower. You could smell mildew. Almost taste it.

"I just got back from there," she said. "Miami."

"Yes, we know," Ernesto said.

"I went over to identify the body," Annie said.

"Yes, that's required," he said.

The other one, the big one with the slick little mustache and the darting eyes, said nothing.

"It was horrible," Annie said, and shook her head. "Have you ever been in a morgue? Well, of course you have," she said.

"Yes," Ernesto said.

"Horrible," she said. "The smell in there."

"Yes," he said. "Mrs. Santoro, can you . . . ?"

"Excuse me," she said, "I didn't get your names."

"Oh, excuse *me*," Ernesto said. "Detective Garcia." His

true surname was Moreno. "And my partner, Detective Rodriguez." Domingo's surname was Garzon. "I was wondering if you could tell us where we can locate your stepdaughter?"

"Jenny? Why do you want her?"

"Mrs. Santoro," Ernesto said, "we want to make sure nothing happens to her like happened to your poor daughter in Miami Beach."

"Was this drug-related?" Annie asked.

"Your daughter?"

"Yes. Did her death have something to do with drugs?"

"Perhaps," Ernesto said.

"I thought so. But I don't think Jenny's into drugs. I mean, she's into *enough*, believe me, but—"

She suddenly cut herself off.

"Yes?" Ernesto said.

"Nothing," Annie said.

"We know she's a prostitute," Ernesto said.

"You do?"

"Yes. That's not why we want to find her. We want to protect her, Mrs. Santoro."

This all came out in Señor-Wences English.

"Thass nah why we wann to fine her. We wann to protec' her, Meez Santoro"—well, the *Santoro* came out beautifully, of course, but everything else was dipped in guacamole. She thought Miami must be really overrun with them if they were hiring *policemen* who couldn't even speak English.

"Who told you Jenny was a prostitute?" she asked.

Ernesto almost said "Alice," forgetting for a moment that unless he had talked to the Miami daughter *before* she got killed, she couldn't have told him *anything*. "Your daughter in Orlando," he said, and then realized *that* was a mistake, too. The daughter in Orlando was *also* dead. The only difference was that Mrs. Santoro didn't know about her yet.

78

Chances were, not even the police knew about her yet. They would know about her when the body began stinking. Which in this heat should be very soon.

"I spoke to her yesterday," Annie said. "She said she'd call back, about meeting me in Miami, but she never did. Well, Katie. Always unreliable," she said, and made a dismissing gesture with her hand.

Ernesto knew they had spoken. That was why the daughter would soon be stinking up the neighborhood. "She was the one who gave us your address," he said. Which was the truth. "Because she is concerned about your stepdaughter." Which was a lie.

"Really?" Annie said. *"That's* a surprise."

Which is the bad thing about lying, Ernesto thought.

"Those two *never* got along," Annie said. "Katie *hates* her, in fact. And you tell me she's *concerned* about her? That's hard to believe."

"Well, people's feelings sometimes change," Ernesto said, and thought Lady, please don't make this hard for us, okay? "Anyway, we'd like to know where she is," he said. "Your stepdaughter Jenny."

He said it "Henny."

She almost laughed.

Instead, she said, "Last I heard, she was in Calusa."

Good, Ernesto thought.

"Where in Calusa?" he said.

"I don't know," Annie said.

Ernesto looked at her. He glanced at Domingo. He was hoping she was not going to make this difficult for them. There had been enough blood.

"Why don't you know?" he asked.

"Why don't I know?" she said. "What do you mean, why don't I know? If I don't know, I don't know."

"You said she's in Calusa . . ."

"Yes."

". . . but you don't know where."

"That's right."

"How can that be?"

"She called me when she got there. She hadn't found a place yet, she was just calling to say she was okay. I haven't heard from her since."

"Ah," Ernesto said. "When was this, please?"

"When she called me?"

"Yes, when she called you to say she was okay."

"Early in April," Annie said.

Ernesto nodded. He was thinking that was about right, she had disappeared around the end of March. She had probably gone straight to Calusa from Miami. While they were still trying to find her in all the hotel bars on the beach. So. Calusa. That was near Tampa, wasn't it?

"Where's Calusa?" he asked.

"Not far from here. Near Sarasota."

"Tell me," Ernesto said. "Does she still go by the name Jody Carmody?"

"Well, she uses a lot of names," Annie said. "I never heard that one before, though, Jody Carmody. Why would she have used *that*, she hates her sisters, hates the Carmody name. I know she was using Angela West and Cheryl Blake, but Jody Carmody? That was my first husband's name, Carmody. Not Jenny's father, Jenny's father was my second husband, he's dead now, he died of a heart attack four years ago. I always thought it was him finding out about Jenny gave him the heart attack. That she was a prostitute, you know."

Ernesto nodded impatiently. He did not want to hear this bullshit.

"Write down the names for me, please," he said. "All the names she goes by."

"Well, there's just the ones I told you," Annie said.

"Write them down, *por favor*. Please."

She went into the kitchen, took a pad and pencil from where they were resting near the phone, and carried them back into the living room. She switched on a floor lamp near the couch, leaned over onto the coffee table, and began writing. As she wrote, she spoke. Ernesto had always admired that, people who could talk and write at the same time.

"She may be a redhead by now, who knows?" Annie said. "Or back to her real color, which is brown. Well, more like . . . well, yeah, brown I guess you would say. She was a blonde the last time I saw her. But who knows what she is now? Did I mention Virginia Darrow? Did I give you that name?"

"No," Ernesto said.

"That's one of the names she uses. Virginia Darrow. I like that one a lot. That and Melissa Blair. The last time I saw her, she was Virginia Darrow and she was a blonde. She looked terrific. Well, she's a beautiful girl, would you like to see some pictures of her?"

"That would be helpful," Ernesto said.

"These are all the names I can think of," Annie said. "Oh wait, there's one more she used to use, but that was when she first went to Los Angeles. When she was still trying to get in pictures. She used this very young name, it was Mary Jane Hopkins. But I don't think she's used that in a long time. Do you want me to put it down?"

"Put it down, please," Ernesto said.

Annie wrote down the name, and then tore the sheet of paper from the pad and handed it to Ernesto. "Here you are,

Detective Gomez," she said, and then frowned. "I'm sorry," she said, "is that what you told me?"

Ernesto had forgotten what he'd told her.

"Yes, that's right," he said, "Gomez."

Domingo looked at him sharply.

Lady, Ernesto thought again, please don't make this hard for us.

"Would you like to see the pictures?" she asked.

"Por favor," he said, and remembered that he'd told her Garcia.

They went into the bedroom. She opened the closet door, and reached up onto the shelf. "Can you help me here?" she said. "It's the gray box."

Ernesto hefted the box down from the shelf. They went back into the living room again, and she began leafing through the pictures, proudly displaying them.

"These are my two daughters when they were little girls," she said. "And this is my first husband. And this is when we used to live in New Jersey. And this is the four of us in Vero Beach, which is the first time we came to Florida. That was when Al decided he wanted to come live down here. My first husband. And this is—"

I don't want to hear this bullshit, Ernesto thought.

"—my second husband, Dom. Well, Dominick Santoro. Do you know Santoro Brothers Construction in Miami? That used to be my husband. Ah, here's Jenny," he said.

Por fin, Ernesto thought, and almost sighed in relief.

He looked at the picture of a six-year-old girl.

"Have you got anything more recent?" he asked.

What it sounded like was, "Ha' you gar anytin' more rissin?"

"Oh sure, just a second," she said, and began rummaging in the box. "The thing is, you know, there aren't very many because she left home so young, she was only sixteen when she left for California. Wanted to be an actress. Well, she was very good, you know, ask anybody. She was the star of *The Crucible*, do you know that play? By Arthur Miller? When they did it at the school. She was the star. The dramatics teacher said she was a very talented young lady. Those were his exact words. A very talented young lady. Still, it broke her father's heart when she went out there. Well, you know, he had a heart attack two years later. Here she is, look, she must be fifteen in this picture, isn't she beautiful?"

She showed them a photograph of a girl in a bikini, good breasts in the skimpy top, wide hips, long legs, standing on tiptoe like a model, a grin on her face, dark hair blowing in the wind.

"I'll tell you the truth," Annie said, "she's my stepdaughter and all, but she's my favorite. Of all the three. The others are my natural daughters, but I like Jenny best. Is that a terrible thing for me to say? I'm supposed to be the wicked stepmother, I know, but I always thought of myself as her real mother, and I loved her better than my own daughters, still do. Here's another one of her on the beach, this was taken in Florida, too, we were living in Bradenton at the time. She was very well developed at an early age, so beautiful. And smart, too, she used to get A's even in mathematics, which is difficult for a girl. I don't know what happened out there, I'll never be able to understand how she became a prostitute, never. Well, listen, Alice, poor thing, was a drug addict, you know. And Katie's been divorced twice, who knows *what* she'll make of *her* life. She sent this from Los Angeles, this is fairly recent. It was a party at a producer's house. In Hollywood. They give big parties, the producers out there in Hollywood."

Ernesto looked at the photograph.

Blonde, good, that was more like it. Sexy *chiquita* grinning into the camera, silky low-cut dress, tits spilling over the top, one hand on her hip, the other holding a drink, long legs in high-heeled sandals.

He handed the picture to Domingo and then said, "Have you any more like this?"

"I think she sent some from Seattle when she was up there, let me see." She began rummaging through the box again. "Is that wrong of me?" she asked. "To love her the most?" She turned to look into Ernesto's face. "Detective Garcia?" she said. "Is that wrong of me?"

Domingo suddenly tensed.

"One cannot dictate to the heart," Ernesto said, and tapped his chest.

"I'm sorry," Annie said, puzzled. "You *did* say Garcia, didn't you?"

Domingo was perched on the edge of the couch now, the picture of Jenny Santoro at a Hollywood party in his left hand, like Fay Wray in King Kong's huge paw.

"Gomez," Ernesto said, and placed his hand gently on Domingo's right arm.

"Gomez, yes," Annie said, and smiled. "I have a terrible time with names."

"If you can find those other pictures," Ernesto said, and returned the smile. *"Por favor."*

In his pocket, Domingo loosened his grip on the switch-blade knife.

7

Luis Amaros was known as El Armadillo to those in the drug trade. This was not because he *looked* like an armadillo. Not many people looked like armadillos. In fact, not many people *knew* what armadillos looked like. Most people confused armadillos with anteaters. An anteater had a long narrow snout, and a long sticky tongue, and a long shaggy tail, and it looked like a hairy flying saucer with legs. An armadillo, on the other hand, had a covering of armorlike, jointed, bony plates, and it looked like a small tank with legs. Luis Amaros did not look like a tank. He looked more like a fire hydrant. Short and squat and a bit chubby. An amiable fire hydrant was what he looked like. A good-natured fire hydrant. He looked like Baby Doc Duvalier of the island Haiti, was what he looked like, but he was not a member of the Duvalier family. Luis was a fire hydrant member of the Amaros family of Bogotá, and he was into dealing drugs. Well, that was a given. If you were Colombian, and you lived in Florida, you were not moving coffee beans.

The reason Luis Amaros was called El Armadillo was because, like the armor-plated burrowing mammal that was his namesake, Luis was very well-armored. There was hardly any way anyone could get to him. Anybody took a fall for dealing dope, it wasn't going to be Luis. It was going to be a dozen other people lower in the echelon, but it was not going to be Luis. That was why so many other Colombians lived in shitty prison cells and Luis lived in a luxurious house on Key Biscayne.

Luis smiled a lot. He had a chubby little face, and an infectious Bugs Bunny sort of grin. It was a wonder people didn't call him El Conejo, which meant "the rabbit" in Spanish. Because actually, he resembled a chubby little rabbit more than he did either a fire hydrant or an armadillo. Women thought Luis was cute. Even some men thought he was cute. "You some sweetheart, baby," customers would often say to him, which Luis took to mean he had a nice friendly smile and chubby cheeks everybody wanted to pinch. Actually, his customers meant he drove a hard bargain. "You some sweetheart, baby." And he would slit your throat for a dime. Or get someone else to do it for a nickel.

Luis prided himself on the size of his penis.

He would often ask girls if he was bigger than Johnny Holmes. Johnny Holmes was a porn star who couldn't act at all, but he had this enormous organ. In the movies Luis had seen with Johnny Holmes in them, Holmes always looked a little soft, as if the damn thing was too long to stay hard all the way to the head. Luis would play a Johnny Holmes movie on the VHS, and ask whichever girl he was with who was bigger, him or Johnny Holmes. They all said he was ten times bigger than Holmes, and also a lot cuter.

On Thursday morning, when the call came from Ernesto Moreno in Calusa, Luis was showing a twenty-year-old black girl a trick with an apple and a handful of cocaine. Luis himself was very light-skinned, but he had a terrific yen for black girls. He also had a terrific yen for apples. Cocaine, he could take or leave, mostly leave. Cocaine was business. The trouble with Al Pacino in that movie *Scarface*—aside from the fact that he was ugly and wanted to fuck his own sister—was that he mixed business with pleasure. Every time you saw Pacino, he was snorting a bucketful of coke. Luis rarely touched the stuff. But there were a lot of girls who enjoyed coke a lot and Luis always kept some in the house to meet the need. Coke-snorting girls were often very grateful girls, except when every now and then you came across a cheap cunt who needed to be taught a lesson.

Luis spoke with a Spanish accent that a lot of girls thought was cute. Not Hispanic girls. They didn't think the accent was cute, they thought everybody talked that way. Anglos, though, slender young things in thin little dresses, flitting around the hotel bars, they thought his accent was cute. They also thought he might have some coke. They heard a Spanish accent, they automatically figured coke. Young girls nowadays, you said, "Hello, how do you do?" they answered, "Hi, my name is Cindy, you got any blow?" That was one of the names for cocaine. Blow.

Before he'd come to Miami, even though he was in the business, Amaros hadn't known there were so many names for cocaine. Americans were so inventive. C, coke, snow, he knew. Happy dust, too, he'd heard it called that and also gold dust. But star dust, no, that was new to him, and so was white lady and nose candy and flake. The names he found most peculiar were Bernice, Corinne, and girl. For cocaine. People calling cocaine Bernice, Corinne, or girl. As if they were equating sniffing a noseful of dope with fucking. Calling the dope *girl*. Maybe they *were* fucking when they sniffed the stuff, the looks on their faces, some of them.

He impressed girls with the cobalt thiocyanate trick. Mix it in with the dope, watch it turn blue. The brighter the blue, the better the girl. Always kept three, four kilos in the house, never knew when there'd be a party. The brighter the blue, the better the girl. Luis had his own expression. The better the *girl*, the better the girl. Meaning you gave a girl good dope, you got good action in return. Except every now and then a cunt got too smart for her own good.

"What you do," Luis said, "you scoop out the middle of the apple like so."

The black girl watched him, eyes wide. Her hair was done like Bo Derek's in the movie *10*. She had informed him last night that this particular hairstyle was really African in origin. According to the blacks, everything these days was African in origin. Even the Torah was African in origin. She had sniffed coke like she was a vacuum cleaner, sucked cock the same way. When he asked her was he bigger than Johnny Holmes, she said, "Man, you are bigger than *God!*"

He worked the apple with a corer.

"What's that do, what you're doin'?" the girl asked.

Her name was Omelia. Black people, they made up names, the names were never right on the money. Like Omelia *sounded* like Amelia, but it wasn't. He'd balled black girls named Lorenne, Clorissa, Norla—none of them real names at all, just names that *sounded* like they could be names. He *loved* black girls with their funky sounding names.

"What we're doing here," he said, "is we're making a hole in the apple here. Right in the center of the apple."

"What for?" she said.

She was sitting Indian style on a chair at the kitchen table.

Knees up, ankles crossed. Naked. High sweat-sheen on her skin.

"Put the dust in it," he said.

"In where?" Omelia said. "The apple?"

"Right here in the hole," he said.

"Gonna mess up real good blow," she said.

"No, give it a good flavor."

"Who tole you that?"

"Trust me," he said, and poured cocaine into the cored apple. He took a plastic straw from a glass on the counter. He stuck the straw into the apple and then handed the apple across the table to her.

He watched her sniffing coke.

Eyes closed.

Legs slightly parted.

"When you finish," he said, "I'll eat the apple."

"We should put some of this in *my* hole," she said, and looked up and giggled.

"You want to do that?" he said.

"Anythin' you want, man. This is *some* shit you got here. Where you get such shit, man?"

"I have connections," he said.

"*Purify* my hole, shit like this."

The telephone rang.

"Excuse me," he said. "I won't be long."

"You better not be," she said. "We got things to *try*, man."

He walked into the library, closed the door behind him, and picked up the ringing phone. Through the window, he could see out over Biscayne Bay, southward to Soldier Key. The sky was clear and blue, but it would turn cloudy by afternoon, and then it would rain again.

"Hello?" he said.

"Luis?" the voice on the other end said.

"Yes?" he said.

"Ernesto."

They talked for almost five minutes.

Their conversation was entirely in Spanish.

Ernesto reported that he and Domingo were now in Calusa and were staying at a motel called the Suncrest.

He said they now had seven different names for Jody Carmody, but they were pretty sure her real name was Jenny Santoro.

Luis asked if the name was Spanish, she hadn't looked Spanish.

Ernesto told him it was Italian.

Luis said nothing to this. He did not like Italians. He equated Italians with the Mafia, and the Mafia with people who would kill him in a minute to get at his business.

Ernesto told him this was going to be a very difficult job. All these different names now, and nobody else to ask about her.

Luis told him to stay with it.

He told him to contact a man named Martin Klement at a restaurant named Springtime. In Calusa. Tell him they were looking to buy good cocaine. Tell him to ask around. Martin Klement.

Luis told Ernesto he wanted to hang the girl from the ceiling by her cunt. Put a hook in her cunt and hang her from the ceiling.

Well, we'll do our best, Ernesto said.

Both men hung up. Luis went back into the kitchen, smiling like Bugs Bunny. Omelia was no longer sitting at the kitchen table. For a panicky moment, he thought Not again. He thought this in Spanish. His heart was beating wildly.

"Baby?"

Her voice.

Distant. From the other end of the house.

"Come find me, baby," she said.

He went to find her, wondering if she'd done with the cocaine what she said they should do with it.

At ten minutes to ten that Thursday morning, Cynthia Huellen buzzed Matthew from the front desk to say there was a girl here who wanted to talk to him about Otto Samalson. He asked her to send the girl in right away.

She was no more than seventeen, Matthew guessed, a carrot-topped, freckle-faced redhead wearing blue shorts and a white T-shirt. She came into the office and then stopped stock still inside the door, as though paralyzed. He thought for a moment she would turn and run right out again.

"Won't you sit down?" he said, as gently as he could, and motioned to the chairs in front of his desk.

The girl looked terrified.

"Miss?" he said.

The girl nodded.

"Please sit down, won't you?"

She moved crablike toward one of the chairs, sat in it, and then immediately and defensively folded her arms across her chest.

"I'm sorry," Matthew said, "I didn't get your name."

"Kelly," the girl squeaked, and cleared her throat. "Kelly O'Rourke."

"How can I help you, Miss O'Rourke?" Matthew asked.

She stared at him, her eyes wide. He wondered if he had grown horns.

"Miss?"

"Yes, sir."

"Please relax."

"I'm relaxed," she said.

"I understand you want to talk to me about Otto Samalson."

"Yes, sir."

"What about him?"

"I read in the paper that he worked for you."

"Well, he was *doing* some work for us, yes."

"The paper said investigator with the firm of Summerville and Hope."

"Yes, well, that wasn't quite accurate," Matthew said.

"That's why I came here," Kelly said, sounding disappointed, like a child who'd been promised the circus only to have it rain. "'Cause the paper said he worked for you."

"Well, maybe I can help you, anyway," Matthew said. "What was it you wanted to tell me?"

She hesitated.

Then she said, "I saw him."

"When?" Matthew asked at once.

"Sunday night."

"Where?"

"At the Seven-Eleven where I work. He came in and asked for a pack of cigarettes."

"Where's that?"

"On Forty-one. Just over the Whisper Key bridge."

"Which bridge? North or south?"

"North."

"What time was this?"

"About a quarter to eleven."

"Are you sure it was him?"

"Yes, I recognized his picture in the paper. He seemed like a nice man."

"He was," Matthew said. "Did he say anything else?"

"Just that he didn't need matches. When I handed him the cigarettes. Said he had a lighter, thanks."

"Was he alone?"

"Yes."

"Came in alone?"

"Yes."

"Went out alone?"

"Yes. But . . ."

Matthew was writing. He looked up sharply.

"Yes?"

"I watched through the front window, you know? The big window? Because he was such a cute little man. And there was nothing to do, the place was empty."

"And?"

"He got in his car, and started it, and backed out."

"Yes, go ahead, Kelly."

"This other car backed out right after him. Like it was waiting for him to pull out, you know? Backed out and followed him."

"You're sure it followed him?"

"Made the turn at the light, same as he did."

"Heading in which direction?"

"South on Forty-one."

"What kind of car was it, Kelly?"

"A black Toronado," she said, "with red racing stripes and tinted windows."

"Did you happen to notice the license plate?"

"No, I'm sorry. I would've looked if I'd known he was gonna get killed. But I didn't know that."

"Did you notice who was *in* the car?"

"No. I told you, the windows were tinted."

"You couldn't tell if it was one person . . . or two?"

"I couldn't see in."

"Anything else you can remember? Anything Mr. Samalson said or did?"

"Yes, sir," Kelly said, and suddenly smiled. "He made a joke about my hair. He said it looked like my head was on fire."

The moment she was gone, Matthew called Cooper Rawles at the Calusa P.D. He had first met Rawles when he was working on what the police files had labeled the Jack and the Beanstalk case but what Matthew would always remember as the Bullet in the Shoulder case. Unfortunately, the shoulder in question had been his, and the bullet had been traveling at enormous velocity, trailing fire and pain behind it.

Rawles had been there on that memorable night in August, upstairs with Bloom, questioning a suspect named Jack Crowell who'd made a break for it when the cops started demolishing his alibi. Crowell burst out of the front door of the building, barefoot and barechested, a gun in his right hand, shoving his way through the handful of people cluttered on the front steps, almost falling over the lap of a woman who sat Haitian-style, her knees wide, her dress tented over her crotch. Matthew, waiting outside on Bloom's explicit instructions, heard Bloom's voice shouting from inside the building—"Stop or I'll shoot!"—and shoved himself off the fender of the car, moving to intercept Crowell, figuring Bloom was right behind him with his own gun, and never once stopping to think what might happen next.

What happened next was that he'd got shot for the first time in his life, and he never wanted to get shot ever again because not only was it embarrassing, it also hurt like hell. Rawles hadn't said much that night. He was a man of few words. He'd just shaken his head, and then walked over to the car to radio for a meat wagon. Matthew visualized him now as the phone rang at the Public Safety Building. A huge man, black as the Arctic night, wide shoulders and a barrel chest. Massive hands. Stood at least six feet four inches tall and weighed possibly two-forty. No one to mess with.

When he came onto the line, Matthew said, "Detective Rawles? This is Matthew Hope. I have some information for you."

Rawles listened silently as Matthew repeated everything Kelly O'Rourke had told him not five minutes earlier.

There was a long silence on the line.

"You've been busy," Rawles said, and for a moment Matthew thought he'd only imagined the reprimanding note in his voice. But then Rawles said, "Maybe you ought to make application for the Police Department, Mr. Hope."

Matthew said nothing.

"Understand you were out to see Mrs. Nettington before *we* got to her," Rawles said.

His meaning was unmistakable now.

"Mrs. Nettington was my client," Matthew said.

"Is that why you asked all kinds of questions about where her husband was Sunday night when Samalson was boxed?"

"What is this?" Matthew said.

"I think you know what this is, Mr. Hope," Rawles said. "I don't think you'd be acting this way if Morrie wasn't on vacation 'cause Morrie'd have called you as a friend and told you to bug off. What I want to know is why you think you can get away with conducting your own personal little investi—"

"No one's conducting a personal—"

"No? I hear from David Larkin that you went to see *him*, too. And that you had access to a file on a case Samalson was working for him. Now you weren't by chance representing Mr. *Larkin*, too, were you?"

"No, Detective Rawles, I was not representing David Larkin."

"Yeah, get huffy, go ahead," Rawles said. "You just go gettin' huffy on me."

Matthew said nothing.

"Who else you been talking to?" Rawles asked.

Matthew did not answer him.

"Don't talk to anyone else, you hear?" Rawles said.

Matthew still said nothing.

"Thanks for the Toronado shit," Rawles said, and hung up.

What it was, they called him The Armadillo.

When she first heard this, she said Please, you're making my flesh crawl. That's like a snake, isn't it? An armadillo? Doesn't it have scales and everything? Like a snake?

He told her No, an armadillo was an animal ate ants.

She said Terrific. What kind of creep is this, he eats ants?

He explained that the guy's name was Luis Amaros, his real name, and he lived in this great house on Key Biscayne, looking out over the water, a gorgeous house must've cost him a million, a million-two. He had a sailboat parked behind the house *plus* a motor cruiser, and there was a Jag and a Rolls in the garage, the guy was what a person might consider well off, believe me. There was no question that he was a pro, she was right about that, he was very definitely moving cocaine, which accounted for the solid gold fixtures in the toilet and the safe with six, seven kilos he kept for entertaining his lady friends. But that was no reason to be afraid of him. Because what they were going to do was leave Miami the minute they had the coke. Amaros wouldn't bother coming after them, why would he? For a lousy two, three keys, whatever? Besides, how could he ever find them? This was a big state and an even bigger country.

He thought of himself as a ladies' man, Amaros, keen eye for the ladies, wouldn't have anything to do with hookers, which is why Jenny was perfect for the job. You don't look anything like a hooker, he told her, which she supposed he intended as a compliment though she couldn't see anything wrong with the way hookers looked. In L.A., the hookers she knew dressed like college girls whenever they went out to turn a trick. Out there, it was the *straight* girls who looked like hookers. Your movie stars looked like the biggest hookers of all. They went to the Academy Awards, you'd think they were giving out prizes for who was showing the most tits and ass.

It still bothered her that she'd never made it as an actress. Whenever she watched the Academy Awards on television, it made her sad that it wasn't her up there making an acceptance speech. Made her want to cry, watching the Academy Awards. Thank you, thank you, I'm so moved I could cry. Oh, thank you. I would also like to thank my marvelous director, and I would like to thank my wonderful co-stars and my kind and understanding producer, but most of all I would like to thank my mother, Annie Santoro. For giving me so much love and understanding. Mama?

And at this point she'd hold up the Oscar.

Mama, this is really yours.

Tears in her eyes.

Still bothered her.

And yet she was sort of pleased that he didn't think she looked like a hooker. She guessed that meant she looked *pure*, you know, the girl next door, the *virgin*, which was what she'd played to good effect in California when she was still Mary Jane Hopkins. Little pigeon-toed stance, hands twisting the hem of her skirt, Gee, Mister, I never had one of *those* in my mouth before. Long time ago, that was. Mary Jane Hopkins was dead and gone now. But she was flattered that he thought she still looked pure as the driven snow.

This customer of his who'd shared the coke with Amaros was a working girl just like Jenny, only Amaros hadn't known that. He'd known it, he wouldn't have had anything to do with her. What happened was he'd picked her up in the Kasbah Lounge out there in Bal Harbour at the Morocco Hotel, which was his favorite hangout on the beach. Very fancy hotel up there, combo playing like supposed to be mysterious African-style music in the lounge there, all beaded curtains and waiters in red fezzes, very dimly lit, hookers cruising, but Amaros wouldn't know a genuine hooker if she came complete with a scarlet letter on her chest. Didn't tip to the fact that Kim—which was the name this girl went by, her real name was Annabelle—was a hooker, began moving on her the way he would a straight girl, what kind of work you do, you been in Miami long, where you from originally, like that.

Kim was getting a big kick out of it, to tell the truth, this pudgy little guy with the Spanish accent and the big diamond ring on his pinky and the Bugs Bunny grin never suspecting for a minute that she got a hundred bucks an hour for her time. When he asked if she did cocaine, she began to get really interested. Because sometimes, you found a guy had great coke it was worth more than the C-note to spend some time with him. So she went along with it, all big-eyed and innocent, Oh gee, Mr. Amaros, I'm just a little girl from the state of Minnesota, I wouldn't know about cocaine and all those bad things, him holding her hand while the waiter in the fez brought lavender-colored drinks.

So finally Amaros convinced her to come take a look at his big house out on Key Biscayne, which really knocked Kim's eyes out, I mean this was *some* house. And he opens the safe, and takes out a big plastic bag looks like sugar and he puts it on the dresser and opens it, and she dips her finger in it and oh, yes, daddy, it is cocaine of the nicest sort. He does a trick with some chemical, it makes a sample turn blue, and he tells her the brighter the blue, the better the girl, but she's already snorting through a rolled-up twenty dollar bill, and she doesn't need *him* to tell her how good this stuff is.

In the safe, she spots six more bags.

He tells her he just keeps it around to entertain his friends.

She is very happy he is such a fine entertainer. She tells him he ought to go into the catering business.

He is having a jolly old time, Amaros, introducing this nice little girl from Minnesota to all the wicked, wicked ways of the big bad world. He shows her a movie starring Johnny Holmes, the porn star with the enormous cock, and asks Kim who's bigger, him or Johnny Holmes. She says Oh, *you*, my dear, without question, which isn't really a lie because he is in fact rather well hung for such a short guy.

So the idea is for Jenny to go to this same Kasbah Lounge and sit at the bar there drinking something purple or pink, waiting for her dream boy to walk in one night, after which she will catch his eye and play the innocent little girl from Dubuque, Iowa. He will whisk her away to his castle on Key Biscayne, and he will open the safe and take out a bag of coke and do his Brighter-the-Blue trick and show her his Johnny Holmes movie and his own humongous weapon and she will put a little bit of chloral hydrate in his drink and knock him out and run off with the rest of the stuff in the safe, how does that sound to Jenny?

Jenny thinks it sounds terrific.

Because to her this is still the way out.

This was now like the last week in March when they were planning this.

8

Matthew was still steaming.

Back some time ago, before they'd got to know each other better, he'd had the same kind of confrontation with Bloom. Twice, in fact. The first time was while Bloom was investigating the murder of Vicky Miller and the kidnapping of her daughter, Allison. Bloom had told him—on the phone, in much the same way Rawles had told him on the phone—to bug off. What he'd said, actually, was:

"Counselor" (and the word *counselor* rankled because it was more often than not used sarcastically even among contesting attorneys in a courtroom) "it would be nice to have your word that from this minute on you won't be running all over the city of Calusa questioning anybody you think might have some connection with this case, as I would hate to have the blood of a six-year-old girl on my hands if I were you, Counselor."

Matthew had said, "Stop talking to me as if I'm a fucking Los Angeles private eye."

That was the first time Bloom had felt it necessary to chastise Matthew. The second time was more recently. It had, in fact, been shortly before Matthew took the bullet in his shoulder. And yesterday morning was the third time, only it hadn't been Bloom, a *friend*, delivering the warning, it had been a detective Matthew knew only casually. And he was still annoyed. He had not, to his knowledge, done anything to jeopardize or compromise the police investigation into the death of Otto Samalson. He had not spirited away evidence, he had not forewarned witnesses or suspects, he had done nothing whatever to warrant Rawles's blunt reprimand. "You've been busy." It occurred to him that Bloom had once used those exact words. With much the same sarcastic lilt. "You've been busy." Maybe all cops said "You've been busy" when they meant "Fuck off." And the reprimand was even more annoying because Matthew had been calling to give the man *information*, the make and color of the automobile that had followed Otto out of the Seven-Eleven parking lot last Sunday night. Matthew hadn't *sought* this information, it had *come* to him. And he had immediately turned it over to the police. And had been told not to talk to anyone else. He was tempted to call Grown-ups Inc. and ask them to please get Rawles off his back.

Grown-ups Inc.

Another game he and Susan had invented. Long long ago. When they were still in love. On the way to her house that Friday afternoon, he thought about that game. And wondered if Susan remembered it.

His annoyance began to dissipate as he drove out toward Stone Crab Key. It was impossible to stay angry on a day like today. A day like today reminded him of a Chicago summer. The sky clear and piercingly blue, the sun shining, the temperature back to what it *should* have been in June, a pleasant eighty degrees at 5:35 P.M. (or so his car radio had just informed him), the humidity a comfortable forty-two percent. Driving westward across the Cortez Causeway, Calusa Bay billowing with sails on either side of the bridge, he thought for perhaps the thousandth time how wonderful it was to be living down here. And thought of the plans he'd made for himself and Joanna this weekend. And grinned from ear to ear.

He felt peculiar going up to the front door of the house he used to live in. Usually, he parked at the curb and tooted the horn and Joanna popped out a moment later. Today, he went up the walk, and rang the front doorbell, and looked over at the orange trees he himself had planted six years ago, and wondered if old Reggie Soames still lived next door, and rang the bell again, and Susan's voice came from the back of the house, where the master bedroom was, "Matthew? Is that you?" She sounded surprised. Had she forgotten she'd invited him for a drink?

"Yes!" he called back. "Am I early?"

A long silence. Then:

"The door's open, come in."

He twisted the doorknob, and the door sure enough wasn't locked, and he walked into a living room he remembered, different furniture in it now, she'd completely redecorated after she kicked him out, but familiar nonetheless. He'd been in this house only once since that night two years ago. He stood in the living room now, and looked out through the sliding glass doors to where he used to dock his sailboat. *The Windbag.* He had named it over Susan's protests. She hated sailing and had wanted to call it *The Wet Blanket.* The boat had cost seven thousand dollars used, which hadn't been bad for a twenty-five-footer that slept four comfortably. The boat and the Karmann Ghia he still drove were virtually the only two things he'd got out of the divorce. Susan had got everything else: the house, the Mercedes-Benz, his daughter, his clock collection, everything. Matthew had the Karmann Ghia repainted and sold the boat a month after the final decree. Oddly, he hadn't been sailing since.

"Matthew," Susan called, "fix yourself something, will you? I'll be right out."

"Where's Joanna?" he shouted, but got no answer. He went to the bar, found it still well-stocked, poured himself a Canadian Club on the rocks, shouted "Can I fix *you* something?" and was surprised when he heard her voice behind him, almost at his shoulder, saying, "I'm here, don't yell."

He turned.

She was wearing a white terry robe.

Her hair was wet.

She was smiling.

No lipstick on her mouth.

No makeup at all.

Susan fresh from the shower and smelling of soap.

"Hi," she said, "didn't Joanna call you?"

"No," he said, puzzled. "Why? Is something wrong?"

"Well, that depends. Damn it, she promised."

"What is it?"

"Well . . . she's on her way to Palm Beach."

"She's on her way to *where*?" Matthew said. He was almost amused. This was beginning to sound like the old Susan. Keep the kid away from him any which way possible, make Life with Father as difficult as . . .

"This wasn't my idea," she said at once, "I promise you, Matthew. She called me from Diana Silver's house all excited because Diana's parents were going to Palm Beach for the weekend, and they'd invited her along, and she wanted to know could she go with them. This was eleven o'clock or so, I would have called you myself, but I was already late for an appointment, and I had an open house to set up and a hundred other things to do. I told her to call you and get your permission. When I got back here tonight, there was a note on the kitchen table saying she'd be home late Sunday night. I assumed she'd called you and you'd said it was okay."

"Well, I had three closings today," Matthew said. "I was out of the office till four-thirty. Maybe she—"

"I'm sure she would have left a message."

"I didn't get any."

"Then she *didn't* call."

"Maybe she was afraid I'd say no." Matthew shrugged. "The Father's Day weekend, you know."

"Maybe." Susan really did look troubled. "Anyway, I wasn't expecting you. I figured . . ."

"Don't worry about it," he said, and put his drink down on the bar. "If you've made other plans . . ."

"No, that's not it," Susan said, "it's just . . . I was in the shower . . . I must look like a drowned cat."

"You look beautiful," he said.

"Sure, sure, sweet talker."

There was an awkward silence. She made an abrupt motion, as if she were about to raise her hand to fluff her hair, the way women will do when they feel they are being observed or admired or both, and then aborted the motion and shrugged girlishly and said, "Did I hear you offer me a drink?"

"Name it," he said.

"A Beefeater martini, on the rocks," she said.

He looked at her.

"Yeah," she said, and grinned.

When they were married, their most frequent argument was what Matthew had labeled the Beefeater Martini Argument. It had been Susan's contention that Matthew never got drunk when he drank, for example, two Scotches with soda or two *anythings* with soda, but that he always got drunk or fuzzy or furry or slurry (these were all Susan's words) when he had two martinis, especially two Beefeater martinis. The magic word Beefeater somehow added more potency to the drink.

But now, two years and much gin under the bridge later, here was Susan asking for the evil potion that changed men to furry, fuzzy beasts and worked God knew what transformation on nice Presbyterian girls from the state of Illinois.

"Very dry, with two olives," Susan said.

He began mixing the drink.

"I hate it when she breaks her word," Susan said. "She's growing up so fast, isn't she? She'll be a woman before we know it. *Then* will we have troubles," she said, and rolled her eyes.

He did not miss the word *we*.

Silently, he mixed the drink.

"You're right, it must have been because of Father's Day," Susan said. "She was probably embarrassed to ask."

"I'm sure," Matthew said, and handed her the glass.

"Thank you," Susan said. "What it is, Matthew, Diana's brother is home from Duke for the summer, and *he* was going to Palm Beach with the family, and I think Joanna has a bit of a crush on him, and *so* . . ." She rolled her eyes again, let the sentence trail, shrugged, raised her glass, and said, "Shall we drink to Electra's demise?"

Matthew smiled.

"But you didn't pour one for yourself," she said.

"I'm drinking Canadian," he said and lifted his glass from the bar.

"I thought you drank—"

"They make me furry and fuzzy," he said.

"Don't be ridiculous," she said. "Did you mix enough for two?"

"I did."

"Then join me," she said. "If we're going to get furry and fuzzy, we ought to do it together."

He poured himself a martini, and dropped two olives into the glass.

"That's much better," she said, and nodded.

They raised their glasses. They clinked them together. They drank.

"Shall we go outside?" Susan said. "Sit by the pool?"

There did not used to be a pool here when Matthew shared the house with her. The settlement money had bought one. Or the alimony payments. Or both. He tried not to feel bitter about the alimony payments. Bitterness could spoil a good martini. He followed her out to the pool. She was wearing only the terry cloth robe, hardly the sexiest garment in the world, and she was barefoot, no heels to give her ass and her breasts a perky, sexy lift—but somehow she looked sexy enough.

They sat in lounge chairs beside the pool. Matthew figured the pool and patio had cost at least eighteen grand.

"You really think she was afraid to call me, huh?" he said.

"Oh, no question."

"She should've put Grown-ups Inc. on the case."

"Oh my God!" Susan said. "Do you remember that, too?"

"I was thinking of it on the way out here," he said, smiling, nodding.

"Grown-ups Inc., that was a century ago," she said, and fell silent.

On the canal beyond the pool, a fish jumped.

He couldn't remember now who had first come up with the notion. As with most of the games they had played when they were married (had they really played games, had there really been fun?), it had probably been a collaborative effort, one of them saying something that led to an elaboration that led to an embellishment that led to a fillip, and there you were! Grown-ups Inc.

The way Grown-ups Inc. worked was really quite simple. If, for example, your building superintendent wasn't sending up enough heat, and you were either afraid or embarrassed to call him and demand more heat, you called Grown-ups Inc. instead, and you said, "I don't know what I'm going to do, there's not enough heat in the apartment, and I have a three-year-old daughter—"

That would've been about right for when they'd invented Grown-ups Inc. Joanna *had* been about three, and they were still living in Chicago where it got damn cold in the wintertime and where if you didn't have heat you could freeze to death.

"—and the apartment is like an igloo."

"We'll take care of it," the man from Grown-ups Inc. would say.

And he would call the super and tell him, "This is Grown-ups Inc., we're calling for Matthew Hope, we want the heat turned higher in his apartment at once, thank you very much."

The uses of Grown-ups Inc. were manifold.

Need theater tickets? An indoor tennis court from five to six? A dinner for eight served on your veranda? A birthday telegram, Valentine's Day chocolates, Mother's Day flowers, Father's Day tie?

Grown-ups Inc. would take care of all or any of these things painlessly. Grown-ups Inc. was premised on the sound concept that everyone needed a grown-up he could turn to. Marine generals needed grown-ups they could turn to. Women activists needed grown-ups. The president of the United States needed a grown-up. Terrorists needed grown-ups. In Grown-ups Inc. there was a grown-up for everyone, a grown-up to serve every need. Want to ask for a raise? Grown-ups Inc. would call your boss. Want to plan a trip to Bombay or Siam? No need to call a travel agent. Grown-ups Inc. would take care of it because Grown-ups Inc. took care of *everything*.

In fantasy, they had used Grown-ups Inc. more times than they could count. There was once a rat the size of a zeppelin in the Chicago apartment and the moment Susan saw it, she yelled, "Call Grown-ups Inc., quick!" Out on *The Windbag* one day, they were caught in a sudden squall that threatened to capsize the boat, and Matthew—clinging to the wheel for dear life—grinned weakly, and told Susan to get on the radio to Grown-ups Inc.

There was nothing Grown-ups Inc. could not do.

"Do you know . . . ?" Susan said softly, and then stopped, and shook her head.

"What?" he said.

"When . . ." She shook her head again.

"Tell me."

"When I . . . when I found out that night about you and . . . shit, I still can't say her name."

"Aggie," he said.

"Aggie, yes," Susan said, and sighed. "When I found out about her that night, I . . . I . . . went all to pieces, you know, I didn't know what to do. And I . . . I thought . . . when Matthew comes home, we'll have to call Grown-ups Inc. They'll solve it for us." She nodded bleakly. "But of course that's not what happened, is it? Because there *isn't* any Grown-ups Inc."

"*We're* Grown-ups Inc.," Matthew said.

"The way we used to be Santa Claus," Susan said. "For Joanna."

"Yes," he said.

They were silent for several moments.

"Do you think Grown-ups Inc. could have saved it?" she asked. "Do you think *we* could have saved it, Matthew?"

"I don't know," he said honestly. "There was so much anger."

"There still is, don't kid yourself," Susan said and smiled. "I still think of her as The Cunt. Aggie What's-Her-Name. The Cunt."

"You're different," he said.

"How?"

"Two years ago, you never would have used that word."

"Maybe you didn't know me two years ago."

"Maybe not. You used to call your period The Curse."

"I still do. Some things never change, Matthew."

"We've changed, Susan."

"Older," she said.

"For sure."

"I'm thirty-six," she said. "That makes me middle-aged, doesn't it?"

"Hardly," he said, and smiled.

"You should see some of the gorgeous creatures in my exercise class," she said. "If you ever want to feel ancient, go to an exercise class."

"Frank says the reason exercise classes are so popular is because of the costume. It makes women feel like Bob Fosse dancers. Tell them they'd have to come to class in faded blue jeans and a gray sweatshirt, and enrollment would drop off by half. That's what Frank says."

"Frank," she said, and nodded, as though fondly remembering someone half-forgotten.

They both fell silent again. A bird called somewhere. Another bird answered.

"Are there any more of these little mothers?" she asked, and extended her empty glass to him.

"Jack Lemmon," he said. "*The Apartment*. The scene in the bar."

"We were still living in Chicago when we saw it."

"Yes."

She nodded again. Taking her glass he went into the house familiarly, as if he had never left it, and walked to the bar, and poured what was left of the martinis equally into her glass and his. When he came back out onto the patio again, she was sitting with her face turned toward the pool and the canal beyond, one leg extended, one leg bent at the knee. He felt an extraordinarily sharp urge to place his hand on the inside of her thigh. He sat instead, in the lounge beside hers, and handed her one of the glasses.

"We musn't drink so much that we won't know what we're doing," she said, sipping at the drink.

"We can always call Grown-ups Inc. later on," he said.

"Yes, and ask *them* what we did."

"The eyes and ears of the world."

"The *mouth* of the world," Susan said.

"I felt like calling them yesterday," he said, and told her all about his telephone encounter with Detective Cooper Rawles. She listened intently. It was like the old days, when he used to come home from the office and relate to her one problem or another and she listened because she *cared*, she still *cared*. It was like then.

"So what are you going to do?" she asked.

"Just what I've *been* doing," he said. "If there are questions I want answered, I'm going to ask them."

"Despite the warning?"

"I don't feel I'm interfering with his case," Matthew said.

"But that's not it," Susan said. "Even if you *were* interfering, you'd continue, wouldn't you?"

"Well," he said, smiling, "as an officer of the court, I don't think I'd knowingly obstruct justice or impede the progress of an investi—"

"But you'd continue."

"Yes."

"Because you enjoy it," Susan said.

"Well, I . . ."

"You do, Matthew."

"I guess I do."

"Why don't you simply learn all there is to learn about criminal law—?"

"Well, there's a lot to—"

"—and start practicing it?"

He looked at her.

There was a shrug on her face.

Eyebrows lifted.

Brown eyes wide.

Questioning.

Why not practice criminal law?

The simplicity of it.

"Just like that, huh?" he said.

"Why not?" she said. "I have a feeling you find it more interesting than real estate."

"*Anything's* more interesting than—"

"Or divorce or negligence or malpractice or—"

"Yes, but . . ."

"So do it," she said, and this time actually shrugged.

Why not, he thought, and leaned over and kissed her quickly on the cheek. "Thank you," he said.

"That's a thank-you?" she said, and reached up to him, and

put her arms around his neck and drew him down to her on the lounge. For a moment, they teetered awkwardly, Matthew on the edge of the lounge, struggling for purchase, Susan trying to make room for him, the normal clumsiness of foreplay exaggerated by the suddenness of her move and his unprepared reaction to it. Like groping adolescents—and perhaps this was good because it, too, reminded them of another time long ago—they shifted weight, bumped hips, tangled arms, and finally settled, or more accurately collapsed onto the lounge in an approximate position of proximity, Susan on her side, the robe pulled back to expose her left flank, Matthew seminestled into her, his left arm pinned under his body, his right arm draped loosely over the curving arc of her hip, their lips at last meeting abruptly and in surprise.

Later, he would try to understand that kiss.

They had kissed many times before. Kissed as true adolescents in steamy embrace, when kissing was all she would permit and therefore the sole expression of their passion. Kissed after kissing had become a prelude to heavy petting, something to be got through hastily, like the dull passages of a novel, something to be skimmed or skipped entirely, merely the necessary overture to nipples and breasts and the exciting electric touch of nylon panties and the crispness beneath and the moistness below. Kissed only perfunctorily in the waning years of their marriage, on the cheek in greeting or farewell, passionlessly on the lips in bed before what had become a mechanical act. Kissed last Sunday night hurriedly and somewhat frantically, eager to get to the real thing, both of them fearful of what they were about to do and simultaneously afraid they wouldn't *get* to do it before one or the other had a change of mind or heart.

Now . . .

It was in many respects a first kiss.

First in the sense that it brought back to each of them, in a rush of memory, the *actual* first time they kissed in Chicago, on the doorstep of her house, a porchlight glowing, the sounds of summer insects everywhere around them, I had a good time, Matthew, So did I, their lips tentatively brushing, clinging, her arms coming up around his neck, his hands in the small of her back, pulling her close, into his immediate erection, Jesus, she said breathlessly, and pulled away and looked fiercely into his eyes, and kissed him again quickly and hurried into the house.

But first in another sense as well.

First in that for perhaps the only time in their separate adult lives, they brought to the simple act of kissing each other an expertise they had learned not only from each other but from others as well, so that the mere anatomical joining of two orbicularis oris muscles in a state of contraction became something much more intense and heated and all-consuming.

They broke away.

She said what she had said back in Chicago, more years ago than he could count.

"Jesus."

Breathlessly.

And then:

"Let's go inside."

Ernesto figured what they should do first thing this morning was start spreading the word around. This was Monday already, they'd been here in Calusa four days already, this was ridiculous. They had contacted this Martin Klement person at his Springtime restaurant, just the way Amaros had told them to, but they hadn't heard anything from him since, so what they had to do now was let the word out they were looking to score. Ernesto figured unless the girl was a pro, she wouldn't know how to get rid of four keys of coke, she'd be looking for buyers.

"She'll be shopping around looking for a buyer, am I right?" he said to Domingo. He said this in Spanish. Whenever the two were alone together, they spoke Spanish.

Domingo said, "Maybe she plans to snort the whole four keys all by herself."

Ernesto said, "That isn't why a person steals four keys of

coke, to snort them. A person steals four keys to *sell* them is what a person does."

Domingo said, "Maybe, but even so I think it's risky to say we're looking for big cocaine. We don't know what the narcotics situation is here in Calusa."

It looked to him like a very clean town on the surface, but in Spanish there was a proverb that said, *Las apariencias engañan.* In English, this meant, "You can't judge a book by its cover." Domingo didn't know what was going on here in the city of Calusa, Florida. Perhaps it was a very strict town, policewise, in which case they could find the Law on their motel doorstep if word got around that they were looking to buy dope in quantity.

On the other hand, it could very well be the kind of town where you could buy four keys of coke right on Main Street, in which case somebody already had the trade nailed down and they might not like the idea of two Miami Beach dudes strolling in talking a big dope deal.

"These are all things to be considered," Domingo said, "if a person is interested in staying alive and staying out of jail."

Actually, the most recent figures from the Florida Department of Law Enforcement didn't mention anything about narcotics in Calusa County or in the city of Calusa itself. It reported that the crime rate in the entire state of Florida had begun to climb again only recently, after two years of decline, and it defined "crime rate" as the number of "serious" crimes committed per 100,000 people. Serious crimes included murder, rape, robbery, aggravated assault, burglary, larceny, and motor vehicle theft. Selling four keys of cocaine on Main Street either wasn't a serious crime or else the FDLE had no figures on it. In any case, there were 13,236 serious crimes committed in Calusa County in the year just past, an increase of 11 percent over the 11,928 reported during the year before that. Sixteen murders, most of them involving people who knew each other, had been committed in the county during the past year. Rapes went up from 97 to 127. There were similar increases in every category except auto thefts.

Calusa County Sheriff Alan Huxtable said that rapid population growth might have accounted for the increase in the number of crimes. He also pointed out that completion of the interstate highway might have been another contributing factor.

"We've traced some of these crimes back to I-75," he said. "People come into Calusa to commit a crime, and then go back into the other counties. The interstate just brings a lot of undesirable people through."

Ernesto and Domingo hadn't read the newspaper article in which Sheriff Huxtable was quoted, otherwise they might have taken offense. They did not consider themselves undesirable people. They were here, in fact, *looking* for an undesirable person who had stolen four keys of cocaine from their employer, taken the stuff *out* of Dade County, in fact, and *into* Calusa County, where for all they knew it had already been sold to someone who'd already run it up to New York in the back of a pickup truck carrying lettuce and tomatoes.

Ernesto and Domingo were merely two righteous citizens trying to correct an outrageous wrong.

It didn't sound like a warning until a moment before he walked out of Matthew's office.

At the start of their conversation—this was at ten-fifteen on Monday and Matthew was feeling too good to be bothered by anyone or anything—Daniel Nettington was quietly telling him that he'd been visited by a big black detective at eight o'clock last night—a goddamn *Sunday,* could you believe it? Cops had no respect.

Daniel Nettington was Carla Nettington's philandering husband.

Daniel Nettington was the star of the porn show Otto had recorded in the bedroom of a woman named Rita Kirkman.

Carla had told Matthew her husband was forty-five years old. He looked a good deal older. His graying hair was combed sideways across his forehead in a vain attempt to hide his encroaching baldness. His teeth and the index finger and middle finger of his right hand were nicotine stained. His small brown eyes were embedded deep in puffy flesh. He was an altogether unattractive man, and Matthew could not for the life of him imagine why: (a) Rita Kirkman kept pressing him to leave his wife and/or at least take her out to dinner, and (b) Why Carla Nettington would care if he was sleeping with the entire state of Florida.

"This black detective," Nettington said, "informed me that the man who was killed had been *following* me. That my wife had gone to you, and that you had hired this man to *follow* me."

He seemed inordinately fond of the verb "to follow" in all its declensions. The verb "to follow" incensed him. He was outraged by the fact that Otto Samalson had been *following* him. That Otto had been *killed* was a matter of only secondary importance.

"This was all in the file this black detective got from Otto Samalson's assistant, a *Chinese* lady from what I understand. A regular little United Nations, huh?"

Matthew said nothing.

"According to what I was told by this black detective, whose name is Cooper Rawles . . ."

"Yes, I know Detective Rawles."

"Yes, I gathered that. According to what he told me, I was being *followed* for something like ten days before this man met with his accident. Is that true, sir?"

"It wasn't an *accident*," Matthew said. "Otto Samalson was murdered."

"Yes," Nettington said. "And because he was *following* me, it now appears I'm a goddamn suspect here."

"Is that what Detective Rawles told you? That you're a suspect?"

"I don't need a black detective to tell me I'm a suspect when he comes to my home—on a Sunday night, no less—and begins asking questions about where I was the *previous* Sunday, June eighth, at a little before eleven, which happens to be when the man who was *following* me got shot and killed on U.S. 41. Now what I want to know, Mr. Hope . . ."

"Yes, what exactly is it you want to know?" Matthew said.

"And I don't want to hear any bullshit about the confidentiality of the lawyer-client relationship," Nettington said, "because it so happens I'm an attorney myself."

"I'm sorry to hear that," Matthew said.

"What's that supposed to mean?"

"Only that I'm sorry to hear it. What law firm do you work for?"

"*I'll* ask the questions, if you don't mind," Nettington said, and then immediately answered the question anyway. "I don't work for a law firm," he said, "I'm house counsel for Bartell Technographics."

"I see," Matthew said. "And does your work ever take you out of town?"

"Rarely," Nettington said.

"A pity," Matthew said.

Nettington looked at him.

"That's exactly what I want to talk to you about," he said.

"My wife tells me she's got some kind of tape—she hasn't *heard* the tape yet, but there's some kind of tape supposed to be between me and some woman, God knows *what* she's talking about—*is* there such a tape?"

"I'm not in a position to discuss that, Mr. Nettington."

"There's either a tape or there isn't one," Nettington said.

"That is a safe assumption," Matthew said.

"So is there one?"

"I can't answer that, and you know I can't."

"If Carla's already *told* me—"

"That's *your* allegation, Mr. Nettington."

"It's what Carla said."

Matthew said nothing.

"That there's a tape."

Matthew still said nothing.

"Where is this tape?" Nettington asked.

Silence.

"I don't think the police have it, 'cause the black detective didn't mention it. It was only Carla who mentioned it. Said you'd told her there was an incriminating tape."

Silence.

"I'd like that tape," Nettington said.

Silence.

"If it exists."

Silence.

"Does it exist?"

Silence.

"What I'm prepared to do," Nettington said, "is pay a goodly sum of money for that tape. If it exists."

"*If* the tape exists," Matthew said, "it's already been paid for, Mr. Nettington."

"Which means it *does* exist," Nettington said. "What you just admitted is that my wife already paid for it when she hired

119

you to put a private detective on me, which means the son of a bitch *did* manage to plant a bug in there somehow, didn't he?"

"In where, Mr. Nettington?"

"In Rita's house, you know damn well where, Mr. Hope. If you told Carla the tape's incriminating, then you know what's on it, and you know where it was made."

"In any event . . ."

"I want that tape," Nettington said.

"Mr. Nettington . . ."

"Do you hear me? I want that tape."

"Yes, I hear you," Matthew said. "Tell me, Mr. Nettington, when Detective Rawles asked you—"

"Don't change the subject," Nettington said.

"When he asked you where you were on the night Otto was killed, what did you tell him?"

"I told him *exactly* where I was."

"Which was where?"

"If you're so curious about that, ask him. Or don't you two get along?" he said, and grinned wolfishly. "Would you like to know what he said about you?"

"Not particularly."

"He said you enjoyed playing cops and robbers. Said if you ever came to visit me, I should call him right away."

"So you came to visit me instead," Matthew said.

"I called first," Nettington said.

"So you did."

There was a long uncomfortable silence.

"But if there's nothing further," Matthew said.

"Will you let me have that tape?" Nettington said.

Matthew sighed.

"You ought to reconsider," Nettington said.

Which was when it sounded like a warning.

He looked at Matthew a moment longer, his gaze unwavering, and then he got up and walked out of the office.

They had decided between them, he and Susan, that it might be best if their daughter didn't find him there when she got home. Joanna was a very smart cookie, and she was apt to put two and two together if she came home and found Mummy and Daddy munching crumpets and sipping tea together in the living room.

They were neither of them ready to answer questions about what had happened this weekend or about just what the hell was going on here. Neither of them *knew* just what the hell was going on here, but even if they suspected—after two nights and days of making love around the clock and never once leaving the house—that something was in the wind, they didn't feel like sharing it with Joanna just yet. Anyway, what could you say to your fourteen-year-old daughter about something like this? Mummy and Daddy have been fucking our brains out all weekend, darling, how nice to see you? No. Better for Daddy to disappear in the night like a terrorist with an unexploded bomb, handle the questions later, if and when they came up. Matthew knew the questions would come up sooner or later.

In Calusa this year, school had ended on the ninth. Last year, it had ended on the twelfth. Each year in Calusa, the kids were out on the second Monday in June, and back again early in August, which should have been a criminal offense. Joanna was sleeping late now that school was out; she called him at the office shortly after Nettington left. The moment he came onto the line, she began singing "Happy Father's Day to You," to the tune of "Happy Birthday to You," the lyrics a bit strained but the sentiment heartfelt.

"Hi, baby," he said. "What time'd you get back?"

"Around eleven, I figured it was too late to call. Dad," she said, "I want to apologize about the weekend."

"No need," he said.

"It's just that Mom was so insistent . . . well, you know how she gets when I'm about to see you."

"No," he said cautiously, "how does she get?"

"Well, she's always trying to finagle me out of it. Well, you know."

"Uh-huh," he said.

"I told her I'd be embarrassed to death, calling you and telling you I was going away for the *Father's* Day weekend, so she said she'd call and square it with you, which I know she did, but I still feel rotten about it."

"Did *what*, honey? *Called* me, did you say?"

"Well, yeah. I almost called you, anyway. When I went home to pack. But Mom said she'd already taken care of it, and it might be best to leave well enough alone—what she said, actually, was 'Let sleeping dogs lie,' referring to you, Dad, the sleeping dog—that you'd taken it calmly, and I might wreck it if I called."

"Called me a sleeping dog, huh?"

"Well, you know Mom," Joanna said.

"Said I'd taken it calmly, huh?"

"I *hope* you did, Dad. Were you very angry?"

"No, no. Mom was there when you went home to pack, huh? You didn't just leave a note on the table or anything?"

"What?" Joanna said. "A note? No. What note? What are you talking about?"

"Nothing. Nothing."

"I should have called myself, I'm such a coward."

"Well, don't worry," Matthew said, "Grown-ups Inc. took care of it."

"Who?"

"Grown-ups Inc. Don't you remember? When Mom and I used to—"

"No," Joanna said. "Grown-ups Inc.? Is that real or something you made up?"

"Well, something we made up, actually."

"You and Mom?"

"Yes."

There was a sudden silence on the line.

"So how was the weekend?" Matthew asked.

"Good," Joanna said.

"I understand Diana's brother went along."

"Did Mom tell you that?"

"Yes."

"She shouldn't have. I wish she hadn't, Dad. She probably said I have a crush on him, am I right?"

"Well, she hinted that might be the case."

"I wish she hadn't," Joanna said again.

"Don't worry about it."

"Well, she shouldn't have."

There was another silence.

"When am I going to see you?" he said.

"Can you take me to dinner tonight?"

"I'd love to. What time shall I pick you up?"

"I'll check with Mom. I think she has a date with Peter the Pest, maybe I can spend the night."

"Oh?" Matthew said. "Does she?"

"I think so. I'll call you later, okay?"

"Fine," he said.

"I bought you a nice present," Joanna said, and hung up.

In most civilized cities, people didn't begin drinking until four-thirty at the very earliest. In New York, for example—

according to Frank Summerville—the bars didn't start filling up till about five-thirty. But Calusa was a resort town in season and a retirement town all year round, and tourists and senior citizens sometimes discovered time weighing heavily on their hands. So what better place to while away the late afternoon hours than in a bar where, during Happy Hour, you got two drinks for the price of one? Happy Hour in Calusa began at 4:00 P.M.

At four-oh-seven that afternoon, at which time Joanna was on the phone again to say it was okay for tonight, Jimmy Legs was in a bar called The Yellow Bird, listening to a piano player slaughtering some very good Cole Porter tunes, and waiting for a man named Harry Stagg to join him. Jimmy was not here to while away the time. Jimmy had business to discuss with Harry, and the business was finding a hooker who had copped his brother's gold Rolex.

Stagg came into the bar at about four-ten, five minutes earlier than he was due. He was a very punctual person, Stagg, and he was also very tall—though, actually, *everybody* looked tall to Jimmy. He was wearing a white linen jacket over pastel-colored slacks the same color as his open-throated shirt. He was wearing white Italian-looking shoes with no socks. He looked like one of the cops on "Miami Vice." Needed a shave, too, just like that cop on "Miami Vice." That was a show Jimmy hated because it made cops look like heroes instead of the pricks they really were. "Hill Street Blues," too. Propaganda. He stood up as Stagg approached the table.

"Hey, how you doin'?" he said, and took Stagg's hand. The men shook hands briefly. Stagg looked over at the piano as if wondering what had died inside it. He ordered a Johnnie Walker Red on the rocks from the waiter who came over to the table and then looked over at the piano again.

"Where'd that guy learn to play?" he asked Jimmy.

"San Quentin, sounds like," Jimmy said.

"It *does* sound like it," Stagg said. "They remodeled this place, din't they? This used to be called Franco's, dinnit?"

"I think so."

"Yeah, Franco's, I think. So now it's The Yellow Bird, huh?"

"Yeah."

"That's a big difference, Franco's and The Yellow Bird."

"Yeah."

The waiter brought two Johnnie Walker Reds on the rocks to the table.

"I only ordered one," Stagg said.

"The second one is complimentary, sir," the waiter said.

"I'da known that, I'da ordered the black," Stagg said.

The waiter smiled. "Next time, sir," he said, and walked off.

"They should tell you in advance it's two for one," Stagg said. "Give you a chance to order premium stuff."

"Nobody tells you nothin' nowadays," Jimmy said.

"Whole fuckin' world's fucked up," Stagg said. "Terrorists, all kindsa shit." He sipped at the Scotch and then said, "So what's on your mind?"

"There's somebody I'm lookin' for," Jimmy said. "She's a hooker stole my brother's watch."

"Oh, okay," Stagg said. "Because first, when you said you were lookin' for somebody, I thought Why's he comin' to me, am I the Missing Persons Bureau? But then you say she stole your brother's watch, and I get it." He took a pad from the inner pocket of the white jacket. He took a pencil from the same pocket. "What kinda watch?" he asked.

"A gold Rolex," Jimmy said. "It cost eight grand in Tiffany's, New York."

"That's some watch," Stagg said.

"Solid gold," Jimmy said. "The band and everything. Eight grand in Tiffany's."

"That ain't cornflakes, eight grand."

"My brother's ready to kill her," Jimmy said, "a watch like that."

"Well, let me see I can find it for you, the watch. Maybe he won't want to kill her once he gets the watch back. Lots of people, they say they're gonna kill people, they only mean they want their goods back, you know? Let me ask around, see what I can find out, okay? I give it my best shot, we see what happens, okay?"

"His initials are on the back of the case," Jimmy said.

"Good, I'm glad you told me that," Stagg said. "What are his initials?"

"D. L. For David Larkin."

Stagg wrote down the initials, and then said, "There's a Larkin Boats on the Trail. Is that the same Larkin?"

"Yeah, that's my brother."

"No wonder he can afford a watch costs eight grand," Stagg said. "What'd he do, change his name? 'Cause *your* name's Largura, ain't it?"

"*I'm* the one changed my name," Jimmy said, and smiled.

"So did I," Stagg said. "My name used to be Stagione, that means 'season' in Italian, I changed it to Stagg. That's better than Stagione, Stagg. Harry Stagg, I like that better than Harry Stagione, don't you?"

He blinked at Jimmy and then said, "Whattya mean *you* changed your name? From Larkin? To Largura?"

"Yeah, I wanted an Italian name," Jimmy said. "I didn't like havin' a Wasp name."

Matthew picked up Joanna at seven o'clock.

No sign of Susan anywhere around the house.

In the car, he casually asked, "Did your mother go out with Peter?"

"Yes," Joanna answered.

Peter the Pest.

Suddenly jealous of Peter the Pest, né Peter Nelson Rothman, the main man in Susan's life for the past . . . what? Two, three months? None of Matthew's business, of course. She was no longer his wife, she was his *former* wife, his *ex* wife. Still, it wasn't right, was it, for a situation to have become *so* transparent that your fourteen-year-old daughter could automatically assume that if Mommy had a date with Peter the Pest then she'd be free to spend the night at *your* house because when Mommy dated Peter *she* spent the night at *his* house.

Well, listen, it was none of his business.

Free country, woman wanted to date the town's . . .

The thing he couldn't understand, though, was how she could *do* this the very night after they'd . . .

Well, listen.

No strings on her, she was entitled to whatever . . .

But, damn it, she was the one who'd . . .

Well, what the hell.

But truth was truth, and she was the one who'd engineered their weekend together. Told Joanna she'd call him to explain about the Palm Beach trip, never called, was waiting instead to pounce when he got to the house Friday evening, fresh out of the shower and looking good enough to eat. Oh my, didn't Joanna call you? She said she would call. Well, just so it shouldn't be a total loss, let's go to bed together, okay?

So tonight she was seeing Peter the Pest.

Who once, on the tennis court, told Matthew he could beat him no matter *what* Matthew did.

"Here's what we'll do," Peter said. "You can hit the ball

wherever you want, anyplace on the court. When I hit the ball back, I'll hit it directly to your forehand, right where you're standing. And I'll *still* beat you."

Matthew was offended.

He told Peter he didn't want to play with him anymore, and walked off the court.

But that wasn't why she shouldn't be dating him tonight. It was simply . . . well.

Well, damn it.

Really.

"So will you be sleeping over?" he asked.

"No, she'll be coming home early," Joanna said.

Matthew tried to keep from smiling. It was not easy.

He thought Jesus Christ, I'm falling in love with my own wife!

All through dinner, Joanna was uncommonly silent.

Matthew had known this kid for a long, long time, and he knew better than to pry when she was in one of her dark and pensive moods. Usually, he waited her out. Eventually, she told him what was bothering her. Tonight she did not seem about to tell him anything.

She had ordered clam chowder and the soft-shell crabs. He had ordered oysters on the half shell and the broiled swordfish. That was at seven-thirty. It was now close to eight-thirty. She had said perhaps three dozen words in the last hour.

"Could we get some lemon wedges?"

And . . .

"My fork is dirty."

And . . .

"Can I have a little white wine or will they take a fit?"

And . . .

"Please pass the salt."

And . . .

"I wonder if they have brewed decaf."

Silence now as they drank their coffee.

He decided to break his own cardinal rule.

"Something wrong?" he asked.

"Nope."

"You haven't said much all night."

"I'm tired," she said. "Too much sun. I was on the beach all day."

"Sure there's nothing you want to tell me about?"

"Nothing."

Silence again.

"Did you enjoy yourself in Palm Beach?"

"Yep."

More silence.

"Joanna, what is it?" he said.

"What is what?" she said.

"Whatever it is."

"It's nothing."

"Well, I know it's something."

"Okay, you want to know what it is?"

"Yes."

"I found your tie."

"My *what*?"

"Your tie. I found your tie at the house."

"What house?"

"*Mom's* house, whose house do you think?"

"What tie? You found my . . . ?"

"The blue tie with the pony on it, the blue Ralph Lauren tie."

"Oh."

"Do you know the tie I mean?"

"Yes, I know the tie."

"I found it out by the pool," Joanna said. "You know where the two lounge chairs are? That's where I found the tie. On one of the lounge chairs."

"Uh-huh."

There was a long silence.

"Were you at the house this weekend?" Joanna asked.

He hesitated.

"Dad?"

"Yes," he said. "I dropped by after work Friday."

"Mom didn't mention it," Joanna said.

"Well," he said.

"Did she ask you to come over or what?"

"Joanna," he said, "what business is this of yours?"

"Well, I just think it's *odd*, that's all."

"It is," he said.

"I mean, was there something you had to discuss with her? Something about me?"

"No," he said, and hesitated. "Joanna," he said, "this really is none of your business."

"'Cause you usually discuss things on the *phone*, you know?"

"Yes, I know."

"In fact, you usually wait outside in the car for me, you toot the horn and *wait*, you know? So it just seems *odd* that you'd go to the *house* to talk to Mom, if that's why you went there. I mean, it's not exactly a *secret*, Dad, that you don't get along too well, you know what I mean? I mean, a person wouldn't exactly call you *pals*, you know what I mean? So I think it's really *strange*, I mean actually *peculiar* that you'd go over to the house while I'm away in Palm Beach!"

"Lower your voice, please," he said.

"I'm sorry," she said, and looked quickly around the room to see if any of the other diners had reacted to her somewhat strident outburst.

"There was some kind of mix-up," he said calmly. "I didn't know you were going to Palm Beach. I went to the house to pick you up. Your mother invited me in, and we had a few drinks together. Okay?"

"Then why is that none of my business?"

"Because it isn't," he said.

"And also, why didn't you tell me on the phone when I talked to you earlier today that you'd seen Mom over the weekend? And how come you're saying there was a mix-up and you didn't know I was in Palm Beach when on the phone you didn't seem too surprised when I was talking about her calling you and telling you all *about* Palm Beach? So what's going on, Dad?"

"Nothing's going on," he said.

"Okay, fine," Joanna said, and took her napkin off her lap and put it on the table. "Could you get the check, please, Dad? I want to go home. I'm really very tired."

"Joanna . . ." he said.

"Get the check, okay?"

They rode out to Stone Crab Key in silence. The house was dark when they got there.

"Have you got your key?" he asked.

"Yeah, I've got it. You want your tie?"

"There's no hurry, I'll—"

"Maybe you can pick it up some other time," she said, "when I'm not home again," and got out of the Ghia and ran to the front door.

He watched as she put her key into the latch.

She unlocked the door, opened it, and went into the house.

The lights came on.

He realized all at once that she'd told him she'd bought him a nice present.

Apparently she'd decided not to give it to him.

He waited another moment, and then pulled the car away from the curb, trying to remember what Susan had said about Electra.

10

Andrew Hacker was a detective who probably stood six feet two inches in his stockinged feet and maybe weighed a hundred and ninety pounds, but standing alongside Cooper Rawles he looked stunted. Hacker hadn't said a word since they'd entered the office. Matthew wouldn't even have known his name if Cynthia Huellen hadn't announced them both on the phone before she led them down the hall and showed them in.

Rawles in person was a mountain of a man, intimidating by his very presence, more intimidating because Matthew knew he was a good cop and a tough cop, and he was here now laying down all kinds of law. Hacker just stood beside him, looking small and being silent, shock of red hair hanging on his forehead, freckles all over his face, all he needed was a piece of hay in his teeth to look like a shit-kicking redneck. This was Rawles's show, and Hacker knew it. He just kept listening to his partner, his face expressionless. It was raining outside. Really raining. What they called a frog-strangler here in Calusa. Outside Matthew's window, the pavements were sending up steam. Rawles was doing a little steaming of his own.

"What I understand," he said, "is she called you first."

"I guess she did," Matthew said.

"There was a burglary, so the first person she calls is *you*, not the police. That's the first thing pisses me off, Mr. Hope," he said, and poked a thick forefinger toward Matthew's desk. "The second thing pisses me off is there was a tape stolen from that office and the first time I heard about it was when the Chinese lady told me it was gone."

"I don't know which tape you mean. A *lot* of tapes were stolen, Detective Rawles. As well as file folders and uncashed checks and petty cash and—"

"I'm talking about the Nettington tape," Rawles said. "Did you know this tape existed?"

"Yes."

"Why didn't you tell me about this tape?"

"The last time I told you anything . . ."

"Never mind the last time, which by the way we located that Toronado."

"Oh?" Matthew said, and waited for more. Nothing more came.

"I'm talking about *this* time," Rawles said, "where we're concerned here with a tape that may have had something to do with Samalson's murder, and you *knew* about this tape, and you didn't see fit to tell the police about it. Did you *hear* this tape, Mr. Hope?"

"Yes."

"We listened to it a half-hour ago," Rawles said. "The *original* of it, which was in the safe. Whoever busted in there stole a copy the Chinese lady made."

"*Plus* a lot of other things. Including a tape deck and two typewriters."

"That's a very interesting tape, Mr. Hope. It's also a tape that makes your Mr. Nettington—"

"*My* Mr. Nettington?"

"His wife is your client, isn't she?"

"Yes?"

"Well, this tape nails him to the wall where it concerns adultery, which by the way is a crime in the state of Florida, I refer you to Chapters 798.01, 02, and 03. Living in Open Adultery, Lewd and Lascivious Behavior, and Fornication, all second-degree misdemeanors punishable by terms of imprisonment not to exceed sixty days. Did your Mr. Nettington know that tape could send him to jail?"

"He's not *my* Mr. Nettington," Matthew said.

"Admittedly on a bullshit violation, but sixty days ain't hay when you're an attorney and not a professional burglar, huh? Did Nettington know this tape existed?"

"Yes."

"How did he know?"

"His wife told him."

"She informed you of this?"

"No. He did."

"What?" Rawles said.

"Yes."

"When?"

"Yesterday morning."

"Said his wife had told him about the tape?"

"Yes."

"You went to see him? I goddamn well told you to—"

"He came here," Matthew said.

"For what purpose?"

"He wanted the tape."

"So now Samalson's office is busted into and the tape is gone."

"Yes."

"What time did she call you?"

"Who?"

"The Chinese lady."

"Oh. Nine this morning, a little after nine."

"To tell you somebody'd busted in, huh?"

"Words to that effect, yes."

"So she called you."

"Yes. She called me."

"Why?"

"I think she didn't like the condition of the files you returned."

"What?"

"I think she feels you messed up her files."

"We didn't mess up any files," Hacker said.

It was the first time he'd said anything. Matthew looked at him, surprised.

"All we done was Xerox 'em," he said. "And bring 'em back to her. That's all we done with her files."

"She should've called *us*," Rawles said. "That was her obligation. Not a lawyer. There's a burglary, you call the police."

"That's what I advised her to do. As soon as I got there."

"No, *not* as soon as you got there," Rawles said. "As soon as you found out the *tape* was gone."

"As soon as I recognized the extent of the burglary. On the telephone, it didn't sound—"

"Whatever it sounded like, you should've called us immediately," Rawles said. "This is just another example of your running around us, doing things your own way, sticking your nose where it doesn't belong. Maybe you're not much impressed with homicide, but *we* are."

"I can assure you—"

"You can assure me this is the end of your butting in, okay? That's what you can assure me. Keep your fucking nose out of this fucking case from now on, okay?"

"Which is also a misdemeanor," Matthew said.

"What?"

"I refer you to Chapter 847.04. Open Profanity. Whoever—having arrived at the age of discretion—uses profane, vulgar, and indecent language in any public place or upon the private premises of another is guilty of a second-degree misdemeanor. Punishable, as you mentioned earlier, by sixty days in jail."

Rawles blinked.

"Yes," Matthew said.

"I think you heard me," Rawles said, recovering at once.

"Yes, I heard you," Matthew said.

"Let's go," Rawles said to Hacker, and both men went off in a huff.

There was no question in May Hennessy's mind that whoever had broken into the office was a pro. Whatever else Daniel Nettington could do well—and he seemed to be an ace in the sack—he did not seem to be the kind of man who could pick a lock without leaving a scratch anywhere on it. Moreover, and May had told this to the police, she wasn't at all sure the Nettington tape was what the burglar was really after. May had worked too many cases with Otto not to recognize a possible smokescreen when she saw one. She had told this to Rawles and his freckle-faced partner. The Larkin file was missing, too, wasn't it? Plus a dozen other files, some of them on cases only recently closed out. Not to mention seven or eight *other* tapes that could've got a lot of people in trouble with their spouses if somebody was looking to make trouble. So she had suggested to Rawles that he shouldn't jump to conclusions when he heard the tape—which she was lucky to have the original of, and which was pretty hot and incriminating stuff—but should instead keep an open mind.

She had reported all this on the phone to Matthew not twenty minutes before Rawles and Hacker came barging in. Matthew doubted that Rawles was keeping an open mind. Rawles was smelling real meat, and Rawles was eager to close in. That was what Matthew sensed. That was why Rawles wanted him to keep out of the way. He didn't want his case screwed up on any technicality. Rawles was going to find Nettington, sit him down, have him listen to the tape, and then ask a hundred questions about the burglary of Samalson's office and incidentally the murder of Samalson himself.

Hacker and Rawles—both of whom had been cops for a good many years, Rawles in both Cleveland *and* Calusa— should have realized that honest people and thieves do things in different ways. If an honest person, for example, knew that there was something he needed or wanted in Otto Samalson's office, he would simply go to the office and ask for it. A thief, on the other hand, doesn't think that way. A thief thinks *There is us and there is them, and they are the ones who are on our backs and keeping us from getting what we want and need*, that is the way a thief thinks, *so we will steal it from them*. Even if it's possible to get the thing by *asking* for it politely, the thief will steal it anyway. That is his nature. That is why honest people go around shaking their heads in bafflement over what thieves do. They can no more understand the psychology of the thief than they can the theory of relativity. Cops, however, are *supposed* to understand the psychology of the thief.

It was surprising, therefore, that it never once occurred to Hacker or Rawles—though it did occur to May—that perhaps they were dealing with a bona fide thief here and not an amateur like Nettington.

It never occurred to Matthew, either.

Matthew had a good excuse; he himself was an amateur.

Rawles and Hacker had no excuse at all, unless eagerness to close out a case could be considered an excuse.

Not understanding the way a thief's mind works, Matthew concluded that an amateur like himself had broken into Otto's office. But Nettington seemed too obvious a choice— the man wasn't *that* stupid, was he?—and so Matthew, still thinking like an amateur, tried to think of any other amateur who might have wanted that tape desperately enough to have stolen it.

The only other amateur who came to mind was Carla Nettington.

You mean the police *will be listening to that tape?*

And . . .

When can I hear it?

And . . .

I wish the goddamn police *weren't in this.*

And . . .

Thank you very much, Mr. Hope, please send me your man's report, and *the tape, and of course your bill.*

Carla's words.

Eager to get that tape.

Worried about the police hearing it.

He went out to see her that afternoon.

It was still raining when he got to the old house on Sabal Key. He made a forty-yard broken-field run—skirting puddles and fallen palm fronds—from the Ghia to the front door, and then stood under an ineffective shingled portico that dripped gallons of water down the back of his neck while he rang the doorbell.

"Yes, just a minute!" Carla called from somewhere in the house.

He waited.

He was going to drown.

The door opened.

So did her eyes. Wide in surprise.

"May I come in?" he said.

"Yes, certainly," she said. She was not happy to see him. Her voice and her body language told him that. Voice chilly and distant. The words saying "Yes, certainly," the tone saying "Who the hell invited you?" Her body half-turned away from him as she stepped aside to let him in, her posture suggesting that she would have preferred showing him her back but was too polite for such blatant rudeness.

The house had the musty smell of all Florida houses. Mildew and dust and fetid growing things. Air plants hanging near the windows. Orchids with their gnarled roots. Silvery slashes of rain hit the louvered windows, rattled on the roof. There was an enclosed feeling, almost claustrophobic, moist and dim. He remembered hiding in closets when he was a boy, overcoats covering his face, boots and galoshes underfoot. The smell of a closet on a rainy day.

She was wearing black. Black designer jeans and a black crew-neck sweater. Pale oval face and dark lipstick. Eyes as green as the plants in every corner of the room. Black enameled earrings. Barefooted. Her feet very white in contrast to the black. Fingernails and toenails painted the same color as her lips.

"What is it you want?" she asked. Facing him now. But her posture still denying him, excluding him. "The police have already been here," she said.

"Looking for your husband?"

"Yes. I told them I didn't know where he was. I'm telling you the same thing. Now if you'll forgive me, Mr. Hope . . ."

"That's not why I'm here," Matthew said.

"Then why are you? I thought I told you your services were no longer—"

"Otto Samalson's office was broken into last night."

"So?"

"Someone stole the tape he made of your husband and Rita Kirkman."

She looked at him in puzzlement for a moment, seeming not to understand the innuendo. And then her green eyes widened in recognition and surprise, and the corners of her mouth turned up in faint amusement.

"Please," she said. "Don't be absurd."

"The tape was stolen, Mrs. Nettington."

"And you think I stole it, or had it stolen?" She still looked amused. "You really don't understand, do you?" she said.

"I'm sorry, I don't," Matthew said.

"Mr. Hope," she said, as slowly and as patiently as if she were instructing a backward child, "the moment Otto Samalson was killed . . . the moment that tape became virtually public knowledge . . . it was no longer of any possible use to me."

"I assumed, Mrs. Nettington—"

"Yes, I know what you assumed. You made that clear the last time I saw you. You assumed I was looking for a divorce."

"That's what you led me to believe."

"Yes." The amused look still on her face, annoying now because it seemed to be mocking him. "But you see, Mr. Hope, things are not always what they appear to be, are they?"

"Apparently not," he said.

"What I told you when I first came to see you," she said, "was that I wanted my husband followed because—"

"Yes."

"—I suspected he was having an affair. And I further said—"

"Yes."

"—that if indeed we could prove this, I would initiate divorce proceedings."

"Yes."

"Yes. But I was sort of lying, you see."

"Lying?" Matthew said.

"Yes. About divorcing him."

"You didn't plan to divorce him?"

"That's right."

"Then why did you ask me to hire a private detective?"

"To follow him."

"Yes, why?"

"To get the goods on him."

"Yes, *why?*"

"Mr. Hope, you're an attorney," Carla said, "so I know you're familiar with Chapter 61.08 of the Florida Statutes. Regarding alimony?"

"Yes, I'm familiar with it," Matthew said.

"The part about determining a proper award? That would be Section One, do you know it?"

"Yes, what about it?"

"Where it says, 'The court may consider the adultery of a

spouse and the circumstances thereof in determining whether alimony should be awarded to such spouse and the amount of the alimony, if any, to be awarded'? Do you know the section I mean?"

"Yes, I know the section."

"Well?" she said.

"Well what?"

"Well, that's why I wanted to get the goods on Daniel."

"I think you read the section wrong," Matthew said, shaking his head.

"No, I read it correctly. I once had à friend who was a lawyer."

"If you were thinking . . . well, I don't know *what* you were thinking, actually, since you just told me you weren't planning on a divorce at all. But if you *had* been planning one, and you were thinking your husband's adultery would increase the amount of alimony . . ."

"No, I wasn't thinking that."

"Good, because you'd have been mistaken. The section was designed to protect a husband with an adulterous wife. The chapter says the court may grant alimony to *either* party, but very few men ever ask for alimony. In practice, it's the wife who normally gets alimony, and if a husband can prove his wife was playing around, alimony will often be cut substantially and in some instances even denied."

"Yes," Carla said. "That's my understanding of the chapter."

"So you see—"

"I *am*," she said.

"You are what?" he said.

"Playing around," she said.

Behind her, rain lashed the windows, and the palms and pines outside tossed fitfully in the wind.

"I *have* been playing around for a long, long time," she said.

Matthew looked at her. Green eyes still amused. Mouth turned up in a smile.

"And I figured if my husband ever decided to divorce me, I wouldn't get a cent in alimony unless I could show that he was *also* playing around, which would sort of balance the scales of justice, don't you think?"

You lift a rock, Matthew thought, and there are all sorts of fat, white-bellied slugs twisting and squirming under it.

"Which is why I decided to protect myself," she said. "Get the goods on *him* before he got the goods on *me*. Make sure I had insurance if he ever told me he wanted a divorce. Show him the pictures, here you go, Charlie, here's you going down on the fat lady in the circus."

She was smiling broadly now. Her amusement had turned to absolute glee.

"You see," she said, "I *never* want to get divorced, not *ever*. I like things just the way they are. Daniel paying the bills and never bothering me about where I go or what I do. That's where I was the night your man was killed, Mr. Hope. Not out with a girlfriend but in bed with a boyfriend." Her smile was wider now. "That's what I call having your cake and eating it, too, Mr. Hope. That's what I call a real good life."

"That's what I call . . ." Matthew started, and then simply shook his head and turned his back, and walked to the front door and out into the rain.

What he called it was a triumph of illusion over reality.

Or something.

We're going to turn you into a Wasp princess from Denver,

Colorado, he told her. Daughter of a rich rancher. Spoiled rotten, there's nothing any man on earth can possibly give you. It'll flatter Pudgy to death to think you *might*, if he minds his fat little spic manners, actually deign to *talk* to him.

We won't do anything with your hair, you truly have lovely hair, long and blonde, is it natural? Well, Pudgy'll find out, won't he, dear? Put it up in a bun, perhaps, to give you an elegantly glacial look. We're going for an image, darling. It's the image that'll get you into that palace of his and into his bed and into his safe.

And then we'll find a gown, he told her, sexy enough to cause Pudgy to drool, but not *cheap*, do you follow me, darling? Something in an ice-blue, don't you think, to echo those gorgeous peepers of yours. Enough bust showing to entice, but careful, careful, mustn't touch, Pudgy, uh-uh-*uh*. Something very clingy, ice-blue, yes, and slit very high on one leg, thigh showing whenever you choose to show it, a long-legged stride into the Kasbah Lounge, Pudgy's eyes will pop.

Jewelry, we'll have to get you something that *looks* genuine, he's a fool when it comes to telling a hooker from a nun, but I'm sure he knows Tiffany's from Woolworth's. We'll find something small but tasteful, run up to Bal Harbour one day, shop the better stores. One piece is all we want. Something for just here, do you see? Right where the cleavage begins. Draw his eyes to the bust, not that you need any help, darling, don't be offended. And shoes. Wonderful shoes to go with the gown. I want you to come into the lounge all starry-eyed and aghast, virtually *popping* out of the gown, tits, tits, *wonderful*, looking for someone who *should* be there but isn't, Miss Colorado who's been stood up, searching the room, Oh my goodness where *is* he, slippers that look as if they're made of glass, they do wonderful things with plastic nowadays, we'll find something in Bal Harbour, this will cost us a penny or two, but well worth it.

And we'll rent a black Caddy, it shouldn't cost more than twenty, thirty an hour, should it? And of course a chauffeur will accompany you into the lounge. Oh, Charles, where *is* he?—that's the chauffeur, Charles—he *promised* he'd be here. And then a Wasp snit, Oh, wait for me outside, this is *so* annoying . . .

Exactly the way it worked.

She came in all breathless and starry-eyed, Junior Prom time except there was a chauffeur in gray behind her, who'd have dreamt she was a hooker going after four, five, six, who-the-fuck-knew keys of cocaine? Ice-blue gown, cost twelve hundred dollars, slippers looking like glass for another three, brooch that looked like a sapphire surrounded by tiny diamonds, fake but gorgeous, who'd have known? You walk in trailed by what looks like a real chauffeur, everything else looks real.

They were going for the gold.

She sits at the bar, looking at her watch. Seventy-five dollars, but it looks expensive. If the chauffeur looks real, the sapphire looks real, the watch becomes real, too. Only real thing here is a hooker from L.A. who knows this is her ticket out of the life. One last trick. No more hands on her after this one. After this one, she won't have to *look* rich, she'll really *be* rich. Meanwhile, she's the fake rancher's daughter from Colorado. Annoyed. Tapping her foot in the looks-like-glass slipper. The chauffeur pops in every six minutes, wants to know is she going to wait any longer or should they start for the party? She keeps telling him another five minutes, that's *all* I'll give him, waiting for Pudgy to make his move. Pudgy keeps watching her. Does he suspect a scam? He's sort of cute, actually, with cheeks you want to pinch and a Bugs Bunny smile. She is not going to give him much longer. If she sits here at the bar another two minutes, he'll know she's a hooker with a gimmick and he'll run for the hills.

The girl, Kim, the one who tipped them to this, she said she gave him twenty minutes before he made his move. Sat at the bar like an actress-singer. Talking about clubs she'd played, off-Broadway shows she'd done. Took him twenty minutes before he got off his fat ass, sitting on one of the brocaded banquettes—the Kasbah Lounge, right? Red embroidery with little mirrors sewn in—twenty minutes to make his move.

Jenny's about to leave. The chauffeur pops in yet another time.

"Miss Carmody?" he says.

Note of servile impatience in his voice.

She looks at her fake watch supposed to cost seventy-five hundred dollars, cost only seventy-five, she sighs in exasperation, and swings the bar stool around, long ice-blue gown slit to Siberia, you can see all the way to eternity if you care to look because she isn't wearing any panties. And all at once— will miracles never?—Pudgy comes off the banquette just as she's heading for the door, and he says something like, "What a pity, has your friend been delayed?"

Spanish accent.

She looks at him like he's a roach flew up into her face.

"I *beg* your pardon," she says.

Nose smelling something vile in the gutter.

From the door, the chauffeur says, "Miss Carmody, shall I bring the car around?"

"Yes, please," she says.

Pudgy says, "Forgive me."

She says, "Excuse me, but would you please get out of my way?"

He says, "I know you must be upset . . ."

"*Please,*" she says, playing it to the hilt, the single word saying Who wants anything to do with *you*, you greasy little spic?

He says, "Perhaps a liqueur would make you feel a little better."

She thinks of the joke about the waiter saying to the prudish British lady "Liqueurs, madame?" and the lady swats him with her purse because she thinks he said "Lick yours, madame?"

She looks deep into Pudgy's eyes, as though trying to fathom his intentions, trying to determine whether he is a pimp or a pusher or a South American rancher and from the door the chauffeur says again "Miss Carmody?"

"Come," Pudgy says, "let's have a liqueur. My name is Luis Amaros, I am a banana importer," and she thinks Yeah the way I am a research scientist at IBM.

A half-hour later, she starts telling him how at the University of Denver when she was the Snow Festival Queen, some guys brought in some cocaine from Los Angeles, and oh wow, that was the most exciting time in her life though Daddy would have killed her if he'd found out.

Pudgy looks at her. She knows he is thinking that all Anglo girls will suck his dick to oblivion if he lays some coke on them.

He says, "Will you still be going to this party?"

"What party?" she says.

"Your friend . . ."

"Oh, *him,*" she says, her heart leaping because she's such a dumb cunt. "The hell with *him,*" she says, and wonders if she's using language too strong for a rancher's daughter from Denver. "Forty minutes late already, I mean fuck *him,*" she says, figuring it's only hookers who watch their language until they're in bed, ladies say whatever the fuck they feel like saying.

He buys it.

She must be a lady.

She just said fuck.

"If you want to come to my place," he says, "I have something that might interest you."

She says, cautiously, "Oh?"

"Would you like to come home with me?" he says, and smiles. "Cenicienta? Would you like to come home with me?"

"I'm not that kind of girl," she says, and wonders if she's playing too much Doris Day. "And what does that mean, what you just said?"

"*Cenicienta?*" he says. "That means Cinderella." He glances at her legs. "In your glass slippers."

"They do look like glass, don't they?" she says, and smiles.

"So?" he says. "What do you think?"

"I really don't know," she says.

"It's entirely up to you," he says.

"You *are* awfully cute," she says.

He says nothing.

"What is it that you have?" she asks. "That might interest me?"

"Blow," he says.

She blinks at him.

"Blow? What's that, blow?"

She's thinking if you come from Denver, you're not supposed to know blow means coke, right?

He lowers his voice.

"What you had in Denver," he says. "What your friends brought from L.A."

"Oh," she says.

Comes the dawn.

"Mmm," he says.

"Gee."

"Mmm."

"Wow."

"So?"

"Sure," she says.

And she's home free.

11

Jimmy Legs showed Stagg the picture.

"Where'd you get this?" Stagg asked.

"I found it in somebody's office," Jimmy said.

"This is what she looks like, huh?"

"Yeah," Jimmy said.

"Like to take a run at *that* sometime," Stagg said.

"We find her," Jimmy said, "nobody's gonna wanna take a run at her no more, believe me. Some broads they gotta be taught you don't steal a person's watch."

"Be a terrible waste, you mess her up," Stagg said, looking at the picture and shaking his head.

"Maybe just bust her nose," Jimmy said. "You break somebody's nose in a coupla places, it hurts like hell. She'll look terrific with a smashed nose like a gorilla's, huh?" Jimmy laughed. "Squash it right into her face, we find her. Face like she's gonna have, she'll be lucky to get half a buck a blow job." He laughed again. Stagg was still looking at the picture.

"The thing is," Stagg said, "nobody heard nothing about this Rolex. I think I must've contacted every fence in town, none of them—"

"Whattya mean you *think*?" Jimmy said.

"What?" Stagg said.

"*Did* you contact every fence or *didn't* you?"

"Well, I . . ."

"'Cause either you done the job right or you didn't do it at all. You miss one fence you might as well not've talked to *any* of them."

"I maybe missed one or two," Stagg said.

"I'm surprised at you," Jimmy said, shaking his head.

"I'll see I can find them this afternoon. You gonna need this picture?"

"I got the picture especially for you," Jimmy said.

"'Cause maybe it'll help, I can show a picture."

"Yeah, but take care of it. You come up blank, I'll prolly have to make some prints, you know?"

"They can do that, huh? You don't need the negative?"

"No, they can do it right from what you got in your hand there."

"It's amazing what they can do nowadays, ain't it?" Stagg said.

He rose from where the men were sitting on the deck at Marina Lou's, looking out over the sailboats on the water. Nobody in the place would have dreamt they'd been discussing the rearrangement of a beautiful girl's features.

"I'll get on this right away," he said, putting the picture in the inside pocket of his "Miami Vice" sports jacket, "see what I can do, okay? I'll give you a call later."

"Yeah," Jimmy said.

This was at eleven o'clock on the morning of June 17.

At exactly eleven-ten, May Hennessy called Matthew to say that every cloud had a silver lining.

What had happened was that she'd been trying to put together the shambles the burglar had made of the office—papers strewn everywhere, drawers overturned, books thrown helter-skelter—when she'd come upon a spiral bound notebook of the sort Otto used when he was on surveillance. She figured he'd tucked the book into his desk drawer on the Friday before he was killed, intending to give his notes to her for typing on Monday morning.

There had been no Monday morning for Otto.

The notes were still where he'd left them, still in his handwriting.

They were the notes he'd made for the last week of activity on the Larkin case.

Did Matthew want to see them?

Matthew's partner Frank believed that the best writers in the world wrote exactly the way they spoke, their style being a sort of voice-print. Which further meant, Frank said, that a great many highly acclaimed writers were boring conversationalists. Frank was probably wrong; he was wrong about a lot of things. In any event, Otto wasn't writing for publication, and the prose style in his notes was indeed somewhat like his speaking style, condensed into a rapid shorthand and sounding far different from the typed reports Matthew had earlier read. Perhaps May Hennessy edited for client consumption as she went along.

The typed reports had been a chronicle of futility.

Small wonder that Larkin had been dismayed by the lack of progress on the case. Otto had first checked the telephone directories for Calusa and all the neighboring towns. No Angela West. He had checked every motel and hotel. Nothing. He had checked all the condominium rental offices. He had checked all the car rental companies. He had checked all the banks. Nothing anywhere. If Angela West was living in Calusa, Sarasota, or Bradenton, he did not know where.

But the handwritten notes . . .

On Monday afternoon, June 2, after more than a month on the case, Otto spent a harrowing morning with a supervisor from the telephone company, trying to learn whether or not Angela West might have an unlisted telephone. The supervisor was adamant in protecting the rights to privacy of any telephone company customer. Otto wanted to strangle her. Or so he had written in his notes for that day, a comment May undoubtedly would excise when later typing them.

On Tuesday, June 3, Otto had gone to see a friend of a friend who worked at the airport, and the friend's friend was going to see what he could do about checking the various airline manifests for a possible Angela West traveling to or from the tri-city area. He was having lunch later in a hamburger joint in the South Dixie Mall on Smoke Ridge and 41 . . .

Sitting at a table in a place across the corridor from a games arcade and a bookstore . . .

When a girl carrying a shopping bag walked out of the bookstore and . . .

Holy shit!

It was the girl in the picture Larkin had given him.

Long blonde hair trailing down her back, high heels clicking as she glided past him not four feet from where he was sitting, he almost jumped out of his socks.

He followed her out of the mall and into the parking lot where she got into a white Toyota Corolla with the license plate 201-ZHW and a yellow-and-black Hertz #1 sticker on the rear bumper. She made a right turn on 41, Otto on her tail, and continued north till she got to Egret Avenue where she made a left heading west and finally pulled into the parking lot of the Medical Arts Building on Egret and Pierce, a two-story, red-brick complex with what Otto figured had to be at least twenty or thirty doctors' offices in it. Otto ran in after her, but she was already wherever she was going by the time he got into the lobby, and he had no way of knowing which of the doctors she was going there to see. He copied down the names of all the doctors listed on the lobby directory board—it turned out there were only sixteen—and then went out to wait for her in the parking lot.

She was in there about an hour.

In his notes at this point, Otto did a bit of editorializing on doctors in Florida, who figured everybody here was old and in no hurry and who overbooked more outrageously than the airlines did. You sometimes waited an hour and a half before a nurse led you into a little cubicle where you undressed and waited another half-hour, reading last year's *Sports Illustrated* until a doctor walked in and said, Hello, how are we feeling today? We are feeling *annoyed*, Otto wrote in his notes. Matthew suspected that some of this was for May's benefit, keep his assistant smiling and shaking her head as she excised any extraneous material from the typewritten report.

Anyway, Cinderella was in there for an hour, with Otto sitting in his car waiting for her to come out. When she finally did, he followed her out of the parking lot and across Egret to the traffic light on Sea Breeze. She made a left just as the light was turning. A traffic cop waved Otto down as he started to follow, so he was forced to stop at the light, and wait for it to change, by which time he'd lost her heading east on Sea Breeze.

He went back to the office, called Hertz, told the young girl who answered the phone that he was a private detective working for an insurance company, and that he was trying to trace a girl who'd been named beneficiary of a substantial policy. It was his belief that she may have rented a Toyota Corolla from Hertz, and he wondered if she could check her files for the license plate 201-ZHW and let him have the name and address of the renter.

The young girl—eager to help a working girl like herself inherit a zillion dollars—checked her files and came back five minutes later with the information that on April 3, at the tri-city airport, Hertz had rented the Toyota Corolla with the 201-ZHW license plate to a woman named Jenny Santoro who had since renewed the rental twice.

Otto asked how she was paying for the car.

The girl told him American Express.

Otto asked if that was the name on the card, Jenny Santoro.

The girl told him Yes.

Otto asked if Jenny Santoro had given an address here in Calusa.

The girl told him No, but that wasn't unusual. Lots of people rented a car before they'd found a place to stay. She had given her home address, though, as 3914 Veteran Avenue in Los Angeles, California.

Jenny Santoro.

More editorializing here. Otto was astonished that she was Italian. That long blonde hair? Those blue eyes? Italian? Well, now he had a name, and now he had to start all over again with the new name.

By the end of the next day, Wednesday, June 4, Otto was

beginning to think the Jenny Santoro was a phony, too, this despite the fact that you had to show a driver's license before any rental company would let you drive off with a car. Otto noted gratuitously, however, that you could buy a phony driver's license for a hundred bucks anyplace in America, and since the work he'd been doing all day long—the same routine checks he'd made for Angela West—were coming up blank for Jenny Santoro, there was a strong likelihood that the lady was carrying queer documents.

On Thursday, June 5, Otto went back to the South Dixie Mall.

He went back there because Cinderella (or Angela West or Jenny Santoro) had been carrying a shopping bag, and it was safe to assume there'd been something *in* that shopping bag and reasonable to expect she'd made a purchase in the mall, perhaps in the bookstore, perhaps in one of the other shops.

He showed the bookstore clerk the picture Larkin had given him and asked if this girl had made any purchases and if so how she had paid for them. He was praying for a check with a name and an address printed on it. He told the clerk, by the way, that he worked for a credit-card verification agency, whatever that was, and was trying to track down a stolen card.

The clerk recognized the photo, said Yes, this girl had bought a book just the other day, and then checked her receipts. The book was something entitled *A New View of a Woman's Body*. It cost $8.95, and Cinderella had charged it to MasterCard. The name was another name entirely.

Jody Carmody.

Otto showed her picture in every store in the mall, using the same credit-card verification routine, wanting to know if she'd bought anything, and if so whether she'd used either a credit card or a check. He was still hoping she'd used a check in one of the stores. A saleswoman in a record shop recognized the picture, told Otto she'd bought some tapes and paid for them by credit card. Visa, this time.

The name on the card was Melissa Blair.

Otto went back to the bookstore, bought a copy of the book for himself, and drove to his office where he asked May to check all the tri-city phone directories for either a Jody Carmody or a Melissa Blair. May came up blank. Otto continued reading the book Cinderella had bought.

It was, he discovered, a sort of illustrated guide with chapter headings like "Self-Examination" and "A Woman's Reproductive Anatomy" and "Universal Health Problems of Women" and "Feminist Abortion Care" and so on.

Otto wondered if the choice of this particular book had any connection with the visit Cinderella had made to the Medical Arts Building.

Had she gone to see an obstetrician/gynecologist?

On Friday, June 6—two days before his murder—Otto went back to the Medical Arts Building, carrying with him the picture of Cinderella. He spoke to four OB-GYNs, the last of whom—a man named Dr. Schlemmer—identified the picture and said Yes, he had examined the girl, who had given her name as Mary Jane Hopkins and her address as 1237 Hacienda Road on Whisper Key. She had paid for the visit in cash. When Otto asked why she had come to see him, Dr. Schlemmer said that was privileged information.

Otto wondered if she was pregnant.

That same afternoon, Otto drove out to 1237 Hacienda Road, which turned out to be a place called Camelot Towers, which was a six-story condominium with ten apartments on each floor. He checked in the resident manager's office for the name Mary Jane Hopkins. No such person living there. He showed the picture of Cinderella at the Jacaranda Ball, the one Larkin had given him. Ice-blue gown. Long blonde hair, bright blue eyes, wide smile on her face. The resident manager said she did not recognize the girl in the picture. By eight o'clock that night, he had knocked on the doors of seventeen apartments and showed Cinderella's picture to eleven people.

Five of those people said she looked familiar but they hadn't seen her around in a while.

Three of those people said they'd never seen her in their lives.

Two said they may have seen her, but they weren't sure.

One said he'd seen her in the parking lot only yesterday, but he couldn't remember which space she was parked in.

Otto got home at about eight-thirty.

He planned to go back to the condo on Saturday morning—and again on Sunday if necessary—to knock on more doors, showing the picture and trying to learn why she had given this particular address to Dr. Schlemmer.

That was the last of the handwritten notes.

Otto was killed on Sunday night.

"What are you talking about?" Larkin said, and leaned toward Matthew. "He *found* her? And he didn't *call* me?"

"No, no, he—"

"You just said he spotted—"

"Yes, but—"

"So why didn't he. . . ?"

"What happened was—"

"Yeah, how about it? I'm the man was paying his bills, and I'm the last to—"

"The notes were still in his handwriting," Matthew said. "They hadn't been typed yet. I'm sure Otto planned—"

"So what'd the notes say?"

Matthew told him what the notes had said. They were sit-

159

ting on the deck of Larkin's house, looking out over the water. It was three o'clock in the afternoon, and thunderclouds were already massing.

"You're kidding me," Larkin said.

"No, I'm serious."

"Cinderella?"

"Yes."

"The picture I gave him?"

"Yes."

"I don't believe it," Larkin said.

"It's what happened."

"I don't believe in coincidences like that," Larkin said, shaking his head.

"Well," Matthew said.

"I just don't believe it."

"Anyway . . ." Matthew said, and began telling the rest of the story.

Every now and then, Larkin interrupted.

"Did he get the license plate?"

And . . .

"Italian, I can't believe it. She looked like an Indiana wheatfield."

And . . .

"*Another* name? What is she, a *spy*?"

But mostly he listened. And when Matthew finished telling him that Otto had planned to check out that condominium again on Monday, Larkin shook his head and said, "Fuckin' bad break."

"Mr. Larkin," Matthew said, "the reason I'm here, I know you went to Otto because you considered this a confidential matter—"

"Very," Larkin said.

"—and I assure you I'm well aware that I've already

160

breached your privacy by reading Otto's reports. I wouldn't have done that if I didn't feel so strongly about this. I don't like the idea of someone killing him, Mr. Larkin. I don't like it at all."

"Neither do I."

"The reason I'm here . . . is there anything you can add to what you already told Otto? Anything that might shed some light on why he was killed? Because you see—"

"I told him everything. The girl stole my watch, I wanted him to find her."

"Because you see, in his notes, Otto seemed to think there might have been some significance to the girl's visit to a doctor's office and her purchase of a book about a woman's body. What I'm asking . . . is there anything Otto *didn't* know, anything you *didn't* tell him, that might have had some bearing on his murder?"

"Like what?"

"Like . . . Mr. Larkin, was the girl pregnant?"

"What?"

"Was she pregnant? Angela West, Jenny Santoro, Jody Carmody, Melissa Blair . . . Cinderella? Was she pregnant?"

"How the hell would I know? I only saw her that one night."

"Never saw her after that, is that right?"

"Never."

"Do you have any reason to believe she might have *become* pregnant that night?"

"Why would I believe that?"

"Well . . . forgive me . . . but was any sort of contraception used?"

"What kind of question is that?" Larkin said angrily and rose suddenly and began pacing the deck. Beyond him, out over the water, there were distant flashes of lightning.

"I'm sorry I have to ask such a personal question, believe me," Matthew said. "But in his notes Otto speculated that perhaps the girl's visit to an OB-GYN's office, coupled with her purchase of the body-book, might indicate she suspected she was pregnant. Otto's intuitions were usually pretty sound, Mr. Larkin. And since this happened almost two months ago, it *is* possible, after all, that—"

"The girl was a pro," Larkin said. "Pros don't get pregnant."

"Well, you don't know for a fact that she was a professional."

"Amateurs don't fuck a guy's brains out and then steal his watch," Larkin said.

"Maybe not," Matthew said.

"Anyway, what if she *is* pregnant, which I doubt. What does that have to do with Otto's murder?"

"I don't know," Matthew said.

"I don't see any connection at all. Even if she . . ."

He suddenly stopped pacing.

"Or is *that* it?" he said. "Is *that* why you're here?"

"I don't know what you mean," Matthew said.

Larkin was standing before him now, hands on his hips, looking down at him. Lightning streaked the distant sky again. "You think *I* might've killed Otto, don't you?" he said. "Or *had* him killed."

"No, I don't," Matthew said.

"You come here asking me did I knock her up . . ."

"You're misunderstanding my—"

"Bullshit. What is it you're thinking? That Otto was about to *learn* the fuckin' bitch got herself pregnant? That it was me who decided to take him off the case? Permanently? Is that what you're thinking?"

"No. But if she *is* pregnant . . ."

"Who gives a shit *what* she is?" Larkin said. "I *hope* she is, you want to know. With a fuckin' Mongolian *idiot!*"

His vehemence startled Matthew. Out over the water, there was more lightning, and now the sound of distant thunder.

"I'm trying to say if Otto was close to making such a discovery, then it's possible that *someone*—maybe even the girl herself—wasn't too keen on having the information made public."

"Well, the *someone* wasn't me. And you know something? You're right, you *did* breach my privacy by reading those reports and I'm starting to get a little bit pissed, okay? So maybe you oughta just get the fuck out of here, okay? Do me that favor."

"I was hoping—"

"You were hoping wrong."

"Sorry to've bothered you then," Matthew said and rose, and started for the steps leading down to the side of the house.

"And let me tell you something else," Larkin said. "I've already put somebody else onto finding little Cinderella, and he's not the gentleman Otto was. So I don't think he'd appreciate your snooping around."

"Thanks, I'll remember that," Matthew said.

"I think you better," Larkin said.

Lightning flashed far out over the water.

From where they sat on a deck overlooking Calusa Bay, Ernesto and Domingo and the two other men glanced up briefly at the jagged yellow streaks and then turned away from the water and continued talking. They were conversing in low, controlled voices because they were discussing dope.

The two men with Ernesto and Domingo took turns addressing Ernesto. They had figured the other one didn't have any English at all. If they'd been a bit more astute, they'd have realized Domingo was listening to every word and not missing very much. Instead, they kept everything going to Ernesto.

The one who was talking now was a hefty man wearing a short-sleeved sports shirt, tan slacks, and loafers with no socks. He was something like thirty years old, Ernesto guessed, and he brought to the selling of his dope the intensity an IBM salesman might have brought to the selling of a typewriter or a computer. He enjoyed his job, this man. He enjoyed the big bucks to be made in his job. His name was Charlie Nubbs. Ernesto didn't think that was his *real* last name, Nubbs. But that was how the man introduced himself, "Hello, I'm Charlie Nubbs, we hear you're looking to buy some heavy machinery."

Heavy machinery was cocaine, Ernesto guessed.

Ernesto and Domingo had spread the word around cautiously. Told a few people here and there that they had cash and were looking to spend it on choice blow. Let it be known they were looking for at least ninety-percent pure, which is what the girl had stolen from Amaros. Two, three keys, they said. Actually, the girl had stolen *four* keys, no wonder Amaros wanted to hang her from the ceiling. Four keys of nine-oh pure? Shit, man!

Nobody knew they were looking for Jenny Santoro, of course. All anybody knew was they were looking for dope. What they were hoping was somebody would say "Hey, there's this chick in town she fell into some very good stuff and she's looking for buyers." That's what they were hoping. So far, nobody knew such a chick.

Charlie Nubbs was telling them that this Friday night they were expecting a shipment of very good stuff. Charlie Nubbs didn't know how many keys would be on the boat when they met it. They never knew until it arrived, it was different each shipment. What they had to do, he said, taking Ernesto into his confidence, was be prepared to pay cash on delivery for however many keys were on the boat. The price depended on how pure the coke was. It had been running a very high pure-content lately, he was expecting the new shipment would be at least ninety-percent pure, which was about as good as you could get.

"I understand you're looking for very rich stuff," he said to Ernesto.

"That's all we will accept, yes," Ernesto said.

"And in what quantity?"

"Two, three keys."

"That's all, huh? 'Cause I was hoping you might want to take more than that. We sometimes get ten, twelve keys in a shipment, that's a lot of cash to come up with. We could lay some of it off, you know, it'd be easier for us."

Voices lowered. The men facing the water, looking out over the water. Women eating salads at a nearby table. Sailboats out there on the water. All tranquil and lovely, white sails against the pale blue sky and deeper blue water. Sea gulls hovering. Tuesday in Paradise.

The men continued talking dope.

"What we're talking here," the man with Charlie Nubbs said, "is seventy-five a key, something like that. if it's as rich as it's been running lately."

The man with Charlie Nubbs was called Jimmy Largura. Ernesto thought he was Latino at first, he looked Latino. Turned out he was Italian, though. Jimmy Largura. Though Charlie Nubbs referred to him every now and then as Jimmy Legs. Jimmy Legs this, Jimmy Legs that. Jimmy Legs was now telling them how a speedboat, one of those cigarettes like the black one out there, would run out to meet the bigger boat this

Friday night, take the shipment. It would be nice if Ernesto here could guarantee say the purchase of at least half a dozen keys, come up with say four-fifty for six keys, that would take a big load off their minds, knowing six keys were already committed.

"We could perhaps go to six keys," Ernesto said. "But not at the price you're talking."

"That's a fair price," Charlie Nubbs said. "For ninety-pure? That's a very fair price. Ain't that a fair price, Jimmy?"

"For ninety-pure?" Jimmy said. "You gotta be kidding. It's a steal. For ninety-pure, it's a steal."

"If it's *really* ninety," Ernesto said.

"Even if it's only eighty-*five*," Charlie Nubbs said.

"Or even eighty," Jimmy said. "It's a bargain even at eighty."

"I can get ninety-percent pure for forty K," Ernesto said, lying.

But he was thinking if he could come up with a good deal for Amaros . . . then if they couldn't find the girl, which he was thinking might turn out to be the case, Amaros wouldn't be so angry. If Ernesto could get him, say, six keys of ninety-pure at forty a key, that was very low.

If these men were that stupid.

"If that's how much you're talking," Jimmy said, "there's no sense talking. Forty K? You're kidding. Tell me you're kidding, please."

"Forty sounds right," Ernesto said.

"Say you paid seventy-five for it . . ." Jimmy said.

"That's too high," Ernesto said.

"I'm only sayin' *suppose* you paid seventy-five . . ."

Ernesto was shaking his head.

"*Suppose*, okay?" Jimmy said. "It won't kill you to suppose for a minute. You want another drink? Or you want to order some lunch?"

"Let's have another round," Charlie Nubbs said, and signaled to the waiter for drinks all around the table.

"I'm saying *suppose* you went in for seventy-five a key," Jimmy said. "You give it a full hit, you already double your price. With ninety-pure it can stand a full hit, you know that. You could even step on it more, if you felt like it."

"Well, I wouldn't advise that," Charlie Nubbs said. "You step on it too hard . . ."

"You're right, you're right," Jimmy said. "So say just a full hit, okay? You pay seventy-five . . ."

The waiter was approaching the table. Jimmy immediately changed the subject.

"The one out there with the blue sails," he said, "that's got to run you at least seventy-five thousand, don't you think?"

"Maybe even more," Charlie Nubbs said.

The waiter put down the fresh drinks and asked if they'd care to see menus now. They told him to give them a few more minutes. The moment the waiter was gone, Jimmy lowered his voice again.

"Say seventy-five a key," he said, "and you take six keys, you commit for six, okay. That comes to four hundred and fifty, you give the shit a full hit, you walk away with twice that. Nine hundred K. That ain't bad on my block."

Ernesto was thinking that in today's market, seventy-five was in fact a fair price if the shit really *was* ninety-percent pure. But he wasn't looking for *fair*, he was looking for a bargain. If he went to Amaros with a bargain, maybe he wouldn't be too angry that they hadn't found the girl.

"Forty is a fair price," he said.

"Come on," Charlie Nubbs said.

"You're kidding," Jimmy Legs said.

"Forty, forty-five *tops*," Ernesto said. He turned to Domingo. *"Cuarenta o cuaranta y cinco esta bien, no? Por noventa por ciento de pureza?"*

Domingo nodded. *"Sí, por supuesto,"* he said.

"How does *seventy* sound to you?" Charlie Nubbs asked Jimmy.

"No, no, we can't do it for that, that's out of the question. Look," he said, "let's finish our drinks and go, okay? No hard feelings."

He smiled to let them know he really meant there'd be no hard feelings.

What was going on here was the same kind of bargaining that went on in any business negotiation, except that the business here happened to be narcotics. Both Jimmy Legs and Charlie Nubbs knew exactly how many keys were coming in on that boat this Friday night, never mind the bullshit about the shipments varying. Twenty keys were coming in and they had agreed to pay a million flat for the twenty. That was fifty thousand a key. If they could get four hundred and fifty thousand for only *six* keys, that meant they'd be getting the remaining fourteen keys for only five-fifty, which came to something like thirty-nine, forty a key, which was dirt cheap.

Jimmy was sure the spics knew the going price for cocaine that was ninety-percent pure, which this actually was. Either they knew or they were amateurs. *He* knew for sure that they were jerking him around when they offered forty. Seventy-five was a good price, it really was. Well, not a *good* price—nobody was giving anything away at seventy-five—but a fair price. He and Charlie were getting a very good deal on the twenty keys because the South Americans they were dealing with were new people trying to establish a foothold in Florida. Fifty thousand a key was, in fact, a *damn* good deal. But in this business it was cash on the barrelhead, mister, and they were having a tough time coming up with the million. So they wouldn't have minded laying off some of it on the spics. Not at forty a key, though. That was ridiculous.

Ernesto and Domingo both knew that forty was ridiculous. That was why Ernesto had immediately modified this to "forty, forty-five," which was also ridiculous. A fair price was seventy-five. But Ernesto figured the wops were telling the truth (always a bad failing) when they said they wouldn't mind laying some of the deal off on somebody else, which meant they weren't about to lay it off at *cost* but were trying to make a little bit *above* cost for putting the deal together and so on. The question was how much they had agreed to pay for the dope. If they were paying sixty a key, for example, which is what it sounded like if they were asking seventy-five, then there was no way Ernesto was going to get a bargain here. He'd either have to find the girl or risk Amaros's anger. Amaros might even hang *him* from the ceiling if he didn't find the girl. He was thinking Ai, *muchacho*, it would be nice to get this shit for fifty a key, make Amaros very happy.

He didn't have a chance of getting it for fifty; fifty was what they were paying for it. But he didn't know that. Anyway, nobody was leaving just yet.

The waiter brought menus.

The men ordered.

Domingo kept eyeing the two women at the nearby table, both of whom were all dressed up for their Tuesday lunch.

"So what do you say?" Charlie Nubbs asked.

"I told you," Ernesto said. "The highest I can go is forty-five. And even that, I'd have to check back with Miami."

"Then we can't talk business," Jimmy said. "'Cause the lowest we can go is seventy."

Ernesto noticed that a few minutes ago Jimmy had considered seventy out of the question. They were making progress.

"This snapper is delicious," Charlie Nubbs said.

"Yeah, they get it fresh every morning in this place," Jimmy said.

"You get good fish over in Miami, too, don't you?" Charlie said.

"Oh, sure," Ernesto said.

"How about sixty-five?" Jimmy said. "And you take eight keys. That's we're talking five-twenty, that's a good deal."

Ernesto suddenly knew they were paying fifty thousand a key.

"Sixty-five is too high," he said. "I could never clear that with Miami."

"Must be a real high roller there in Miami," Jimmy said, "he can't go to sixty-five."

Ernesto said nothing. He looked at Domingo. Domingo shook his head. Jimmy suddenly wondered if the big guy with the slick little mustache wasn't the *real* boss here.

"What *could* you go for?" Charlie Nubbs asked. "I mean, what do you think your man in Miami would okay?"

"I told you," Ernesto said. "Forty-five." He hesitated and then said, "Maybe fifty absolute tops."

"Tell you what we'll do," Jimmy said. "You take ten keys for sixty a key, you've got a deal. That's *cost*, amigo, believe me. That's exactly what we're paying for it."

Ernesto knew he was lying.

The question was whether they'd be willing to come down to fifty-five. He was afraid that if he offered fifty-five they might become offended and walk. Italians had pride. At the same time, he wondered how desperate they were for cash.

"What we're talking is six hundred thou," Charlie Nubbs said.

Jimmy was doing arithmetic in his head. Sell off ten for six hundred, that meant they were paying only forty a key for the remaining ten keys. That was very good. *If* the spics went for it. If not, he didn't know what he would do. They were probably looking to pay fifty-five a key, which was why they'd started at forty. Sell them ten keys for fifty-five, that meant the remaining ten keys were costing forty-five a key . . . no, that sucked. Sixty a key, he thought, take it or leave it.

"Take it or leave it," he said aloud.

Ernesto knew he meant it.

So did Domingo.

"I have to call Miami," Ernesto said.

"There's a phone booth in the lobby," Charlie said.

"I want to call from the motel," Ernesto said.

Everybody understood the need for privacy. They would not be discussing soy beans or hog bellies on the phone.

"Okay," Jimmy said, "get back to us tomorrow sometime. I don't hear from you by three o'clock, I figure you're out."

"Good," Ernesto said.

"Good," Jimmy said.

12

The headline on Wednesday morning's newspaper read:

MURDER CAR FOUND

The article under it described a black Toronado that the police had found deep in the palmettos off Bay Point Road, near the old Adderby place. The car, the police said, was registered to a woman named Florence Goodel, who had reported it stolen on June 7, the day before Otto Samalson was murdered. The police said that Miss Goodel was definitely not a suspect. The article did not mention whether the police had found any latent fingerprints or spent cartridge cases in the automobile. Neither did it say how the police had *known* the black Toronado in the palmettos was the car driven by Otto's murderer.

Matthew nodded sourly, threw the newspaper into his trash basket, picked up the telephone receiver, and dialed Jamie Purchase's office.

Jamie Purchase.

Forty-six years old on the night of the Goldilocks murders, ten years older than Matthew. In the pale moonlight, he'd seemed much younger, or perhaps only more vulnerable. He was wearing a faded blue T-shirt, white trousers, and blue sneakers. Matthew had introduced himself to the patrolman at the scene as Dr. Purchase's attorney, which indeed he was.

Two years ago Jamie Purchase was a client for whom Matthew had reviewed and revised a pension plan. He was also a man who came home one night after a poker game to find his wife and his two little daughters brutally murdered. He called the only attorney he knew: Matthew Hope. On the phone that night, Matthew first asked him if he'd committed the murders, and then asked if he wouldn't prefer a criminal lawyer to a man who'd never represented anyone involved in a crime. Jamie had said, "If I didn't kill them, why do I need a criminal lawyer?"—which plunged Matthew headlong into the case.

Just like that.

This past Friday, Susan had said, "Why don't you simply learn all there is to learn about criminal law and start practicing it?" The more he thought about it, the more he liked the idea. But now, as he sat in Jamie's waiting room, he wondered if in actuality he hadn't started practicing criminal law away back then, when the phone call from Jamie had shattered the stillness of the night.

"Mr. Hope?" Jamie's receptionist-nurse. "Doctor will see you now."

"Thank you."

Jamie looked good. Two years ago his world had disintegrated. He seemed all right now, looked all right. He had not remarried. Rumor around town had him dating a twenty-seven-year-old interior decorator. It did not sound too serious.

"I called Nathan," he said. He was referring to Dr. Nathan Schlemmer, who had identified Cinderella as Mary Jane Hopkins but had refused to tell Otto why she'd come to see him. "Do you know him?"

"No," Matthew said.

"Fiftyish," Jamie said. "Gray hair, closely trimmed gray beard, blue eyes so pale *they* look gray." He shrugged. "Dr. Nathan Schlemmer. I know him well enough to be able to state, unequivocally, that if you'd gone to him directly, asking about this Mary Jane Hopkins, he'd have told you—and I quote more or less accurately—'Mr. Hope, this is not information I care to divulge.' That is Dr. Nathan Schlemmer, very uptight, very tight-ass. However . . ."

"Uh-huh," Matthew said.

"Professional courtesy. Plus a slight lie. I told him the girl was a patient. I asked him why she'd gone to see him. I asked him if she was pregnant."

"Was she?" Matthew said.

"She was not," Jamie said.

"Then why *did* she go see him?"

"She suspected she had herpes," Jamie said.

"Uh-huh," Matthew said. "And did she?"

"Yes."

The boat was a huge monster with a flying bridge.

Larkin was behind the wheel, guiding her in toward the dock, careful not to bang her up. A deckhand wearing a Larkin Boats T-shirt ran forward to toss a line to someone on the dock wearing an identical T-shirt, The Way to the Water. Another hand dropped fenders over the side. More lines came over, you'd think this was the QE2 Larkin was docking. Big boat, though, had to cost a pretty penny.

Two people were standing on the bridge with Larkin. Tubby little man wearing a sports shirt as colorful as a Portuguese man-of-war, and a blonde lady wearing yellow shorts, a white shirt, and a pair of sunglasses. Larkin frowned the moment he saw Matthew standing on the dock. He clambered down off the bridge, jumped ashore, walked immediately to him, and said, "What are you doing here?"

"Few questions," Matthew said.

"Get lost," Larkin said. "I'm about to sell a half-million-dollar boat here."

"I'll wait."

"No, just get the hell off my property."

One of the dockhands was helping the couple ashore now. First the lady in the yellow shorts. She was perhaps fifty years old, too stout, too heavily made up, and a bit unsteady in ankle-strapped sandals with very high heels. She come onto the dock with a smile of relief and a murmured "Thank you," and then turned to watch her companion jump ashore. The man was grinning from ear to ear. He was eager to buy this boat. Matthew wasn't sure the lady was half as eager. The man stepped back a pace, hands on his hips, and studied the boat from dockside.

"This won't take a minute," Matthew said.

"My customer's waiting," Larkin said.

"No, he's admiring the boat."

Larkin looked toward where the man was walking up and down the dock, reaching over to touch the boat's teak railing, running his hand over her gleaming white flanks.

"What is it?" Larkin said.

"Mr. Larkin, when I saw you yesterday, I told you that Otto—"

"I don't want to hear another word about Otto. I've already got somebody *else* looking for—"

"Yes, I know. But I've learned something that—"

"I don't care what you learned."

"Mr. Larkin, Otto thought your Cinderella might have been pregnant . . ."

"You already told me that. And *I* told you—"

"But he was wrong. She went to see a doctor because she had herpes."

Larkin glanced quickly down the dock to where the man in the rainbow sports shirt was pointing to something on the boat's transom. He said a few words to the woman, and the woman nodded, an uncomprehending look on her face.

"So?" Larkin said.

"I asked you yesterday if you could've made her pregnant."

"So?"

"I'm asking you today if you could've given her herpes."

"I don't have to answer that," Larkin said.

"Yes, you do," Matthew said. "Because Otto was killed. And there's got to be a reason for it."

"Let's say I *did* give her herpes, okay? I'm the kind of guy who gives herpes to twenty-two-year-old girls. Twenty-three, whatever. When I don't even realize she's a hooker. I'm that kind of rat, okay? What's that got to do with Otto's murder?"

"Well, Mr. Larkin, suppose someone in her family—a father, a brother—*learned* she had herpes and decided to find out who'd given it to her. This is Florida, you know. There're lots of rednecks down here who don't like their kin messed with."

"This girl isn't a redneck."

"But you don't know what her family's like, do you?"

"What's your point?" Larkin said. "She stole my watch, that's all I—"

"Yes, but Otto was killed. And to me that's a bit more important than your watch. What I'm suggesting is that perhaps this father or this brother spotted Otto following her and jumped to the wrong conclusion."

"What conclusion?"

"That *Otto* was the man who'd—"

"Oh, I get it. This *father* of hers . . ."

"Yes, if it was her father . . ."

"Or *brother* . . ."

"Yes."

"Or whoever . . . didn't realize Otto was a private eye, figured he was somebody who *knew* Cinderella . . ."

"Yes."

"Somebody, in fact, who knew her well enough to give her *herpes*, right? And then what? *Killed* him for it? Come on, man."

"This is Florida," Matthew said again.

"No way at all is it even a possibility," Larkin said. "Because to begin with, hookers don't *have* fathers or brothers."

"I'm sorry," Matthew said, "but I don't find any of this even remotely funny. And you *still* haven't answered my question."

"Too fuckin' bad," Larkin said, and glanced quickly down the dock toward his customer. "In case you don't know it, this isn't a court of—"

"*Could* you have given her herpes?"

"Oh, now I *really* get it," Larkin said. "If I'm the guy responsible, if I'm the one infected her, then the wrong man got killed, right? Poor Otto took the rap for *me*, right? So you're here to tell me what an unprincipled son of a bitch I am. Well, let me tell *you* something, Mr. Hope, and then I want you to get the hell out of here before I have Kirk *throw* you out."

He nodded down the dock to where one of the hands was hosing down the boat. Big muscular guy with pecs bulging in the white T-shirt, biceps bulging below the short sleeves, tattoo on the right forearm, a dagger dripping blood.

"The only person selling herpes—and I hope to God nothing *else*—was Cinderella herself. Jenny Santoro or *whatever* the fuck her name is!" He glanced down the dock again, and then lowered his voice. "She's the one selling it, Mr. Hope, she's the one I bought it from. Which is why, the minute I realized what I had, I hired Otto to find her, never mind the gold watch. I can buy another gold watch, I can buy a *dozen* gold watches, but I can't buy a doctor in the world can get rid of what she gave me. Okay, Mr. Hope? You got it now? You think you got it now?"

Matthew sighed heavily.

"Yes," he said. "Thank you."

"Good-bye," Larkin said.

The conversation was entirely in Spanish, and Ernesto was doing most of the talking.

Their private code name for cocaine was "hat."

In Spanish, hat was *sombrero.*

On the phone, Ernesto kept talking about sombreros. Ten sombreros at sixty dollars each, very high quality. If anybody from the DEA had been listening, he'd have known right off that Ernesto was talking about a drug buy. Ten keys of coke at sixty thousand a key. Drug dealers never mentioned the word *cocaine* on the telephone. They hardly ever mentioned it *anywhere.* Cocaine was always something else. To Charlie Nubbs and his pals, cocaine was "heavy machinery." With the Ordinez gang in Miami, if you talked to someone about a typewriter, you were talking cocaine.

"I tried to get the hats for less," Ernesto said, "but that's the lowest they would go. Very good hats, size nine."

A DEA man would have figured in a minute that the coke was ninety-percent pure.

"When do you have to take delivery on these hats?" Amaros asked.

"Saturday. One-thirty."

"Are the manufacturers reliable?"

"We'll examine the merchandise very carefully before payment is made."

"Do they require a deposit?"

"They haven't mentioned one."

"When will you need a check?"

"As soon as possible."

"I'll have one drawn," Amaros said.

The "check" was total bullshit. Nobody ever wrote a check for cocaine. You would have to be crazy to accept a check for cocaine. Cocaine was as good as cash and what you *got* for it was cash. Amaros was merely telling Ernesto that he'd get the cash to him before one-thirty on Saturday. Ten keys at sixty a key came to $600,000. This was Wednesday, Amaros had two full business days to get the cash. He was not anticipating any trouble.

"What about Cenicienta?" he asked.

This was the first time Ernesto had ever heard her called Cinderella, but he knew immediately that Amaros was talking about Jenny Santoro or whatever her name was. Normally, Amaros referred to her as "the girl." But Ernesto guessed he didn't want to use the word *girl* on the phone because "girl" meant cocaine.

"We haven't located her yet," Ernesto said.

"I'm pleased about the hats," Amaros said, "but I very much want to see her."

"Yes, I know," Ernesto said.

"So find her," Amaros said, and hung up.

So now they're inside the house on Key Biscayne, it's like multileveled with decks on each level, all of them looking out over the water, and Amaros is telling her to make herself comfortable, which is not difficult to do in a place like this. A place like this Jenny figures had to have cost him a mill-five, something like that, waterfront property? Sure, at least that. This is what she wants for herself. This is her dream. A place of her own. Just outside Paris. A place with a garden. Her own house. A little house on a quiet little lane. She will be the American lady. She will tell her neighbors she used to be a stage actress. She will tell them she starred in *The Crucible*. She will drive into Paris on weekends, and sit at a table on one of the boulevards, sipping crème de menthe over ice and trying to guess which of the girls strutting by are in the life, the way she used to be. Because this is the last one. If there really is coke here in this house, and if she can take it away with her, then she will never have to make love to a stranger again.

He pours her a cognac, same Courvoisier she had in the Kasbah Lounge and then—big surprise!—the conversation drifts around to movies, has she seen any good movies lately? In his cute Spanish accent he tells her that occasionally he will watch a pornographic film because he feels pornographic films are an art form and that in fact many of them are superior to the films being shown in most theaters today. He's all at once a film critic, Luis Amaros of the *Village Voice*. She tells him she has never seen a pornographic movie in her life—big lie, especially since she had a bit part in an orgy scene in a skin flick they were shooting in L.A., went down on one guy while another guy was humping her from behind—and would probably be embarrassed seeing one. Oh, no, he says, not if it is a tasteful movie, you would not be embarrassed.

Well, one thing leads to another, and he takes her to the bedroom at the other end of the house and shows her his expensive video equipment, and it turns out that the porn flicks he watches "occasionally" are a collection of a hundred or more tapes he keeps on a shelf in his closet, over where his slacks are hanging. The closet is a big walk-in thing. On the left-hand side, there are his jackets and suits, and on the right-hand side, his slacks and some long-sleeved sports shirts and over these the shelf with the porn-flick tapes. The safe is to the left just as you come into the closet. It's a pretty big safe for a private house. Jenny hopes the girl Kim wasn't giving them a fairy tale. She hopes there is really dope in that safe.

He says, "Would you like to see a truly tasteful pornographic movie?"

She says, "Well, yes, I suppose so, if it's really and *truly* tasteful."

"Oh, yes," he says.

"But," she says, eyes wide and innocent, "you told me you had cocaine."

She isn't interested in snorting cocaine just now, in fact she's very intent just now on keeping her wits about her. This man looks like the sweet little Pillsbury doughboy, you push his big tummy and he giggles, but maybe he won't be so cute if he catches her stealing his coke.

If there's coke.

That's what she wants to find out first, whether or not there's coke in the safe and whether or not it's enough coke to make the risk worthwhile.

She is carrying a huge blue tote bag that looks out of place with the ice-blue gown and the Lucite slippers, but she's already covered that by telling him she was supposed to sleep over at this party she was going to, and has brought along a few things. She has even shown him the few things. A peach-colored baby doll nightgown, bikini panties to match, high-heeled pom-pommed slippers.

So now he goes into the closet, and he kneels in front of the safe.

Will he go through the whole four-to-the-left, three-to-the-right, two-to-the-left, turn-back-slowly-to-the-right routine? Or has he simply left the dial a few figures away from the last number in the combination, the way people do who are in and out of a safe every ten minutes, what burglars call "day combination" or simply "day-com."

Kim said the safe was on day-com.

Jenny wonders if it's still on day-com.

She waits, holding her breath.

He gives the dial a simple flick to the right.

Day-com.

Good.

He reaches into the safe.

Her dream could be inside that safe. Her ticket to Paris could be inside that safe, I used to be a stage actress.

She looks over his shoulder.

Oh my God . . .

Oh my sweet loving Jesus!

There are four fucking bags of cocaine in that safe!

So now they sniff a little, talk a little, watch Johnny Holmes unreel his garden hose—

"Who do you think is bigger?" Pudgy asks. "Him or me?"

"Are you kidding, you're *enormous*!" she says, and ten minutes later drops the chloral hydrate in his drink.

The safe is on day-com again, he has given it that little flick to the left, some ten or twelve numbers away from the last number in the combination. She simply goes into the closet and turns the dial slowly to the right, and it stops on the last number—eighty as it happens—and she grabs the handle and yanks open the safe door and reaches in for all that sweet white dust.

Five minutes later, she's got the shoulder bag full, and she's running across the lawn to the front gate.

It's a little after midnight.

The Caddy is gone.

In its place is a blue Ford.

The minute she's in the car, she says, "Four keys."

Vincent—who waved his magic wand and turned her into a princess—is no longer wearing the chauffeur's uniform.

He rolls his eyes and says, "I've died and gone to heaven."

13

The two girls shopping for jeans at Coopersmith's were both in their twenties, one of them with dark black hair cut almost shoulder length, the other with russet-colored hair cut in a wedge.

The brunette was wearing a wide skirt, a peasant blouse, and flat sandals. She had brown eyes and she looked very Italian. Her name was Merilee James.

The redhead was wearing tan slacks, a brown blouse, and low-heeled tan shoes. She had blue eyes, and she looked very Irish. Her name was Sandy Jennings.

Coopersmith's was one of Calusa's better department stores. The girls probably could have found the designer jeans they were looking for at Global, which was a discount clothing store on the South Trail, but neither of them would have dreamt of shopping there.

They were both call girls.

In Calusa, there were very few bona fide call girls as such. This was not a convention town or a gambling town, it was just a rather pleasant family resort town—at least when the weather was good. Not too many men came down here looking for the kind of good time a hooker might show them. The singles who came to Calusa were looking for other singles who'd care to spend a freebie night or two in the hay. The married men were with their wives and children. So a bona fide call girl—the ones who charged a hundred bucks an hour—were as rare as snowflakes. What you had down here were some girls doing ten-dollar blow jobs for teenage kids in pickup trucks behind either of the two topless joints, or else— and this was rare, too—a free-lance, scaly-legged whore in her forties who sat on a bar stool toying with a ginger ale and hoping somebody would find her attractive enough to pay for her favors.

Both Sandy and Merilee were genuine call girls.

This meant that Sandy and Merilee were not their real names.

They had met each other a month ago, at a lounge on 41. Merilee said she was down here on vacation. She worked in New Orleans as a computer programmer for Shell Oil. That was what she told Sandy. But that was okay because Sandy told her she was a graduate student in psychology at UCLA. She was in Florida looking over the universities here because she was thinking of perhaps applying for a teaching job down here after she got her master's.

At the time, Sandy suspected Merilee was a hooker, and Merilee suspected the same thing of Sandy, but neither of them mentioned it until one rainy afternoon when they went to an early movie together—the five o'clock movie in Calusa cost only $2.25—and the movie had a hooker in it, and later on over dinner Merilee and Sandy began discussing the girl in the picture and it turned out *they* were both hookers, too, well, well!

Merilee, in fact, was working pretty steady down here, at night, which was why she had to go to five o'clock movies. She had a couple of old guys she serviced on Fatback Key. She thought one of them was in love with her. Or maybe he was kidding. But he kept saying he wanted to take her out to dinner, maybe go away for a weekend together, buy her jewelry, like that. Only he never did. She asked him once whether he was jealous of her making love to other men. She didn't say *fucking* other men, she never talked dirty when she was with him, he despised dirty talk. He said he was very jealous because he loved her so much. But he never suggested like making this a permanent live-in thing, you know, even though he was a widower. Sandy told Merilee she herself wasn't turning any tricks down here, just taking it easy for a while.

Today, while they were trying on clothes in the dressing room, neither of them discussed their mutual profession, except peripherally. In fact, neither of them even discussed *men* except peripherally, which was odd since a lot of women, when they were alone together, discussed nothing *but* men.

What they were discussing was career moves.

What Sandy was going to do, as soon as she settled a few financial matters here in Calusa, was get out of Florida entirely. Get out of the country, in fact. She had very big plans for the future and they didn't include sucking some married businessman's cock. She was only hanging around here till a few things were settled, that was all. It wasn't a bad place to wait, she told Merilee.

Merilee thought she might stay with what she was doing till she was thirty. She already had fifty grand in Dreyfus Liquid Assets, and it was paying good interest at the moment, and she guessed in the next six years—she had just turned twenty-four—in the next six years, if she kept adding to the account and if the interest rates stayed good, she could maybe hope to have something like five, six hundred thousand in cash. That was a lot of money. You had cash like that, you could do a lot of things with it.

For example, there was a guy she knew here in Calusa, his name was Martin Klement, who'd been born in London but who was now an American citizen with a restaurant on Lucy's Key. Martin had spent a great deal of time down in the Caribbean—first running a hotel on Antigua, and then a restaurant in St. Thomas, and then another restaurant on Grenada—before coming up to Florida and settling in Calusa. His restaurant here was called Springtime, all done up in green and white and fresh with flowers every day of the week, an immediate hit the moment it opened six years ago, perhaps because there was no such thing as a *real* springtime in the state of Florida although longtime residents insisted they could tell when the seasons changed.

Martin was maybe fifty-three years old, a giant of a man some six feet three inches tall with white hair and a white walrus mustache, tattoos on both arms, reputed to have done some shady deals down there where the trade winds played, a keen eye for a quick penny had old Martin Klement. Merilee also suspected that Martin was AC/DC, or at least that was the rumor circulating, not that Merilee cared in the slightest.

Well, last night Merilee dropped in at the restaurant to see what was shaking—Martin sometimes had guys sitting there at the bar who would perhaps be interesting—and he came over and bought her a drink on the house and the two started chatting. Martin liked her a lot, and she liked him, too. He still spoke with a British accent, and sometimes used funny British expressions. When he'd first met Merilee, in fact, he'd tried to teach her Cockney rhyming slang, but it was far too difficult and all Merilee had come away with was "bread and honey"— if she was remembering correctly—which meant "money," which was the only thing in the world that interested her.

They started talking about the unusually hot weather they'd been having and its effect on the restaurant business. It was Martin's theory, and maybe he was right, that extremely hot weather sent people *out* to eat, maybe because a woman didn't want to toil over a stove when it was ninety degrees outside.

One topic led to another and eventually Martin asked, "Have you been out to Sabal Beach since the crackdown started?"

"No, I haven't," Merilee said.

"They're still letting the women go topless, but catch anyone *bare*-arsed, male *or* female, and it's into the wagon with them."

"Awful, the police down here," Merilee said.

"Think they'd find a way to spend their time more profitably, wouldn't you?"

"Really," Merilee said.

"They'll have their hands full soon enough," Martin said, "never mind chasing after nude bathers. Did you read the stories on the big drug arrest in Miami a few months back?"

"No, I didn't," Merilee said.

"Took the DEA almost a year to set it up, but they netted some very big fish indeed. What I'm saying is I wouldn't be surprised if bearing down on the *other* coast won't send the drug people scurrying here to Calusa. The police'll have plenty to do, believe me, without rounding up nudists."

"Well, there's not much of that here in Calusa," Merilee said. "Narcotics."

"True enough, I've yet to see anyone openly smoking marijuana in my place," Martin said. "But I'll tell you, Mer, on occasion I've happened upon a few people doing a bit of coke in the men's room, eh? So it's not as uncommon as you might believe."

"Well," Merilee said.

"I've been asked myself once or twice," Martin said, lowering his voice.

"Asked what?"

"Y'know. Whether I knew where to get any stuff."

"Oh."

"Recently, in fact," Martin said. "Two Hispanics came in the other night, told me they were looking to buy quality cocaine, ready to pay top dollar for it. I'll tell you, I wish I could've accommodated them. I figure the way they got to me . . . I wouldn't repeat this, Mer—"

"Cross my heart," she said.

"—is years ago, when I had the restaurant on Grenada, I was . . . well . . . engaged in what one might call 'redistribution,' eh? Helping merchandise find its way from one place to another. There was money to be made in redistribution, I can tell you. You'd get your banana boats up from South America, they'd be carrying other than bananas sometimes, eh? You accepted whatever cargo you thought you could safely handle, you merely redistributed it to Barbados, and it found its way from there to Guadeloupe or Martinique and then on up the chain to Haiti and finally into Florida, this was, oh, six, seven years ago, Mer. Grenada's a stone's throw from Venezuela, y'know, and once you were past British Customs, you had the whole Caribbean open to you. A great deal of money was waiting to be untrousered back then. Now, too, for that matter. All you need is the merchandise to redistribute, eh? Which is why these two men came to the restaurant, sat at the bar, ordered a few drinks, mentioned they'd heard my name here and there. Hispanics, y'know, the Colombian word gets around, look up

Martin Klement, he used to own The Troubador on Grenada, he's got a restaurant in Florida now, maybe he can help you."

"I can see how that might happen," Merilee said.

"I truly wish I could help them," Martin said, and sighed. "They were talking real commitment. Excellent money, too. If you should hear of anyone, let me know."

Merilee was standing in front of the dressing room mirror as she repeated this story to Sandy. She was pulling up the zipper on a pair of very tight jeans. She sort of did a little leap off the floor as she pulled up the zipper.

"What I'm saying," she said, "is six years from now, I'll be like those two Spanish guys, you know? I'll have myself a real bundle, I'll breeze back here into Calusa, tell Martin I'm looking to make a big dope buy, are these too tight?"

"A little," Sandy said.

"Mustn't look cheap, must we?" Merilee said, and both girls giggled. Merilee took off the jeans and tried on another pair, talking as she smoothed them over her hips and turned this way and that in front of the mirror.

"Martin knows everything," she said. "That's 'cause he owns a restaurant, all kinds of people come in. He was the first one in Calusa to recognize me for a hooker. You were the second one, but you're in the life yourself, so that's understandable. Do you know what *la moglia del barbiere* means? That's Italian. It means the town gossip. Actually, it means 'the barber's wife,' but everybody knows what it *really* means. Because the barber hears everything there is to hear, and he tells it to his wife, and she gossips about it. Well, people tell restaurant owners and bartenders the same things they tell barbers. That's how come Martin hears so much. Which, speaking of barbers, when did you do that to your hair?"

"Two weeks ago come Saturday," Sandy said.

"You got tired of it long?"

"Sort of."

"You like it better red, huh? Than blonde?"

"Sort of," Sandy said.

She was silent for the space of a heartbeat, and then she said, "How much are they looking to buy?" and Merilee's eyes met hers in the mirror.

Yellow flags and banners were flying outside 1237 Hacienda Road when Matthew pulled into the condominium's parking lot that Thursday afternoon. A huge sign outside the sales office read:

CAMELOT TOWERS
THE SALE OF THE CENTURY!
NOTHING DOWN
NO CLOSING FEES
9.9% 30-YEAR FIXED

Frank had told him that Florida State First had been forced to foreclose on the condominium's contractor and was virtually giving away the unsold units in an attempt to get rid of them. Sixty units in the entire complex, twenty-four of them still unsold. Last week, Otto had questioned the occupants of seventeen apartments. Seventeen plus twenty-four came to forty-one. From sixty came to nineteen. Still nineteen apartments to tackle. Assuming Frank was right about the number of unsold units.

Frank had also told him the latest condominium joke:

This man comes down to Florida looking for a condominium. He pulls his car into the nearest parking space and is looking for the sales office when he spots a woman and asks her, "Can you tell me where the sales office is? I'd like to see one of the condominiums."

The woman says, "Why do you need the sales office? I live here, come look at *my* condominium."

"Well, thank you, that's very kind of you," the man says and follows the woman upstairs to her apartment.

"Would you care for a drink?" the woman asks.

"Well, thank you, I wouldn't mind," the man says.

She brings him a drink, and they sit in the living room, drinking.

"Would you care for some sex?" the woman asks.

"Well, thank you, I wouldn't mind," the man says.

"Some kinky sex?" she asks.

"Well, yes, thank you," he says.

"Unzip your fly," she says.

He unzips his fly.

"Put your member on the palm of my left hand," she says.

He puts his member on the palm of her left hand.

She raises her right hand and begins smacking his member, smack, smack, smack, each smack punctuated with the words, "Don't . . . ever . . . park . . . in . . . my . . . space . . . *again!*"

Matthew hoped he hadn't parked in anyone's space.

He looked for the Resident Manager's office, found it tucked in a corner of the building that housed the workout room and the rec room, and knocked on the door.

"Come in!" a woman's voice called.

He opened the door onto a small reception room with a desk and chair in it, no one in the chair, no one behind the desk. This was one o'clock in the afternoon, he assumed the receptionist was out to lunch.

"I'm in here!"

He followed the voice into a larger office with a larger desk in it. An attractive, dark-haired woman sat behind the desk. She was, he guessed, in her late thirties, early forties, a pleas-

ant smile on her face, her brown eyes studying him from behind tortoiseshell glasses. Behind her was a rental calendar
with large blocks of in-season time marked with different col-
ored strips of tape.

"Can I help you?" she asked.

"I'm Matthew Hope," he said.

"Anne Langner," she said. "Please sit down, won't you?"

"Thank you," he said, and took a seat opposite her desk.
"Miss Langner," he said, "I wonder if you remember . . . on
the sixth of June . . . that would have been two weeks ago this
coming Friday . . . a man named Otto Samalson . . ."

"Oh, yes," she said at once.

"You do remember him?"

"Well, of course. With all the stories about him on television and in the papers? Yes, certainly. He was here asking
about a beautiful young woman, I forget her name just now."

"Well, I'm sure he asked about *several* names," Matthew
said.

"Yes, now that you mention it, he did. I'm sorry but I didn't
recognize the girl in the picture he showed me. She isn't one
of our owners, and she isn't renting an apartment here,
either."

"*Would* you have recognized her?"

"Oh, yes."

"Even if she was living here with someone else?"

"What do you mean?"

"Well, *not* an owner, *not* a renter, but living with someone
who *is* an owner or a renter."

"Oh. Well . . . I don't know. There are sixty units here,
twenty-four of them as yet unsold, the others either owner-
occupied or in our rental program. It would be difficult to—"

"How many are owner-occupied?" Matthew asked.

"Nineteen."

"Year-round residents?"

"Not all of them. Seven are owners who only use the apartment two or three months out of the year but prefer not to rent it when they're away."

"That leaves twelve year-round residents."

"Yes."

"Of the seven absentee owners, are any of them here now?"

"I really couldn't say. This isn't a full-service condo, you see, we don't check on the comings and goings of anyone whose apartment isn't in our rental program."

"How many apartments are rented right now?"

"All of the seasonal renters are already gone, they usually disappear just after Easter, the beginning of May at the very latest. We have three summer rentals, but they're unusual. The rest are renting by the year, people who come down here with a job, expect to buy a house, rent a condo while they're settling in and looking."

"So," Matthew said, "right now how many apartments are occupied?"

"Twelve owner-occupied. Three summer rentals. Six annuals."

"Twenty-one in all."

He was thinking Otto had already covered seventeen of those twenty-one. But *which* seventeen?

"Plus any absentee owner who may be in residence just now," Anne said. "They come and go."

Better yet, Matthew thought.

"Would you mind if I knocked on some doors?" he asked.

"It's a free country," she said, and arched one eyebrow. "Will you need any help?"

Matthew knew an arched eyebrow when he saw one.

"Maybe," he said, and smiled. "I'll let you know."

When Matthew was a boy in Chicago, the one thing he'd hated more than anything else in the world was going around with his kid sister Gloria when she was selling Girl Scout cookies. His mother had said she didn't want little Gloria knocking on doors all by herself, you never knew who or what might be behind one of those doors.

So Matthew had gone along with a scowling and embarrassed Gloria—her goddamn big brother leading around a *Girl* Scout who could make fires by rubbing two sticks together and everything—and he'd knocked on doors and listened to his sister giving her spiel, "Morning, ma'am, would you like to buy some delicious Girl Scout cookies?" and he'd felt like a horse's ass. Especially since no one at all tried to rape or kill Gloria.

By three o'clock that afternoon, Matthew had knocked on twelve apartment doors.

At two of those apartments, he'd got no answer at all.

At four of them, he was told that they'd already answered questions about the girl with the long blonde hair. One man asked if this was a contest or something, and if so, what was the prize?

At five of them—after describing the girl known variously as Angela West, Jody Carmody, Melissa Blair, Mary Jane Hopkins, and Jenny Santoro—he was told that maybe the girl sounded familiar, but didn't he have a picture?

And at the last apartment, the door was slammed in his face before he could even open his mouth.

Sighing, he knocked on the door to apartment 2C.

He could hear rock music coming from inside the apartment.

"Who is it?" a voice called.

"My name is Matthew Hope," he said, "I wonder if I might have a few minutes of your time."

"Who?"

"Matthew Hope."

"What do you want, Matthew Hope?"

This from just inside the door.

"I'm trying to locate someone, I wonder if—"

"Try the manager's office."

"I've just been there. Miss, if you look through your peephole you'll see I'm not an ax-murderer or anything."

A giggle on the other side of the door.

Then:

"Just a sec, okay?"

He waited. Night chain coming off. Tumblers falling. Door opening.

The girl standing there was wearing cutoff jeans and a green tank top shirt. She was barefoot. Matthew guessed she was five feet eight or nine inches tall, somewhere in there. Her russet-colored hair was cut in a short wedge with bangs falling almost to the tops of her overlarge sunglasses. There was a faint smile on her mouth. No lipstick. She stood in the doorway with one hand on the jamb, sort of leaning onto the hand. It was difficult to tell her age. She looked like a teenager. He felt like asking her if her mother was home.

"So okay, Matthew Hope," she said.

Very young voice.

"I'm sorry to bother you," he said.

"No bother."

"I'm an attorney . . ."

"Uh-oh," she said.

But not alarmed, just jokingly. Smile still on her mouth. Eyes inscrutable behind the dark glasses.

"I'm trying to locate someone for one of my clients."

A lie.

She kept watching him, smile still on her mouth.

"I'm sorry I don't have a photograph," he said, "but she's a girl of about twenty-two or three—long blonde hair, blue eyes, very attractive—and she may be living here at Camelot Towers. Would you happen to know her?"

"Not offhand." A pause. "What's her name?"

"Well, she uses several different names?"

"Oh? Is she wanted by the police or something?"

"No, no."

"That's right, you said you were trying to locate her for a client." Another pause. "What are these names she uses?"

"Jenny Santoro . . ."

Shaking her head.

"Melissa Blair . . ."

Still shaking her head.

"Jody Carmody . . . Angela West . . . Mary Jane Hopkins . . ."

"Lots of names."

"Any of them ring a bell?"

"Sorry."

"And you haven't seen anyone of that description?"

"No, I'm sorry."

"Going in or out of the building . . ."

"No."

". . . or in the elevator?"

"No place." Shaking her head again. "Sorry."

"Do you live here?" he asked.

"I'm visiting a friend," she said.

"Is *she* home?"

"*He*. No, I'm sorry, he's out just now."

"I was wondering, you see—"

"Yes?"

"—if he might have seen this person I'm looking for."

"I really don't know. I'll ask him, how's that?"

"Would you? Here's my card," he said, reaching for his wallet, searching for a card, never a damn card when you needed one, "he can call me here," handing her the card, "if he thinks he knows her."

She took the card, looked at it.

"I'll tell him," she said.

"Thank you."

"Not at all," she said, and closed the door.

The name plate on it read: HOLLISTER.

14

She did not reach Martin Klement until six o'clock that night. She had called him earlier at his restaurant—Springtime, what a name for a restaurant, it sounded like a place selling plants—and she'd been told that he wouldn't be in till the dinner hour. She asked what *time* that would be. For different people the dinner hour was at different times. The snippy little bitch who answered the phone said they began serving at six-thirty.

Jenny figured she'd try at six, nothing ventured nothing gained.

When Klement came on the line, she said, "Hello, this is Sandy Jennings, I was talking to a friend of mine this afternoon, a girl named Merilee James, she had some interesting things to say about two Hispanic gentlemen."

"Oh?"

Caution in that single word. British caution, but caution nonetheless.

"I think I might be able to accommodate them," Jenny said.

"I'll have to call you back," Klement said.

"No, I'll call *you* back. What do you want to do? Check with Merilee?"

"If you don't mind."

"I'll call you back in half an hour," Jenny said, and hung up.

There was no way she was going to give this telephone number to anybody. Not this one, nor the one at the hotel, either. She didn't want Klement or his two spic friends—or *anybody*, for that matter—barging in looking for coke.

She wondered when Vincent would be home.

When she'd spoken to him on the phone this morning, he'd told her his last appointment was at two-thirty, and he'd be back at the condo by three, three-thirty. She'd come here right after talking to Merilee, hoping he'd be home already, knocked and knocked and finally let herself in with her key. Tried him at Unicorn, they told her he'd already left. So where the fuck was he? Six o'clock already. She desperately needed to tell him what she'd heard from Merilee, first damn good news since they'd come to Calusa.

Sitting on four fucking keys of cocaine, you think there'd be buyers coming out of the woodwork like cockroaches.

Well, you can't take an ad in the paper, can you?

FOR SALE

FOUR KILOS COCAINE

NINETY-PERCENT PURE

CALL OWNER AT . . .

No way.

You kept your ears open, you listened, you didn't trust anybody with the secret. In the state of Florida, you could find yourself on the bottom of the ocean if somebody thought you had four keys of coke. So you had to play your cards very close to your chest. Meanwhile sitting there with what you knew was worth seventy, seventy-five a key. All that shit and no way to translate it to cash.

Until now.

So where the fuck was Vincent?

Thought it might be him when the lawyer knocked on the door.

How the hell did a *lawyer* get into this?

If he really *was* a lawyer.

Man, this was weird.

Well, he'd given her a card, she guessed he was a real lawyer.

Summerville and Hope.

On impulse, she dialed the number—

"Good evening, Summerville and Hope."

—and immediately hung up.

So who hired the lawyer?

Larkin again? It sure as hell wasn't Fat Louie in Miami. You steal a man's cocaine, he doesn't go to any kind of law. No, it had to be Larkin again. Guy coming around with a picture of her. Knocking on the door here at the condo, you know this girl? Vincent later described the picture. Polaroid color shot of her in the ice-blue gown she'd worn first for Amaros in Miami and later here at the Jacaranda Ball. Went there with a girl she'd met at the Sheraton. She hadn't told Vincent about that night with Larkin. Hadn't told him she'd stolen the Rolex. Didn't want to risk his shrill faggoty rage. Didn't want to piss old Vincent off, fags could get meaner than pit vipers.

The look on his face.

"Amaros," he said.

She knew it wasn't Amaros, she knew it was Larkin.

Larkin trying to find her for what she'd given him.

Directly traceable to Amaros.

Nice little present from Amaros, the shit.

She didn't say anything.

She figured four keys of coke was worth getting herpes.

Maybe.

"When did he take your picture?" Vincent said.

"I don't remember."

"Well, damn it, remember! Can't you see he's traced us here?"

Voice high and strident. Very nervous now. Started pacing back and forth. This was like Friday a couple of weeks ago, the fourth, the fifth, somewhere in there. Biting his lip while he paced. Nervous as a cat. Eyes flashing.

"I don't remember," she said again.

Damned if she was going to tell him about Larkin and the Rolex, have to listen to his fuckin' faggoty screams.

Which was why she was a little nervous about talking to Klement now, before she'd had a chance to discuss this. She didn't want Vincent taking another fit. A fag throwing a fit was something to behold. But shit, if there were some real buyers out there . . .

Was the lawyer from Larkin?

Knew names she'd used since she was for Christ's sake sixteen years old!

She looked at her watch. She hoped he'd get home before she had to call Klement again.

When he wasn't there by six-thirty, she started getting a little worried. Had he had an automobile accident or something? Last client at two-thirty, so it was now six-thirty, so where was he?

She dialed the number at the Springtime restaurant.

"Mr. Klement, please," she said.

"Whom shall I say is calling?"

Same bitch from this afternoon. *Whom.* My *ass,* whom, that's whom.

"Sandy Jennings."

Jenny Santoro sort of ass-backwards, she thought.

"Hello?"

Klement's voice.

"Did you check with Merilee?" she said. "Am I real?"

"When can we meet?" Klement asked.

"We can't," Jenny said. "You tell me what your end is, and then you give me a number to call. That's how it works."

Cover your ass. She'd learned all about covering her ass in Los Angeles. It was even more important to cover it here. Four keys of high-grade? Shit, man.

"Sorry," he said, "I don't do business that way."

"You're not the one holding," she said.

"True."

"Do we talk or not?"

"My end is ten percent," he said.

"Five or forget it."

"I hate haggling like a fishmonger."

"So do I."

"Seven and a half then."

"Fine. How do I reach your people?"

"Have we got a deal?"

"Yes. Payment on delivery."

"No. I don't want to be there."

"Then get your end in advance."

"I beg your pardon?"

"From your people. As soon as we set a price."

"Most professionals don't do this sort of business on the telephone."

"Lucky I'm an amateur," Jenny said. "Let me have the number."

Klement gave her the number.

Only once before had Vincent been tempted by a male client, and that was when he was working for Vidal Sassoon in New York. The man's name was Melvyn—with a y, no less— and he was as queer as a turnip, but oh so gorgeous. Great blond locks and cornflower blue eyes and muscles he doubtlessly *flexed* every weekend at Cherry Grove—oh, what Vincent wouldn't have given for a tumble with young Melvyn.

At the time, Vincent was spending his weekends with two good friends of his who owned a house in Pound Ridge, near Emily Shaw's Inn. He made the mistake one Wednesday afternoon, while Melvyn-with-a-Y was in having his golden fleece shorn, to suggest that he might enjoy coming up one weekend, meet some of the boys, party a bit, did Melvyn think he might enjoy that? Melvyn lowered his baby blues and put one hand on Vincent's arm, and said, "Oh dear, that's *so* kind of you, but I'm involved just now."

The person he was involved with, as it turned out, marched in that very afternoon to make certain his sweet little boy was having his hair properly trimmed. The grandest old drag queen who ever lived, wearing a black cape and high-heeled boots and blood-red lipstick that made him look like Dracula.

Vincent swore off that very minute.

Never again would he come on with a client.

Cut the hair, make the chitchat, and let it go.

But at 6:47 that night, while Jenny was on the phone asking for cabin number three at the Suncrest Motel, Vincent was in a room at Pirate's Cove, making love with a man named George Anders, who'd been his two-thirty client.

Anders was a married orthodontist.

Giggling, Vincent told him he had a very bad overbite.

At exactly that moment, Susan Hope walked onto the deck of the restaurant at Stone Crab Shores and spotted Matthew sitting at a table overlooking the water.

A wide smile broke on her face.

Swiftly, she walked to him.

With twenty-five cents and the accent of the man on the other end of the line, you could start a banana plantation in Cuba.

"Sondy Hennings?" he said.

"Yes," she said. "Martin Klement asked me to call you."

"Ah, *sí*," he said.

"Is this Ernesto?"

"*Sí*."

No last name. Martin hadn't given her one, and she didn't ask for one. She didn't care how many names of hers he had, first, last, it didn't matter, the Sandy was a phony and so was the Jennings.

"I understand you're looking to buy some fine china," she said.

This was what Martin had told her to say on the phone. Fine china. What bullshit, she thought. Ernesto was thinking the same thing. Domingo was sprawled out on the bed, looking through the July issue of *Penthouse*.

"That is correct," Ernesto said.

"I have four fine plates that may interest you."

"How fine?" Ernesto asked.

"This is 1890 china we're talking about," she said.

"Ninety?" he said.

"That's right."

Fooling nobody, she thought. We're talking ninety-pure and we both know it and so does anyone listening, fine china my ass.

"How much do these plates cost?" he asked.

"Seventy-five dollars," she said. "I want three hundred dollars for the four plates."

"That's expensive," Ernesto said.

"How much are you willing to pay?"

"Fifty," he said.

"Well, so long then."

"Wait a minute," he said.

And then silence except for static on the line.

It was going to rain again.

She could visualize wheels turning inside his head, gears meshing but she didn't know why.

Was he trying to figure a more reasonable comeback price? Fifty was ridiculous. You sometimes got tricks, you told them it was a hundred an hour, they started bargaining with you. Make it sixty, all I've got is forty, whatever. You said "Well, so long then," they always came back with "Wait a minute."

Only the pause wasn't as long as this one. She waited. She waited some more.

"Where'd you get these plates?" he asked at last.

Funny question, she thought. All that huffing and puffing and this is the question he comes up with?

"Funny question," she said out loud. "Where'd *you* get your money?"

"My money is Miami money," he said.

"So are the plates."

"You got them in Miami?"

"Listen, are you interested at seventy-five a plate or not?"

"We may be interested. But we have to make sure they're quality plates." This came out: "Burr we ha' to may sure they quality place." Another pause. "Where did you get them in Miami? From the Ordinez people?"

"You're asking too many questions," she said. "I'm gonna hang up."

"No, no, please, *por favor*, no, don't do that, *señorita*." Another pause. "How does sixty sound?"

"Low," she said.

"Can we talk about this in person?"

"No."

"It would be good to see you face-to-face."

"When we deliver. First I need a price. So does Mr. K. He's in for seven-and-a-half finder's."

"We?"

"What?"

"Who's we?"

"My partner and me."

"Who is your partner?"

"Who's *your* partner?" she said, and hung up.

She pressed one of the receiver-rest buttons, got a dial tone, and called the Springtime again. When Klement came on the line, she said, "What is this? A setup?"

"What?" he said. "No. What?"

"Your people are asking too many questions. I want a price and no more questions."

"How much are you really looking for?" Klement asked.

"With no bullshitting back and forth?"

"Your best price."

"Sixty-five. With no haggling."

"I'll tell them."

"Times four. Less your seven and a half."

"I understand."

"I want to close this five minutes from now."

"I'll see what I can do."

She called him back five minutes later.

"They've agreed to your price," he said. "They're waiting for your call."

The rain started so suddenly it caught everyone on the deck by surprise. One moment there was sunshine and then all at once raindrops were spattering everywhere. The outdoor diners grabbed for drinks and handbags, sharing for a moment the camaraderie of people caught in either a catastrophe or an unexpected delight. There were cries of surprise and some laughter and the sound of chairs scraping back and a great deal of scurrying until the deck—within moments, it seemed—was clear of everything but the empty tables with their white cloths flapping in the wind, and the empty chairs standing stoically in the falling rain.

The rain came in off the water in long gray sheets.

Susan said, "I'm soaked."

She looked marvelous. Summery yellow dress scooped low over her breasts, cinched tightly at the waist, flaring out over her hips. Not quite soaked, but her face and hair wet with rain, a wide grin on her mouth.

Waiters were bustling about, showing diners to tables inside. There was the buzz of excited conversation, everyone marveling at how swiftly and unexpectedly the rain had come.

"It reminds me of something," Matthew said.

"Yes, me *too*," she said, and squeezed his hand.

"But I can't remember what."

"Mr. Hope?" the headwaiter said. "This way, please."

He led them to a table close to the sliding glass doors. Outside, busboys were hurriedly gathering up glasses and silverware. The wind was fierce. The tablecloths kept flapping, as if clamoring for flight.

"Something in Chicago?" Susan said.

"Yes."

"Something that made us laugh a lot?"

"Yes."

"But what?"

"I don't know. Is your drink okay?"

"I spilled half of it on the way in."

He signaled to the waiter. The place was quieting down now. He kept trying to remember. Or was it something that had happened so *many* times that it had taken on the aspect of singularity?

The waiter took their order for another round.

Susan was silent for a moment.

Then she said, "We have to stop meeting this way," and they both burst out laughing. "Truly, Matthew, this is absurd."

"I know," he said.

"I feel like I'm cheating on your *wife*! That's carrying Electra a bit far, don't you think? You should have heard all the questions she had about why I was all dressed up and—"

"You look beautiful," he said.

"Thank you, and where I was going, and who with, and—"

"What'd you tell her?"

"I said it was none of her business."

"Wrong thing to say."

"Oh, *boy*, was it! Off she went in a huff. How'd you know?"

"I said the same thing to her and got the same reaction."

"Well, what *should* I have said? I mean, I think we've made the right decision about keeping this from her for a while . . ."

"Yes."

"But at the same time I don't want to lie . . ."

"No."

"I guess I *could* have said I was meeting Peter downtown . . ."

"But he normally picks you up at the house, doesn't he?"

"Well, yes."

"And suppose he'd called while you were out?"

"Listen to the expert," Susan said.

"I'm sorry," he said, and the table went silent.

The silence lengthened.

She looked into her drink, eyes lowered.

"You hurt me very much, you know," she said.

This was the first time she'd ever said anything about it. After that night of discovery there'd been no talk except through lawyers. And after the divorce all the conversation was about arrangements for Joanna, more often than not ending in one screaming contest or another. Now, meeting in secret so that Joanna would not know they were seeing each other—God, this was peculiar!—they seemed about to discuss it at last.

"Because I loved you very much," she said.

Loved. Past tense.

"I loved you, too," he said.

"But not very much, did you?" she said, and looked up and smiled wanly. "Otherwise there wouldn't have been another woman."

"I don't know how that happened," he said honestly.

"Was she the first one?"

Her eyes lowered again. Hand idly turning the stirrer in her drink.

"Yes."

His eyes studying her face.

"I knew the marriage was in trouble," Susan said, "but—"

"Even so, I shouldn't have—"

"So many arguments—"

"Yes, but—"

"All the fun gone. We used to have such fun together, Matthew. Then, all at once . . ."

She looked up suddenly.

"What came first, Matthew? Did the fun stop *before* you met her? Or did the fun stop *because* you met her?"

"I remember only the pain," he said.

She raised her eyebrows, surprised.

He did not know how he could explain that he could no longer remember the pleasure. Only mindless passion and pointless pain leading inexorably to more passion and more pain.

"I was dumb," he said flatly.

Her eyes were steady on his face. She did not nod even minutely, there was nothing in her expression to indicate she'd been seeking this confession, this admission in public in a crowded dining room smelling faintly of wet garments while the rain lashed the windows and the white tablecloths turned sodden and gray, she had not led him to this point, this was not vindication time. She merely kept watching him.

"So what do we do now?" he asked.

"I guess we'll have to see," Susan said.

What Ernesto and Domingo figured was that they would have to see.

They were thinking there couldn't be too many young girls in this city—she'd sounded young on the phone—who were in possession of four keys of cocaine, could there? That would have to be a remarkable coincidence, more than one girl with four keys of coke in her pocket? In a Mickey Mouse town like Calusa?

211

The trouble was, the girl didn't want to meet them until it was buy time.

So how could they know for sure this was the girl El Armadillo wanted to hang from the ceiling until they showed up this Saturday with the money she wanted?

As they saw it, there were a lot of problems.

The first problem was that suppose this *wasn't* the girl they were looking for?

They had agreed to pay her sixty-five a key for four keys, which came to $260,000. That was not a terrific bargain. It came nowhere near the excellence of the deal they had made with Jimmy Legs and Charlie Nubbs, whom they had agreed to pay only *sixty* a key for ten keys. That came to $600,000. But for *ten* keys, remember. Whereas for almost *half* that amount, they would be getting only four keys from the girl if she didn't happen to be the girl they were looking for.

In which case—

If they took a look at her and she wasn't the girl with the long blonde hair and the blue eyes—

Well, then, who needed her *or* her expensive coke? It would have to be Goodbye, *hermana*, it was nice knowing you but you can shove your coke up your ass.

In which case, there might be nastiness.

Because suppose the girl was just a telephone talker for some very heavy people who if you didn't buy the coke you *said* you were going to buy would feed you to the sharks?

This was a possibility.

It was Domingo who mentioned this possibility, alert as he always was to the ways and means of staying alive in this profession.

The second problem was that they had agreed to pay the Englishman his seven-and-a-half-percent finder's fee *before* the buy went down. He wanted his money in advance, didn't want to be anywhere near where the transaction took place because that was *his* way of staying alive in this business.

Which was unheard of.

Giving the man his money in advance, before they even knew whether they were buying real coke or just sugar or chalk or whatever the fuck.

They would have to talk to the Englishman about that, work out some way to keep his nineteen-five in escrow till they had a chance to test the shit they were buying.

But that was the third problem.

Because if the girl on the phone really turned out to be Cenicienta then what they would do was grab her and grab the coke, too, without giving her a fucking nickel because this wasn't *her* coke, it belonged to Amaros. And if that turned out to be the case, they certainly didn't want to pay no fucking Englishman $19,500 for what was their own coke.

There were several other problems.

They had agreed to meet the girl and make the buy from her at twelve noon this Saturday.

They had also agreed to make the buy from Jimmy Legs and Charlie Nubbs at one-thirty that same day.

But if the girl turned out to be the girl they wanted then they had no real need to buy the Jimmy Legs/Charlie Nubbs bargain-price coke that was intended only as a consolation prize to calm down Amaros if they *couldn't* find the girl.

In which case, there might *also* be nastiness.

Because both Jimmy Legs and Charlie Nubbs did not look like people who would take kindly to other people backing out of a deal.

Which was just what Ernesto and Domingo were planning to do if the girl turned out to be the one they were looking for.

Grab her, throw both her and the stolen coke in the car, and drive straight to Miami, leaving the wops waiting with their dicks in their hands.

Although maybe, even if she *was* the girl, they should buy the ten keys from the wops, anyway.

Ten keys at sixty a key was truly a bargain.

And what was the big hurry? Once the girl was in their hands, they could take their good sweet time getting back to Miami.

It really was a bargain, sixty a key.

Ernesto told Domingo he wished they didn't have so many problems.

· Also this was already Thursday night, and Amaros hadn't yet called to say when they could expect the money.

In this business nothing moved without money.

It was Domingo's opinion that tomorrow was another day.

He suggested to Ernesto that they go out and try to get laid.

15

Luis Amaros kept his money in a bank where the manager liked doing business with drug dealers. The manager thought they were unusually courteous people with courtly Old-World manners and soft Spanish accents. Like Luis Amaros. Who everyone in town said was the scion of an old Cuban family who'd fled from Castro and invested in Louisiana soybeans, but who Roger Ware suspected was a Colombian thief who was very heavily invested in controlled substances.

This didn't matter to Ware.

Drug dealers brought a lot of money to the bank. Millions of dollars. Always deposited in amounts of less than five thousand dollars so the bank did not have to report them to the IRS. Drug dealers never asked for loans. They let their money sit for long periods of time and, whereas they often withdrew huge sums, they normally gave notice far in advance that such withdrawals were about to occur.

Except on rare occasions.

Like today.

Friday, the twentieth day of June, and raining to beat the band in Miami and Luis Amaros sitting across the desk from him at nine in the morning, smiling and saying he wished $600,000 transferred from his account to a bank in Calusa.

Ware was taken by surprise.

He did not like rainy days to begin with. He had not moved from Pittsburgh, Pennsylvania, for rainy days in Florida. He had also had a fight with his wife this morning. It was never good to approach a banker with an unusual request if he'd had a fight with his wife just before coming to work. Unless you were a drug dealer with zillions of dollars on deposit.

"I'm sure we can handle it, Mr. Amaros," Ware said, "although this *is* rather short notice."

Chidingly but smilingly. The last thing on earth he wanted was for Amaros to take his money across the street.

"Yes, I know," Amaros said, looking extremely doleful. "And I apologize." His pudgy little hands fluttered on the air. "A family emergency," he said.

"Happens to all of us," Ware said understandingly. "Did you have any particular bank in mind? Would our own branch office in Calusa suit you?"

"Where is it?" Amaros said.

He still looked extremely sad, perhaps there really *had* been a family emergency. Everything he said sounded apologetic. Like just now. As though it were somehow *his* fault that he didn't know where their Calusa branch office was.

"Downtown," Ware said. "A block north of Main Street. Very centrally located."

"Is it near the Suncrest Motel?" Amaros asked.

"Well, I . . . I really don't know. I can have my secretary

check if you like. The Suncrest, did you say? I'm sure we can—"

"No, that's all right," Amaros said. "The Main Street branch will be fine."

"If you'd prefer some *other* bank, there'd be no problem at all."

"No, no, that's fine. Centrally located, you said."

"Oh, yes. Not *on* Main Street, but just a block north."

"Fine. I'll need the address . . ."

"Of course."

"So I can tell my cousin where to pick up the cash," Amaros said.

"Had you planned . . . ?"

"Before the close of business this afternoon."

"No problem," Ware said. "So," he said, "as I understand this, you want six hundred thousand dollars transferred immediately for withdrawal later today. A simple wire transfer."

"Yes, I wish you to wire six hundred thousand dollars for withdrawal in cash before the close of business today at your branch in Calusa, yes," Amaros said.

"Can you let me have your cousin's name, please? We wouldn't want that kind of money falling into the wrong hands, would we?"

"No, we wouldn't. His name is Ernesto Moreno."

Ware began writing, talking out loud at the same time. "Ernesto Moreno," he said. He pronounced it Mor-*eeno* even though Amaros had just pronounced it correctly. "That's M-O-R-E-N-O," he said, writing, "I'll just say withdrawal on proper ID. I'm assuming he'll have proper identification."

"Of course."

"Would you want me to add any special instructions? This is a large amount of money, you know."

"Special instructions? Like what?" Amaros asked.

"Well, we could prearrange for the bank to ask your cousin a question that only he would know the answer to. His mother's name, for example . . ."

"I don't know his mother's name."

"Or his birthday . . ."

"I don't know his birthday, either."

"Well, something."

Amaros gave this some thought.

Then he said, "Ask him what we call the blonde girl in Spanish."

"I beg your pardon," Ware said.

"Write it down," Amaros said. "What do we call the blonde girl in Spanish."

"What . . . do . . . we . . . call . . . the . . . blonde . . . girl . . . in . . . Spanish," Ware wrote, speaking the words at the same time. "And what answer do you want him to give?"

"Cenicienta," Amaros said.

"Would you spell that, please?" Ware said.

The wire transfer took exactly seven minutes. It took longer than that for Amaros to get Ernesto on the phone at the Suncrest Motel to tell him that the money was on the way. It was raining in Calusa when the bank on First Street got the wired instructions. In fact, it was raining all over Florida that day. The hurricane season was supposed to be from July to October but people were beginning to say it was coming early this year. They said that every year at about this time.

In his second-floor apartment at Camelot Towers, Vincent paced from sofa to rain-streaked windows to sofa and back again. It's a wonder he isn't wearing a track in the carpet, Jenny thought.

He was very disturbed that this lawyer Matthew Hope had been here yesterday. He kept wanting to know exactly what she had said to this lawyer. She had to repeat word for word, as closely as she could remember, everything the lawyer had said and everything she had said to the lawyer. The last time she'd seen Vincent so upset was when he was talking about the man who came around with the picture of her, the one she figured Larkin had sent but which she didn't say because Vincent didn't even know Larkin existed. Or that she had a gold Rolex in a safety-deposit box at the Sheraton where she was registered as Julie Carmichael. She didn't worry about keeping things from Vincent. She suspected he kept a lot of things from her, too. Listen, they weren't joined at the hip, and after tomorrow she didn't plan to see him ever again.

"We have to get out of this town as soon as possible," he said now. "We do the deal tomorrow, and we split. It's getting too hot here."

She hated it when he tried to sound like a gangster. The words sounded ludicrous coming from his faggoty lips. Though she'd read someplace that homosexual murders were the most vicious of any murders committed anywhere. That sounded ludicrous, too. She could just imagine Vincent trying to shoot somebody, he'd probably shoot himself in the foot. Or stab him. Or anything.

"What time are you supposed to meet them?" he asked.

"Twelve noon."

"Where?"

"They're staying at a place called the Sunset Motel."

"Where the hell is that?"

"On the North Trail, near the airport, they said."

"That's all motels, that stretch near the airport," Vincent said.

"So what's wrong with that? There's nobody here this time of year."

"I'm just saying." He kept pacing. He was wearing very tight jeans, you could see the bulge of his machinery there at the crotch. What a waste, she thought. "Are they expecting *me*?" he asked.

"I didn't say anything about you. They're expecting four keys of cocaine is what they're expecting."

"You told them cash?"

"They *know* cash. If they're in the business, cash is *all* they know. I told them to bring two-hundred-and-forty thousand, five-hundred. That's the two-sixty less Klement's seven-and-a-half percent."

"How?"

"How what?"

"What kind of bills?"

"I didn't specify."

"You should've told them hundred-dollar bills."

"*You* should've been here instead of out sucking some guy's cock," Jenny said.

Vincent shrugged.

"They might bring thousand-dollar bills, something ridiculous like that," he said.

"So what? They don't change thousand-dollar bills in Paris?"

"Paris?"

"That's where I'm going once we unload this shit."

She had never told her dream to anyone before this moment. Well, she'd told Merilee that she'd be getting out of the country, but she hadn't mentioned Paris, the little house on the outskirts of Paris. She was afraid she'd get laughed at if she ever told *that* to anybody. But she was so close now, so close. Vincent looked at her for what seemed a long time, as if trying to visualize her in Paris. She was beginning to think saying it out loud had been a mistake. Not because Vincent was laughing at her, which he wasn't. But maybe God would take it away from her somehow. Steal the dream. Because she'd talked about it,

"Amaros can find you in Paris the same as anyplace else," Vincent said.

"Thanks, that's very reassuring. The son of a bitch gave me herpes, I hope he *does* find me. I'll cut off his cock, the little prick."

"That's redundant," Vincent said. "And *also* grossly inaccurate."

"Don't go fairy on me, okay?" Jenny said. "I hate when you sound like a fairy."

"I *am* a fairy, darling."

"Terrific. Go confess to your mother. Just don't *mince* your fucking words that way."

"I'm heading for Hong Kong," Vincent said. "Let Amaros chase me there if he wants to. I'll hire two Chinese thugs to behead him."

"You keep thinking Amaros is after us . . ."

"Oh, *please*, dear, who *else* is sending around private investigators? And now a lawyer? Everything legal and aboveboard, oh, yes, until he zeroes in on us. Then we can expect a visit from a goon squad. He wants his *nose* candy back, Amaros does. He doesn't like us having stolen his *nose*—"

"Me. *I'm* the one stole it. Never mind us, Kimo-Sabe."

"The private eye came to *this* apartment. That makes it *us*. The lawyer came to this apartment. That makes it *still* us. And if the goons come it'll *still* be us. Which is why I'm going to Hong Kong."

"How do you know he was a private eye?"

"Who are you talking about, darling?"

"The guy who came here with my picture."

"He *said* he was a private eye."

"That's not what you told me."

"When?"

"That day. When I came here that day. The day he showed you my picture."

"I'm sure that's what I told you."

"No, you said some guy had been here with my picture, and you were sure Amaros had sent him."

"Is that what I said?"

"That's what you said."

"Well, who can remember so long ago? Anyway, just let him *try* to find me in Hong Kong."

"I'm more worried about those two spics tomorrow than I am about Amaros," Jenny said. "I don't mind going to this shitty little motel they're staying at, I figure that may be safer than anyplace else, you know? We ask them to come here or over to the Sheraton, they may come back later, you know? Try to steal the money *back*, you know? This way, we give them the stuff, we take the bread, and we disappear."

"Exactly," Vincent said.

"It's just who the hell knows who they are? They may be rip-off artists, drift into town, ask some questions about who's got dope, and then give you a bop on the head and take off."

"Well, you never know who you're dealing with," Vincent said.

"Is just what I'm saying," Jenny said. "In L.A., I had guys you'd go up to their room, fancy hotels, am I right? The Beverly Hills? The Beverly Wilshire? Even the Bel-Air, you can't get fancier than that. Or the Hermitage. You'd go up to their room, they'd get you in the room, big bastards some of them, like gorillas, you know, they'd lock the door, the bastards. I used to carry a single-edged razor blade in my bag, but some of these guys they'd beat the shit out of you before you could bat an eyelash, rape you, steal all your fuckin' money, throw you out in the hall . . ."

"Oooo, that sounds marvelous," Vincent said.

"Cut the fag shit, willya please? I'm trying to be serious here. That's why a lot of girls work with pimps, for protection against these fucking weirdos, you know? What I'm saying is suppose I go in there tomorrow and these two guys haven't even got carfare, never mind sixty-five a key? Suppose what they're planning is a plain and simple Smash-and-Grab? Smash *me*, grab the coke, and it's off to the races. That's what's worrying me."

"Yes," Vincent said.

"So here's what I think we should do," Jenny said.

"The thing is," Jimmy Legs said to his brother, "I think she still has the watch, didn't try to hock it or nothing, leastways according to Harry Stagg, who knows every fence in this city and also there's only two pawn shops."

"Yeah," Larkin said.

He was making the spaghetti marinara sauce he planned to use tonight. He had come home at noon today. Rainy days, he didn't know why it was, nobody came around shopping for boats. Also, what the hell, the owner of the place was entitled to half a day off every now and then, wasn't he? He was chopping onions, which made his eyes tear. Jimmy was sitting on a stool at the kitchen counter, sipping on a gin and tonic. The sliding glass doors that led to the deck were crawling with rain-snakes. Beyond the deck, the sky was gray and ominous.

"Mama made the best marinara sauce in the whole world, may she rest in peace," Jimmy said.

"Yeah," Larkin said. "So you think she's still got the watch, huh?"

"Oh, yeah, no question."

"Then maybe you oughta run over this condo."

"What condo?"

"On Hacienda Road there."

"What about it?"

"This shyster lawyer?"

"Yeah?"

"Matthew Hope?"

"Yeah?"

"He comes here, he tells me the dead guy was—"

"Who, the P.I.?"

"Yeah, Samalson. He tells me he tracked her to this condo. Place named Camelot Towers on Hacienda Road there, I forget the address."

"So whattya mean? She's *there*? Is that what you're saying?"

"Well, I don't know if she's *there* or not. That's an address she gave when she went to see this doctor. Samalson planned to go back Monday morning, but then, you know, he got boxed."

"Yeah."

Jimmy sipped at his drink.

Larkin chopped onions and cried.

"It was the garlic made it so good," Jimmy said. "She used to put in a lot of garlic."

"Yeah, I'm gonna put in garlic," Larkin said.

"Keeps the Angel of Death away, garlic," Jimmy said and burst out laughing. Larkin laughed, too, crying at the same time.

"So what it was," Jimmy said, "he caught it before he had a chance to check it out, huh?"

"Well, Sunday night."

"Before he checked it out."

"Yeah."

"So you want me to run over there, show the picture?"

"You still got the picture?"

"Yeah, Stagg gave it back to me. His real name's Stagione, you know that?"

"No, I didn't know that."

"That's why no *honest* Italian should change his name," Jimmy said.

"What do you mean?" Larkin asked, bridling.

"Because everybody thinks only wanted desperadoes change their names. Or escaped cons. Them and Jewish movie stars. Paul Newman is Jewish, you know. You think that's his real name? Newman?"

"I don't know," Larkin said. "It could be Jewish, Newman." He was still annoyed that his brother had brought up the fucking name change again.

"So's Kirk Douglas," Jimmy said. "His real name is Israel something. Bob Dylan, too. And you remember John Garfield? The pictures he used to make? He was Jewish, too. I gotta tell you, for a Jew he was *some* fuckin' gangster. Bogart, too."

"Bogart was Jewish, too?"

"No, no, who said he was Jewish?"

"I thought you—"

"No, Bogart was a good *gangster*. It's *Garfield* who was Jewish. Jules Garfinkel was his name. Or Garfein. How'd you like a fuckin' name like *that*?"

"Largura's no prize, either," Larkin said.

"Papa just turned over in his grave," Jimmy said.

"Then whyn't you just lay off the fuckin' name, okay?" Larkin said.

"Don't get so fuckin' excited, okay?"

"Okay," Larkin said.

"Okay," Jimmy said.

The men were silent for several moments, listening to the sound of the falling rain and the rattling palm fronds.

"So you want me to run over there or what?" Jimmy asked.

"Well, I don't think it'd hurt, do you? Run over the condo, ask around?"

"No, no, it might be good."

"So when you think you can do that?" Larkin asked.

"Maybe tomorrow afternoon sometime, this rain ever stops. No, wait, it'll have to be Sunday, I got something to do tomorrow. Which reminds me."

Larkin was dropping tomatoes into boiling water now.

"What are you doing there?" Jimmy said.

"Taking the peels off."

"How is that taking the peels off?"

"You'll see."

Jimmy watched.

"I don't see no peels coming off," he said.

"You have to keep them in boiling water for a minute or so," Larkin said.

"Then what?"

Larkin was looking at his watch.

"Fuckin' cheap Timex," he said, shaking his head. "I catch that cunt . . ."

"So where are the peels coming off?"

Larkin drained the hot water from the pot and put the pot under the cold water tap. Jimmy watched as he slipped the tomatoes out of their skins.

"I'll be a son of a bitch," he said.

"Mama used to do it over a gas jet," Larkin said. "She used to put a fork in the tomato and then turn it over the flame to loosen the skin. I only got an electric stove here, though, so I use boiling water."

"I'll be a son of a bitch," Jimmy said again.

He kept watching his brother's magic act, amazed and astonished, shaking his head.

"You got any more of this gin?" he asked.

"Yeah, in the cabinet there," Larkin said, gesturing with his head.

Jimmy went to the cabinet, rummaged around, found an unopened bottle of Tanqueray.

"Okay to break the seal on this?" he asked.

"That's what it's for," Larkin said.

Jimmy poured more gin into his glass. He poured tonic into the glass. He cut a key lime in half, squeezed it into the glass.

"Where'd you get the key limes?" he asked.

"Lady down the street grows them," Larkin said.

"*Salute*," Jimmy said, and drank. "Ahhhhhh," he said, and drank some more. "These key limes are what make a good gin and tonic. Your regular limes suck." He drank again. "Tonight's the twentieth, you know," he said.

"Yeah? So what's the twentieth?"

"The boat."

"Oh, yeah, I forgot."

"One of the cigarettes, remember?"

"I'll run you by the place later, you can pick one you want," Larkin said, "take the key from it."

"Thanks," Jimmy said, and looked out over the water. "I hope this rain lets up," he said. "We got these two spics from Miami, we're layin' off six hundred thousand—"

"I don't want to hear it," Larkin said.

The rain showed no sign of letting up.

Camelot Towers sat tall and gray and ugly on the bay side of Whisper Key, looking more like a federal penitentiary than anything anyone would want to live in—even at nothing down, no closing fees, and a nine-point-nine percent, thirty-year, fixed-rate mortgage.

Matthew made sure he parked the Karmann Ghia in a space marked VISITOR, looked over the checklist of the apartments he'd already visited, and walked into the building. He studied the directory to the left of the mailboxes, wrote down names for the apartment numbers already on his list, and then wrote down names and apartment numbers for the other tenants in the building. He was walking toward the elevator when the doors opened and the redhead he'd talked to yesterday stepped out.

She was not wearing sunglasses this time around.

No mask, so to speak.

Her eyes were as blue as chicory in bloom.

Yesterday—in jeans and a tank top, the sunglasses hiding her eyes—he'd thought she was a teenager.

Today—at three in the afternoon, wearing a short, shiny, fire-engine red rainslicker over a pleated white skirt and shiny red boots, a blue scarf over her short auburn hair—she looked twenty-three or four, all red, white, and blue in rehearsal for the Glorious Fourth yet two weeks away.

"Hello," he said.

The blue eyes flashed.

"Matthew Hope," he said.

"Who?"

But she knew him; he *knew* she recognized him.

"Yesterday," he said.

"Oh," she said. Curtly. In dismissal. "Yes."

And walked out into the rain.

16

The wonder of it. Saturday morning. Rain beating against the windowpanes. Lightning flashing and thunder booming. And Susan in bed beside him.

"Aren't you glad Joanna decided to spend the night with a friend?" Susan asked.

"Yes," Matthew said. "What time do you have to. . . ?"

"Eleven."

"Then we have—"

"Hours yet."

The sound of the rain outside.

A car swishing by on wet asphalt.

"How many women have been in this bed since the divorce?" she asked.

"Not very many," he said honestly.

"How come you didn't buy a motorcycle?"

"A motorcycle would scare me to death. Besides, I couldn't afford one," he said.

"Ah, poor put-upon," she said. "All that alimony. Is that why you're courting me? So you can stop paying—"

"*Courting* you?"

"Well, what? *Dating* me? God, I hate that word, don't you? Dating? It sounds like 'Happy Days.' Don't you hate grown-ups who say I've been dating So-and-so. Dating!" She rolled her eyes. "Courting is much nicer. Anyway, courting is what you've been doing. I looked the word up."

"What do you mean? When?"

"When you started courting me," she said solemnly.

He almost burst out laughing. It was . . .

He was . . .

It was just that he felt so goddamn *happy* lying here beside her, listening to her talking nonsense about courting as opposed to . . .

"I am *not* courting you," he said, and did burst out laughing.

"Yes, you are," she said, and began laughing with him. "You *are*, Matthew, admit it. This is infinitely more serious—"

"Oh, yes, *in*finitely," he said, laughing.

"—than when we were kids. *That* was dating. *This* is courting. Now stop being so silly."

"What was the definition?"

"What def . . . oh. Well, it means 'to woo.'"

"To *woo*? Oh my God," he said, and burst out laughing again.

"That's not *my* definition, it's *American Heritage*'s."

"To *woo*?"

"To woo, yes. Which means 'to attempt to gain the affections or love of.'"

"And that's what I've been doing, huh?"

"Isn't it?"

"Yes," he said.

"Of course," she said. "Do you want to know the derivation?"

"I can hardly wait."

"It's from the Old French *cort*, from the Latin *cohors*, the stem of which is *cohort*."

"Okay, now I get it. Cohorts."

"Courtesan is from the same root."

"What do you think of *my* root?" he said.

"You're the dirtiest man I've ever met in my life, that's what I think."

"You know something?" he said.

"No, don't say it," she said.

"What was I about to say?"

"I don't know. Yes, I do. And I don't want you to say it. Not yet."

"Okay," he said.

They both fell silent.

Rain plopped on the leaves of the palms outside.

"Why won't you let me say it?" he asked.

"Because maybe it's not me, not us, maybe it's . . . I don't know, Matthew, I really don't. Maybe it's the new haircut, maybe it makes me look like someone very different, and maybe you've fallen—"

She cut off the sentence.

"Maybe you've been attracted to someone who *looks* different but who's only the same person underneath and you'll be disappointed when you discover it's still only me after all."

"I love you, Susan," he said.

"Oh, shit," she said, "you had to go say it, didn't you?" and began weeping.

He took her in his arms.

"I love you, too," she said.

231

Sobbing now.

"I've always loved you."

Tears rolling down her face.

"Hold me."

She had left ten minutes ago, and he could not stop thinking about her.

But as he showered, he wondered if what she'd said wasn't perhaps true.

Maybe it *was* only the haircut after all, a surface alteration, the same old Susan underneath, a woman who—by the time the divorce happened—was a stranger to the girl he'd married in Chicago. And a stranger to Matthew. And, by that time, a stranger he didn't very much like.

So here was Susan in the here and now—not physically here, she was already on her way to pick up Joanna, but here in his mind—two years later, give or take, and not an hour ago he'd told her he loved her. He did not think he was the sort of man who used those words as cheap currency in an easy market. He had meant what he'd said, and he was bewildered now by his reaction to a woman he'd known and loved, later known and disliked, still later known and abandoned, and now knew (or did he?) and loved (or did he?) all over again.

Maybe he *was* only in love with a goddamn haircut.

Change a woman's hair, you change the woman.

Cut it short, put her in a yellow dress, she'll come swinging out of church like a hooker.

And yet, the same woman underneath. Had to be. You looked into those dark eyes, wet with tears not an hour ago, and you saw Susan, no one else. People who saw her every day of the week—the people who worked with her, for example—probably hadn't even noticed that she'd cut her hair and had it restyled. But someone like himself—well, look what had happened at the Langerman party. Hadn't recognized her at all until those dark eyes flashed, and there was Susan.

The eyes were always the same.

Cut your hair, paint your toenails purple, it didn't change you except for people who knew you only casually. To anyone else, the eyes were the clue to who you were and who you'd always be. The eyes. Brown, blue, hazel, green, it didn't . . .

The eyes.

Blue.

He wished he had the photograph, but the photograph had been stolen when Otto's office was burglarized.

He wished he could have it in his hand when she opened the door. Look at her face, look at those blue eyes, negate the short red hair, compare only eyes with eyes, nose with nose, cheeks with cheeks, face with face.

Without the photograph, he would have to rely only on memory.

It was eleven-thirty by his watch, still raining here on Whisper Key, the rain sweeping in over the bay and lashing the open corridor that ran along the outside wall of Camelot Towers. He knocked on the door to apartment 2C, knocked again.

"Who is it?" a voice called.

A man. The person she'd been visiting when he was here on Thursday.

"Matthew Hope," he said. "You don't know me."

Silence inside.

He knocked again. "Hello?" he called.

"Just a minute, please."

He waited.

The man who opened the door was wearing designer jeans

and a long-sleeved red shirt, the sleeves rolled up onto his forearms. He was in his late twenties, Matthew guessed, with a pale oval face, hazel eyes, high cheekbones, and a pouting delicate mouth. Black hair swept high off his forehead in a sort of punk hairdo, was he gay?

"Yes?" he said.

One hand on his hip, extremely bored expression on his face.

Was he?

"I was here Thursday," Matthew said. "I spoke to a young woman—"

"There's no young woman here," the man said.

"She told me she was visiting—"

"No, you must have the wrong apartment."

"I'm sure it's the right apartment," Matthew said, and consulted the list he'd copied from the downstairs directory. "Hollister," he said, "2C. Are you Mr. Hollister?"

"I am."

"There was a girl here on Thursday—"

"I'm sorry, you're wrong," he said.

"A young girl with blue eyes and red hair. Short red—"

"No."

"Mr. Hollister . . ."

"You're annoying me," he said, and closed the door.

The nameplate was at eye level.

HOLLISTER.

Matthew kept looking at it.

He debated knocking again. Instead, he went downstairs, walked slowly to the Karmann Ghia, looked up toward the second-floor corridor again, got into the car, and sat behind the wheel thoughtfully for several moments. At last he nodded, started the car, and moved it to a space that afforded a good view of both the staircase *and* the lobby entrance.

He did not know whether or not the redhead was in there with Hollister right this minute.

If so, he intended to wait here till she came out.

He did not know if Hollister was expecting the redhead to visit him again today.

If so, he intended to wait here till she arrived.

The only thing he *did* know was that Hollister had lied to him.

Each kilo of cocaine was packed in a brown paper bag.

Last night, when Jimmy Legs saw the paper bags, he said, "You cheap fucks, you can't afford Baggies?"

You could fit a kilo of coke in a gallon-size plastic Baggie and then tie it shut with a little blue plastic tie. Jimmy and Charlie were doing that now. Transferring the twenty kilos of coke to plastic Baggies from the brown paper bags the fucking farmers had packed it in.

Last night it had taken the Excalibur exactly five minutes to get out beyond the three-mile limit where the ship was waiting. Panamanian registry. Rusting old hulk. Neither the ship nor the cigarette showing any lights, and besides they were out well past the limit. Anyway, if the Coast Guard showed, the cigarette—traveling at close to a hundred miles an hour— would leave them in the dust in a minute. Everybody on the ship was nervous as a cat. Amateurs, all of them. Two bearded guys looking like Castro and his brother. We wann to see d'money firs'. Hardly speak English. Greed in their eyes, fingers itchy. We wann to see d'money.

Jimmy told them they'd get the money after the coke was tested.

Both he and Charlie Nubbs were packing guns. Anybody got frisky here, there was going to be a lot of spics with holes in them. Besides there were three other guys down on the Excalibur where the money was.

They went down to this cabin.

The ship stunk. Of everything. Jimmy could hardly decide what stunk worst, the two bearded dope entrepreneurs or the ship. There were five more guys down in the cabin. Bad odds there in the cabin, seven to two. Jimmy didn't like being way the fuck out here on the Gulf with seven guys who looked liked the *bandidos* in *Treasure of the Sierra Madre*. He was counting on them being new in the business, though, and trying to make a good impression on the big boys. They fucked up this time around, the next time they showed their asses it was *adios, amigos*. Also, they knew the million bucks was still on the Excalibur down there on the water with three guys packing Sten guns. If the coke tested good, they'd work out a step-by-step exchange that wouldn't put either the money or the coke or anybody involved in jeopardy.

Twenty brown paper bags to check.

They used three tests.

Sometimes only one test for any given kilo, sometimes two, sometimes all three in combination. They wanted these raggedy-assed farmers from the wilds of South America to know they were dealing with professionals here.

The first of the tests was the old standby cobalt thiocyanate Brighter-the-Blue. The chemical dissolved in cocaine leaving some kind of blue shit, and if it was a very deep blue, you had yourself very high-grade coke.

The second test was with plain water.

You scooped a spoonful out of the brown paper bag, and dropped a little of it in a few ounces of water. If it dissolved right away, it was pure cocaine hydrochloride. If any of the powder didn't dissolve, the shit had been cut with sugar.

The third test was with Clorox.

You dropped a spoonful of the powder in a glass jar with Clorox in it.

If you got a white halo as the powder fell, the stuff was coke.

If you saw any red trailing the powder, then man, the stuff was cut with some kind of synthetic shit.

It took them quite a while to test the twenty bags.

Satisfied that they were buying good coke, they shook hands with the bearded farmers, transferred the coke to the Excalibur and the money to the rusting tub, and went their separate ways.

Today, Saturday, the twenty-first day of June, they were making some discoveries.

They were discovering, first of all, that you couldn't be too careful when you were dealing with guys who looked like farmers that had never seen or used a toilet in their lives, which was why the ship stunk so bad. What you had to do—no matter how nervous and inexperienced *any* guy selling dope looked—was not take anything at all for granted in the dope business. Because, as they were just discovering, it was possible for certain fucking thieves to fill a bag with three-quarters coke and one-quarter sugar, the sugar wrapped in Saran Wrap on the bottom of the bag.

It wasn't that the fucking farmers couldn't *afford* Baggies, it was that you could see *through* Baggies.

Jimmy recalled now that they had dumped several brown bags of the shit on the tabletop there in the cabin. Show the farmers how careful they were being, take their test samples from anywhere in the pile there on the table.

But Charlie Nubbs recalled it was the farmers who'd handed them the bags for testing, one by one. The first few bags, the ones they knew would be carefully tested, had contained coke right down to the bottom. Go ahead, dump it on the table, we're honest farmers.

Jimmy and Charlie *both* recalled that after they'd dumped three, four bags on the table, they'd stopped doing that. You had twenty keys of coke, it made a hell of a mess you went dumping it all over the table. Besides, how could you not trust these two bearded dopes, bringing their coke up in brown paper bags and nodding and grinning while the tests were being made—thank you for testing our coke, thank you for dealing with such unworthy peasants, nodding, grinning, also smelling very bad.

What they were discovering now was that only five of the brown paper bags were actually filled with coke down to the bottom. Fifteen of the bags ranged anywhere from sixty percent to seventy-five percent coke and the rest Saran-Wrapped sugar.

So what had happened was they'd paid a million bucks for twenty keys of coke, but they'd only got something like *sixteen* keys for their money because the other four keys were Domino, man. So instead of paying $50,000 a key, they had actually paid $62,500 according to Charlie's pocket calculator. Moreover, they had agreed to sell ten keys to the two Miami spics for $60,000 a key, which meant they would be losing $25,000 on those ten keys.

Jimmy said if he ever caught those farmers he would cut off their balls.

Charlie wanted to know what they were going to do about the two Miami spics.

"Pack the shit back in the paper bags," Jimmy said, "the way the farmers done to us. Only we go them one better 'cause *we* ain't farmers. With *us*, it'll be fifty-fifty separated by Saran Wrap. We'll be selling them *five* keys for the six-hundred K instead of *ten* keys, which means we'll be getting a hundred and twenty thou per key, and that ain't zucchini."

Charlie agreed this was not zucchini.

Hollister came down the steps at a run, still wearing the jeans and the red shirt, but with a yellow windbreaker over the shirt, partially zipped up the front, billowing slightly as he came out from the protection of the building and into the wind and the rain.

In one hell of a hurry, Matthew thought, watching him as he ran toward a blue Ford parked in a space some six cars down and diagonally across from where Matthew was parked. He unlocked the door, got in, and started it at once. Matthew debated—but only for the instant it took him to turn the ignition key—whether he should follow him. Suppose the girl was upstairs in the apartment? The Ford moved past on the wet pavement, and Matthew immediately pulled out after it.

Florida license plate.

16D-13346.

Matthew's dashboard clock read 11:40.

Rain lashed the windows, clattered noisily on the roof of the Karmann Ghia. The windshield was fogging. He wiped at it with the heel of his hand, followed the Ford when it took a sharp left onto the southern bridge to the mainland. Over the bridge, not a boat on the water. Another left onto U.S. 41. Heading north into the rain. Just a shade over the speed limit. Headlights on against the rain. Taillights glowing red in the gloom. Passing the northern bridge to Whisper now, still heading north on 41. Steady at fifty miles an hour, five over the limit on this part of the Trail. Causeway to Flamingo Key and Lucy's Circle on the left now, the road to Three Points and the Cow Crossing on the right. Still heading north. Up ahead on the left, the Helen Gottlieb Memorial Auditorium and just past that the new Sheraton sitting on the bay.

The Ford made a left turn.

Matthew's dashboard clock read 11:52.

He watched as the Ford pulled into a parking space.

Hollister got out and walked swiftly toward the entrance to the hotel.

Matthew parked the car some six spaces down from the Ford.

At the Suncrest Motel, further north on the Trail, Domingo looked at his watch and said in Spanish, "It's five minutes to twelve, where's the girl?"

"Don't worry," Ernesto said. "Sixty-five a key is very good money. I'm sure she'll be here."

He had gone to the bank to pick up the money yesterday. When they asked him what they called the blonde girl in Spanish, he was confused at first. Was he supposed to say "*ladrona*," which meant "thief," which was what she was? Was he supposed to say "*puta*," which meant "whore," which was also what she was? And then he remembered his last conversation with Amaros, where he'd called the girl Cenicienta.

He said to the bank manager, "Cenicienta."

The bank manager smiled.

"Yes," he said, pleased. "What does that mean in English?"

"I don't know how to say it in English," Ernesto said, and shrugged. "*Es un cuento de hadas.*"

"Ah, yes, I see," the bank manager said, still smiling.

He didn't understand a word of Spanish.

Now, here in the motel, Domingo lying on the bed and

looking up at the ceiling, the rain sweeping the windows, Ernesto wondered if the girl would turn out to be Cenicienta after all.

As if reading his mind, Domingo said, "We'll have to look at the pictures, *verdad*?"

"Yes," Ernesto said.

She came out of the hotel wearing the same short, shiny, fire-engine red rainslicker she'd had on yesterday, this time over a blue skirt, same shiny red boots, nothing on her short red hair, no sunglasses, either, not on a rainy day, blue eyes flashing as she came down the steps and began walking toward where Matthew was parked.

As she approached the car, he quickly turned his head away.

She went right on by, striding into the rain, stopping at a white Toyota parked some four spaces to the left.

Now what? he thought.

Wait for *Hollister* to come out?

Follow *her*?

Yes. She was the one Otto had been tracking.

He started the Ghia.

As soon as she backed out of her space, he backed out of his. When she pulled out of the hotel parking lot, he was right behind her.

The Florida license plate on the Toyota read 201-ZHW.

A yellow-and-black Hertz #1 sticker was on the rear bumper.

She made a left turn at the light and headed north on 41.

Matthew was right behind her.

A moment later, Vincent Hollister came out of the hotel.

He was carrying a valise.

The Suncrest Motel.

Adorable.

A ramshackle office. A swimming pool the size of a thimble. A gravel driveway leading to eight cabins spaced some ten feet apart from each other. Opposite the cabins, an asphalt rectangle with parking for about a dozen cars.

There was a roadside joint some fifty yards up the road from the motel. It was Vincent's impression—and he'd expressed this to Jenny last night, when they'd booked the room—that the place catered to men and women who wandered over from the bar next door, booked a hot bed, and used it for an hour or two.

Delightful.

He told her he'd be afraid to *touch* anything here for fear he'd catch whatever dread disease was circulating these days. Remembering the herpes she'd caught from Amaros, he apologized a moment later.

On the way back to his place last night, she explained the plan.

She'd show up at twelve noon. Cabin number three, as specified.

She'd ask to see the money.

She'd count the money.

There was supposed to be $240,500, which was $260,000 for the four keys less Klement's seven and a half percent.

If the money was all there and it didn't look like Monopoly money, she'd stay there in cabin number three with one of the buyers—*and* the money—while the second buyer went over to where Vincent would be waiting in cabin number five with the valise full of dope.

Maybe they wouldn't want to test the dope at all, but Vincent doubted that. If you're paying sixty-five a key, you're going to test what you're buying.

If the dope was okay, which of course it was, they would call on the phone—cabin five to cabin three—and Jenny would walk out with the money at the same time the buyer walked back with the dope.

Trains that passed in the night.

No opportunity for funny business.

But just in case, Vincent had a .38 Colt Detective Special tucked into the waistband of his jeans, under the windbreaker.

The Suncrest Motel.

That's what the sign outside the place read. TV, the sign further advised. Swimming pool. Units off road. Air-conditioned. Low rates.

Another sign advised VACANCY.

The Toyota made a left turn across 41 and disappeared up the motel's gravel driveway. Matthew waited till the flow of southbound traffic eased, made the turn across the road and entered the driveway just in time to see the girl knocking on the door to cabin number three. A man opened the door. They exchanged a few words and then the girl stepped inside.

Matthew pulled the Ghia up alongside a small amoeba-shaped hole in the ground that he guessed was the motel's swimming pool, and was looking toward the cabin again when the door to the office opened and a tall, burly man wearing a gray raincoat and rainhat stepped out and walked directly to the car. Matthew rolled down his window.

"Help you?" the man said.

"Uh . . . yes," Matthew said. "I'd like a room, please."

In cabin number three, Ernesto was confused.

The girl didn't look at all like the pictures they had got from her stepmother. In the pictures, the girl was very blonde and very sexy. Here in person, if this was the girl, she had short red hair that was very wet and sticking to her head from when she'd walked over from her car, no makeup on her face, not sexy at all in a red coat and red boots, looking more like Caperucita Roja than Cenicienta.

She was all business.

"I'd like to see the money, please," she said.

"We would like to see the dope, please," Ernesto said.

"The money first."

Ernesto looked at Domingo.

"You afraid I'll bop you on the head and steal it?" she said, and smiled.

The smile made her look more like the girl in the pictures. The smile and the blue eyes.

"So?" she said.

Ernesto was just realizing she wasn't carrying any kind of bag. So where was the dope?

"You don't have the dope?" he said.

"It's coming," she said.

"Coming?"

"A friend is bringing it."

"A friend?"

"In a car. He's only a few minutes behind me."

Ernesto went to the window, spread two Venetian blind slats with his fingers and looked out. He saw a tall, dark-haired man coming out of the motel office and getting into a tan, foreign-looking car. The car door closed behind him. The car started.

"Is that him?" Ernesto asked.

She went to the window, looked out. "No," she said, "he's driving a blue Ford. That's a Karmann Ghia." The car moved

244

past in the rain. She turned away from the window. "So?" she said. "Do I see the money, or do we forget the whole thing?"

She was playing it very hard considering how badly she wanted this deal. She'd been waiting for this deal to come along ever since they arrived in Calusa at the beginning of April. Maybe she'd been waiting for this deal ever since she went to California to become a great big movie star. She would have turned free tricks for the entire Russian army to get this deal. Please God, she thought, don't let anything happen to screw up this deal.

Ernesto was thinking if she isn't the girl, who needs the dope she's selling at sixty-five a key? We've got other people waiting who'll sell for only sixty a key.

Domingo was thinking the same thing.

"So what do you say?" she said. "Do we deal or do we just stand here staring at each other?"

"Get the money," Ernesto said to Domingo.

He wanted to study her face a little longer, make sure.

He could always tell her later to take a walk.

Matthew's cabin smelled of Lysol. There was a dresser with cigarette scars on it and a flaking mirror over it. There was an air conditioner in the window. There was a plaid cover on the bed. There was a telephone on a nightstand beside the bed. In the bathroom, there was a plastic glass on the sink, and a loop of paper on the toilet seat, telling him it had been sanitized. He went to the window and opened the Venetian blinds. He could not see cabin number three from here. All he could see was the asphalt rectangle where he'd parked his car. A red LeBaron convertible was parked there, too, alongside the girl's white Toyota.

He was about to close the blinds again when a blue Ford pulled in alongside his car.

Hollister.

Carrying a valise.

It was ten minutes past twelve by Vincent's watch.

She had told him to give her a half-hour in there. That would be time enough to count the money. There was nothing they could take from her, so she didn't feel herself in any danger. If the money wasn't all there or if God forbid there wasn't any money at *all*, she'd simply say good-bye.

Twenty minutes to go, he thought.

He was in the cabin they had booked last night. Cabin number five. Booked it for two days, paid the man in advance. All she had to do after she counted the money was send somebody over to test the dope.

The dope was in the valise on the bed.

All Vincent had to do was wait.

Which was the hard part.

The money was in hundred-dollar bills, neatly stacked in a dispatch case. Jenny took the bills out of the case and began counting them. Vincent had been hoping for hundred-dollar bills, but this made the counting harder for her. All the while she counted, both men watched her intently. Not her hands riffling the bills as she counted them, but her face.

Kept looking at her face.

The bills were wrapped in narrow paper wrappers, supposed to be a thousand dollars in each stack, but Jenny wasn't taking any chances on being shortchanged. She was counting every bill in each wrapper. Two hundred and forty little stacks of bills, neatly wrapped with $1000 stamped on each wrapper. Plus five loose hundred-dollar bills, which she counted first.

They kept watching her.

One of them said something in Spanish to the other one.

She kept counting.

She had counted a hundred and five thousand dollars when the short one said, "Miss Santoro?"

Her hands stopped.

Her heart stopped.

She looked up from the neatly wrapped bills on the table-top.

The big one with the slick little mustache was standing there with an open switchblade knife in his hand.

The other one had a photograph in his hand.

"This is you, no?" he said.

Twelve thirty-five by Vincent's watch and nobody knocking on the door.

What the hell was going on in there?

How long could it possibly take someone to count two hundred and forty thousand dollars? And some change. Had they brought the money in *singles*? Had they broken into someone's *piggy* bank?

She had to be still counting the money in there because she'd told him she would simply leave if there was any kind of hitch.

So there had to be money in there and it had to be real money or she'd have split right away.

So she had to be counting it.

But what was taking her so long?

"This one, too," Ernesto said, and showed her another picture.

"No, that's not me, either," she said.

It was her, all right. It was her in L.A. at that producer's party where she'd blown him later in the toilet for three hundred bucks. And the other picture was one taken on the beach at Malibu where a girlfriend of hers . . . where'd he *get* these pictures?

"My name is Sandy Jennings," she said. "I don't know who this girl—"

"And this," he said.

Another recent one. At San Simeon when she'd gone up there with the same girlfriend who by the way was a hooker. She'd sent it to her mother last year sometime, dumb picture of her standing in front of—

"None of those are me," she said.

"They're you," Ernesto said.

"Look, you want to deal dope," she said, toughing it out, "or you want to look at pic—"

And Domingo cut her.

When Vincent heard the scream, the only thing he thought was that his money was in jeopardy. He did not give a rat's ass about Jenny. All he cared about was the money they were supposed to get for the dope. He had already done quite a bit to protect the dope and the money he hoped to get for it, and he had not come all this way to have two Spanish gentlemen from Miami walk off with what he considered rightfully his own.

He pulled the .38 from the waistband of his jeans, stepped out into the rain, and started running toward cabin number three.

The owner of the motel was reading that morning's newspaper when he heard the second scream. His gray raincoat and rainhat were hanging on a wall hook to the left of his desk. There was a picture of Madonna in the nude hanging on the wall alongside a calendar. The owner had never heard Madonna sing.

What he decided to do, he decided to ignore the screams.

Because every now and then somebody would smack a girl around in one of the cabins and there was a lot of screaming and fussing but it all worked out later in the sack. One of the things you learned in the motel business was that everything sooner or later worked itself out in the sack. Which was why he never called the police when anybody started screaming or yelling.

One of the switchboard lights popped on.

Cabin number eight.

The one he'd rented to the man with the Karmann Ghia.

The first thing Vincent saw when he burst into the cabin—maybe the first thing he *wanted* to see—was the money on the table. Lots and lots of crisp green bills in little wrappers, the legend "$1000" on each of the wrappers. Open dispatch case beside them.

The next thing he saw was Jenny.

She was lying on the bed. She was bleeding very badly. Her face, her arms, her legs where her skirt was pulled back.

A very big man was standing over her, his back to the door. He turned when Vincent came in. He had a very narrow mustache. There was a knife in his hand. The blade of the knife was covered with blood.

Vincent thought *I've come this far* and shot the man between the eyes. The man toppled backward onto the bed, almost onto Jenny. The other man in the room was reaching into his coat. Vincent figured he was reaching for a gun, so he shot him, too.

He went to the table and started packing the wrapped bundles of bills into the dispatch case. He closed the dispatch case.

From the bed, Jenny whispered, "Help me."

Vincent said, "Ta, darling."

"Please," she said.

But he was already gone.

The last and only time Matthew was shot, Detective Morris Bloom gave him a piece of advice.

"Matthew," he'd said, "never get in the way of a man with a gun. If you see a man with a gun coming toward you, move aside and let him go by. If you feel like being a hero, trip him as he goes by. But never get in his way."

Matthew didn't particularly feel like being a hero.

But he had heard the shots when he was talking to the police on the phone in his room, and the shots combined with the screams he'd earlier heard were enough to propel him out of cabin number eight, into the rain, and sprinting for cabin number three when he saw Hollister coming out of there with a dispatch case in one hand and a gun in the other.

Hollister was running for one of the cabins further up the line.

Matthew did just as Bloom had advised.

He stepped aside to let Hollister go by.

But even though he didn't particularly feel like becoming a hero, he tripped him.

And when Hollister fell headlong onto the gravel, Matthew kicked him in the head.

Which was something else Bloom had taught him.

17

It had started on a Sunday, and it was ending on a Sunday.

But as Daniel Nettington had once pointed out, the cops in Calusa had no respect for Sunday.

Matthew was in the pool when the doorbell rang at ten o'clock that morning. He got out of the water, went walking wet and dripping through the house, and opened the door on Detectives Hacker and Rawles, both wearing business suits and ties.

"Okay to come in?" Rawles said.

"Sure," Matthew said.

They went out back and sat by the pool.

The sun was bright. The three H's—Hot, Humid, and Hazy—were full upon them once again. The detectives sat sweltering in their clothing. Somehow their attire gave them a real or imagined advantage: business suits vs. swim suit; work vs. play.

Nobody thanked Matthew for having called the police last night.

All Rawles wanted to know was whether or not Hollister had said anything to him.

"No," Matthew said.

"Nothing, huh?"

"Nothing at all."

"Tell me again what happened," Rawles said.

"I heard screaming from cabin number three," Matthew said, "and I immediately called the police."

Nobody was yet thanking him for this noble action.

"While I was on the phone, I heard shots. I ran out and was heading for the cabin when Hollister came out carrying a—"

"You knew his name, did you?"

"Yes."

"How'd you happen to know his name?"

"That's a long story."

"I've got plenty of time," Rawles said.

"I haven't," Matthew said. "If you want background . . ."

"We have a right to know how you happened to be at that motel last night, where two men were killed and a woman cut, and another man kicked in the head."

"I kicked him in the head."

"Yes, that's what you told us. Why'd you kick him in the head?"

"It's what Bloom said I should do if I ever tripped a man carrying a gun."

Rawles looked at him.

"Why'd you trip him?" Hacker said.

"I was getting to that," Matthew said.

"I want to know how you knew his name," Rawles said.

"I'll be happy to tell you all that in a deposition," Matthew said. "But not here and not now."

"When?"

"You name it."

"Tomorrow morning at nine," Rawles said.

"I'll be there," Matthew said.

Rawles nodded.

Matthew nodded.

Hacker looked at both men and shrugged.

"You were heading for the cabin . . ." Rawles prompted.

"Yes, when he came out carrying a dispatch case and a gun. He seemed to be heading for a cabin up the line . . ."

"Cabin number five," Hacker said, and nodded.

"Where the coke was," Rawles said.

"Four keys."

"High-grade shit."

"I didn't know about that," Matthew said.

"You just happened to be where a dope deal was going down, huh?" Rawles said.

"I'll tell you all about how I happened to be there when you take the deposition," Matthew said.

"Did you know at the time what was in that dispatch case?" Hacker asked.

"No."

"Two hundred and forty thousand dollars and change," Hacker said.

"So I've been told," Matthew said, though he didn't think of five hundred dollars as "change."

"Did Hollister threaten you with the gun?" Rawles asked.

"No."

"And he didn't say anything to you?"

"Nothing."

"So why'd you trip him?"

"It seemed like the right thing to do."

"Did kicking him in the head seem like the right thing to do?"

"Yes. Unless I wanted to get shot. Which I didn't."

"Because he's claiming now *we're* the ones messed him up," Hacker said.

"Well, that's easily refuted," Matthew said.

"Didn't say a word to you, huh?" Rawles said.

"Nothing."

"Ain't saying a word to us, neither," Hacker said. "Asked for a lawyer right off, started yelling police brutality, and then clammed up."

"On the face of it," Rawles said, "it looks like he's the one killed the two Miami punks, but we won't know for sure till we get a ballistics report."

"How about Otto? Are you running a ballistics—"

"Otto?" Rawles said. "You mean Samalson?"

"That's what this is all about, isn't it?" Matthew said. "Somebody killing Otto?"

"Oh, is *that* what it's all about?" Rawles said.

"That's news to us," Hacker said.

"What *we* thought it was all about was four keys of high-grade coke and two hundred and forty thousand plus dollars, that's what *we* thought it was all about."

Matthew looked at him.

"Detective Rawles," he said, calmly and levelly, "were any bullets recovered in Otto's car?"

"One in the car," Rawles said, "the other still in his head."

"Then compare them with a test-firing from Hollister's gun."

"Why? How do you tie him with Otto?"

"Otto was asking him questions."

"About what?"

"The girl."

"The one who got cut?"

"Yes. Have you talked to her yet?"

"She says she was walking along 41 minding her own business when these two Hispanics pulled up in a red LeBaron convertible, threw her in the car, and drove her to the motel."

"Uh-huh," Matthew said.

"Claims they tried to rape her," Hacker said.

"Uh-huh," Matthew said. "How does she explain the Toyota?"

"What Toyota?"

"The white Toyota with the 201-ZHW license plate. A Hertz rental car. Rented to a woman named Jenny Santoro, which may or may not be her real name."

"How do you know all this?"

"*Otto* knew all this. In any case, she *drove* to the motel. I know because I followed her there."

Rawles looked at him.

"Maybe we oughta take that deposition this afternoon," he said.

"Whenever," Matthew said.

"How's three o'clock?"

"Fine."

"The girl doesn't know anything about a dope deal going down," Hacker said. "Leastways that's what she claims."

"Says she witnessed Hollister killing the two Hispanics, though," Rawles said.

"Then that nails Hollister, doesn't it?" Matthew said.

"I got a hunch she's a hooker," Rawles said, shaking his head. "Juries tend not to believe anything a hooker says. I'd much rather have ballistics evidence."

"When will they be getting back to you?"

"Sometime today. Maybe before you come in."

"Will you ask them to run a test on the other bullets?"

"Sure. But what difference will it make? This is Florida. A homicide committed by a person engaged in robbery is a capital felony."

"I know," Matthew said.

"If we can convict Hollister on two counts of homicide . . ."

"But it'll make me feel better," Matthew said.

Susan called shortly after the police left.

The call surprised him.

He said, "Hey, hi, I was just about to call you."

"Oh?"

"I thought you might like to have brunch with me."

"Well, Joanna's here, you know," Susan said.

"All three of us, I thought."

There was a silence on the line.

"Susan?"

"Yes?"

"I think we've got to stop pretending we're . . . I mean, Joanna's too smart for that. Let's just tell her we've been seeing each other, okay? Tell her I've been courting you. Wooing you," he said, smiling. "Tell her we're exploring the possibility of—"

"That's why I'm calling," Susan said.

"I'm right, don't you think?"

"Yes, but . . ."

"So let's tell her at brunch."

"No, I can't have brunch with you," Susan said, "I'm busy."

"Oh?"

"Yes, I have other plans."

"I thought . . ."

"I know, but . . ."

"Before you left yesterday . . ."

"Yes, Matthew, I know but . . ."

"We said we'd try to get together today."

"But something came up."

There was a sudden silence on the line.

He waited.

It was like sitting in a stalled car on the railroad tracks, waiting for the glaring headlight of a train to come zooming out of the night.

"I'm driving down to Sanibel with Peter," she said.

The train smashing into the car, a ball of fire exploding.

He was happy she could not see his face.

"He asked me to drive down there with him," she said.

He was shaking his head.

"Matthew?"

"Yes, Susan."

"Matthew, I need to think about this, about us, I need to . . . sort things out . . . understand what's . . . I just don't know what's happening, Matthew."

He wanted to say "You said you loved me."

He did not say it.

He wanted to say "You said you've *always* loved me."

He did not say it.

He waited.

"Can you give me a little more time, Matthew?"

He almost said "We have all the time in the world," but that was both a cliché and a lie.

He said nothing.

"Matthew . . . please," she said.

"Sure," he said.

"Just until I can—"

"Sure," he said.

"We'll see," she said.

"Yes, Susan."

"How it works out."

"Yes."

"I want to kiss you right this minute," she said, and hung up.

It never works out the way you expect it to, he thought.

You get your chance, you get a chance finally to make a killing, and something goes wrong to fuck it up.

What possibly could have gotten *into* those two men?

Why on earth had they suddenly *turned* on Jenny?

Cutting her that way! Were they insane?

The lawyer he could understand.

Amaros again.

First the private investigator and then the lawyer.

Fucking big dope dealer with all kinds of money to buy all kinds of legitimate pursuit, but oh just wait till he knew for certain he had the right customers, oh just wait. In would come the gorillas, my dear, to take back the dope and cut off your cock, you do not mess with *Señor* Armadillo, *amigos*, oh no.

Because Amaros had *seen* him.

Amaros knew what he *looked* like.

That night in the Kasbah lounge when he came in every four or five minutes in the gray chauffeur's uniform . . .

Miss Carmody? Are you going to wait any longer? Or should we start for the party?

Miss Carmody?

Miss Carmody, shall I bring the car around?

So here's a little bald-headed guy standing outside the

condo door with a picture of Jenny in his hand, ice-blue gown with the fake sapphire-and-diamond pin on her abundant chest, and he's asking questions and of *course* he's from Amaros, Amaros is closing in.

Gives his name.

Otto Samalson.

Samalson Investigations.

Downtown Calusa.

Yes, Mr. Samalson. Mr. Samalson, you have signed your own death warrant because there is no way *this* person is going to allow you to report back to Amaros, you are too fucking *close*, Mr. Samalson, you have to *go*, Mr. Samalson!

They'd been so damn cautious, too.

She'd flown up, rented a car at the airport, took a room at the Sheraton where he was waiting for her. He'd driven up with the coke in the trunk of the blue Ford, no roadblocks between Miami and here, no danger of who the hell *knew* what if she'd carried the coke in a suitcase on the plane. Met at the Sheraton. Different rooms. She'd stayed on there after he'd taken the summer rental at Camelot Towers—well, of course, the whore princess, you couldn't expect her to rent a *condominium*, could you?

And now a man with her picture in his hand.

Well, yes, it is simple to *find* you, Mr. Samalson, given your address in downtown Calusa, and yes, it is simple to steal a car, Mr. Samalson, and yes, it is simple to *follow* you and to pump two bullets into your car and into your head, bam, bam, good-bye, Mr. Samalson, it was nice knowing you, and good-bye Luis Amaros, too.

The fucking *lawyer!*

Should have finished him last night, but that would have meant either shooting on the run and risking a miss, or else stopping, taking aim, no no my dear. Better to get on with it, move on with it, get away from her, away from the lawyer, grab the dope in the suitcase in the other cabin, mustn't leave all that sweet dust behind, now must we? Dump the dope and the money in the Ford and off we go into the wild blue yonder, riding high into the sun and Hong *Kong*, mister, heaven at last, heaven.

But it never works out the way you think it will.

You sit instead in a six-by-eight cubicle with bars as thick as your cock, and on the wall, prisoners past have written stupid little sayings and there's a toilet you can sit on with everyone looking through the bars at you, and it never works out the way you think it will.

You can never trust women.

Daniel Nettington called Matthew at home at two-thirty that Sunday afternoon, just as he was leaving for the Public Safety Building downtown. Carla Nettington was on the extension.

"Mr. Hope," Nettington said, "sorry to be breaking in on you at home."

Matthew said, "Not at all."

"Daniel and I have had a long talk," Carla said.

"A very long talk," Daniel said.

"What we'd like you to do for us," Carla said, "is draw up a paper saying that in the event of a divorce we will each share everything we own fifty-fifty."

"Uh-huh," Matthew said.

"Not that we're planning on a divorce," Nettington said.

"But this will give us leeway, do you understand?" Carla said.

"Without having to hire private detectives to follow us, eh?" Nettington said.

"A free and open marriage," Carla said.

"So what time can you see us tomorrow?" Nettington said.

"I can't," Matthew said, and hung up.

She had let herself in with her own key.

What she planned to do here at the condo was steal Vincent blind.

Ta, darling.

While she's bleeding on the bed.

He had plenty of jewelry, he wore more jewelry than most women did. She planned to take all his jewelry, carry it back with her to the Sheraton where she would take Larkin's Rolex from the safety-deposit box and then get out of town.

Never mind testifying against Vincent if and when it came to that.

That was something she'd told the cops in anger.

She didn't care *what* happened to Vincent, she only cared what happened to herself.

Ta, darling.

Six stitches in the cut over her eye.

Another four stitches in the cut on the inside of her thigh.

That was what she was afraid of.

That Amaros would keep sending people after her again and again and again because she'd stolen his coke.

She had to get out.

Fast.

Out of Florida, out of America, out of the life.

Take everything Vincent owned that wasn't nailed down, and make her way to Paris, play it by ear from there. Try to make a new start. Find a job in a little theater someplace, out in the country someplace, trees everywhere, rivers, she was still young, still beautiful . . .

A knock sounded on the door.

Jimmy Legs was thinking you couldn't trust spics.

Him and Charlie Nubbs had waited two hours at Charlie's place with the dope that was half sugar wrapped in Saran Wrap and the spics never even showed. You just couldn't trust spics.

So today was a nice sunny day, so here he was at Camelot Towers, knocking on doors and showing the picture of the girl in the ice-blue gown.

The door opened.

He was starting to say, "Excuse me, Miss, I was wondering . . ." when he looked into those blue eyes of hers and never mind the red hair, this was the girl, he knew this was the girl stole his brother's watch.

He shoved the picture at her.

"You recognize yourself?" he said.

She thought in that blinding moment God, another picture, where are they getting these *pictures*!

"My brother wants his watch back," he said, and shoved her into the apartment.

And she thought—as he locked the door behind him—*They always let me in the ballroom but they never let me dance.*

MORE MYSTERIOUS PLEASURES

HAROLD ADAMS
MURDER
Carl Wilcox debuts in a story of triple murder which exposes the underbelly of corruption in the town of Corden, shattering the respectability of its most dignified citizens.   #501 $3.50

THE NAKED LIAR
When a sexy young widow is framed for the murder of her husband, Carl Wilcox comes through to help her fight off cops and big-city goons.
                                                                #420 $3.95

THE FOURTH WIDOW
Ex-con/private eye Carl Wilcox is back, investigating the death of a "popular" widow in the Depression-era town of Corden, S.D.
                                                                #502 $3.50

EARL DERR BIGGERS
THE HOUSE WITHOUT A KEY
Charlie Chan debuts in the Honolulu investigation of an expatriate Bostonian's murder.   #421 $3.95

THE CHINESE PARROT
Charlie Chan works to find the key to murders seemingly without victims—but which have left a multitude of clues.   #503 $3.95

BEHIND THAT CURTAIN
Two murders sixteen years apart, one in London, one in San Francisco, each share a major clue in a pair of velvet Chinese slippers. Chan seeks the connection.   #504 $3.95

THE BLACK CAMEL
When movie goddess Sheila Fane is murdered in her Hawaiian pavilion, Chan discovers an interrelated crime in a murky Hollywood mystery from the past.   #505 $3.95

CHARLIE CHAN CARRIES ON
An elusive transcontinental killer dogs the heels of the Lofton Round the World Cruise. When the touring party reaches Honolulu, the murderer finally meets his match.

JOE GORES
A TIME OF PREDATORS
When Paula Halstead kills herself after witnessing a horrid crime, her husband vows to avenge her death. Winner of the Edgar Allan Poe Award.

#215 $3.95

COME MORNING
Two million in diamonds are at stake, and the ex-con who knows their whereabouts may have trouble staying alive if he turns them up at the wrong moment.

#518 $3.95

NAT HENTOFF
BLUES FOR CHARLIE DARWIN
Gritty, colorful Greenwich Village sets the scene for Noah Green and Sam McKibbon, two street-wise New York cops who are as at home in jazz clubs as they are at a homicide scene.

#208 $3.95

THE MAN FROM INTERNAL AFFAIRS
Detective Noah Green wants to know who's stuffing corpses into East Village garbage cans . . . and who's lying about him to the Internal Affairs Division.

#409 $3.95

PATRICIA HIGHSMITH
THE BLUNDERER
An unhappy husband attempts to kill his wife by applying the murderous methods of another man. When things go wrong, he pays a visit to the more successful killer—a dreadful error.

#305 $3.95

DOUG HORNIG
THE DARK SIDE
Insurance detective Loren Swift is called to a rural commune to investigate a carbon-monoxide murder. Are the commune inhabitants as gentle as they seem?

#519 $3.95

P.D. JAMES/T.A. CRITCHLEY
THE MAUL AND THE PEAR TREE
The noted mystery novelist teams up with a police historian to create a fascinating factual account of the 1811 Ratcliffe Highway murders.

#520 $3.95

STUART KAMINSKY'S "TOBY PETERS" SERIES
NEVER CROSS A VAMPIRE
When Bela Lugosi receives a dead bat in the mail, Toby tries to catch the prankster. But Toby's time is at a premium because he's also trying to clear William Faulkner of a murder charge!

#107 $3.95

PATRICK RUELL
RED CHRISTMAS
Murderers and political terrorists come down the chimney during an old-fashioned Dickensian Christmas at a British country inn.

#531 $3.50

DEATH TAKES THE LOW ROAD
William Hazlitt, a universtiy administrator who moonlights as a Soviet mole, is on the run from both Russian and British agents who want him to assassinate an African general.

#532 $3.50

DELL SHANNON
CASE PENDING
In the first novel in the best-selling series, Lt. Luis Mendoza must solve a series of horrifying Los Angeles mutilation murders.

#211 $3.95

THE ACE OF SPADES
When the police find an overdosed junkie, they're ready to write off the case—until the autopsy reveals that this junkie *wasn't* a junkie.

#212 $3.95

EXTRA KILL
In "The Temple of Mystic Truth," Mendoza discovers idol worship, pornography, murder, and the clue to the death of a Los Angeles patrolman.

#213 $3.95

KNAVE OF HEARTS
Mendoza must clear the name of the L.A.P.D. when it's discovered that an innocent man has been executed and the real killer is still on the loose.

#214 $3.95

DEATH OF A BUSYBODY
When the West Coast's most industrious gossip and meddler turns up dead in a freight yard, Mendoza must work without clues to find the killer of a woman who had offended nearly everyone in Los Angeles.

#315 $3.95

DOUBLE BLUFF
Mendoza goes against the evidence to dissect what looks like an air-tight case against suspected wife-killer Francis Ingram—a man the lieutenant insists is too nice to be a murderer.

#316 $3.95

MARK OF MURDER
Mendoza investigates the near-fatal attack on an old friend as well as trying to track down an insane serial killer.

#417 $3.95

ROOT OF ALL EVIL
The murder of a "nice" girl leads Mendoza to team up with the FBI in the search for her not-so-nice boyfriend—a Soviet agent.

#418 $3.95

DAVID WILLIAMS' "MARK TREASURE" SERIES
UNHOLY WRIT
London financier Mark Treasure helps a friend reaquire some property. He stays to unravel the mystery when a Shakespeare manuscript is discovered and foul murder done. #112 $3.95

TREASURE BY DEGREES
Mark Treasure discovers there's nothing funny about a board game called "Funny Farms." When he becomes involved in the takeover struggle for a small university, he also finds there's nothing funny about murder. #113 $3.95

■ ■